THE BANKER

THE BANKER

Peter Colt

SEVERN HOUSE

First world edition published in Great Britain and the USA in 2025
by Severn House, an imprint of Canongate Books Ltd,
14 High Street, Edinburgh EH1 1TE.

severnhouse.com

Cover and jacket design by Jem Butcher Design

British Library Cataloguing-in-Publication Data
A CIP catalogue record for this title is available from the British Library.

ISBN-13: 978-1-4483-1071-5 (cased)
ISBN-13: 978-1-4483-1072-2 (e-book)

All Severn House titles are printed on acid-free paper.

Typeset by Palimpsest Book Production Ltd., Falkirk,
Stirlingshire, Scotland.
Printed and bound in Great Britain by TJ Books,
Padstow, Cornwall.

Praise for the Andy Roark novels

About the author

Peter Colt is a 1996 graduate of the University of Rhode Island with a BA in Political Science and a 24-year veteran of the Army Reserve with deployments to Kosovo and Iraq as an Army Civil Affairs officer. He is currently a police officer in Rhode Island. He is married with two sons and two perpetually feuding cats.

Suzanne Marie Johnson July 25, 1942 – July 10, 2023
The only woman I ever considered my Aunt.

For Cathy, Henry and Alder.

Acknowledgments

I write the stories but there are a lot of people who make the manuscript into a book.

Cathy and the boys who put up with my spending so much time in the office.

CME who reads and edits the first draft so none of you will ever know how bad my spelling and grammar are.

My agent, the incomparable Cynthia Manson.

My editor Rachel Slatter.

Copyeditor Deborah Balogun.

And the many people at Severn House who work hard to get the book into your hands but never get a shout out.

Acknowledgment

ONE

The rain beat a tattoo against the roof of my battered Ford Maverick. It came down hard enough to have rivaled Art Blakey on good night. If Art Blakey had had a bad night drumming, I wouldn't have heard the difference. It was April 1986, and I was parked across the street from the Merrimack Community Bank, in Amesbury, Massachusetts. Amesbury is the second most northern town in the Commonwealth. It was as close to New Hampshire as you could get without having to 'Live Free or Die.' Amesbury was a nice town, not quite affluent, but most of the people who lived there were strangers to things like welfare cheese and food stamps.

Amesbury had one of the oldest suspension bridges in America that crossed the Merrimack. There were also notable sights such as the Powwow River and Powwow Hill. It had a downtown area that was marked by three-story buildings with no shortage of nineteenth-century brick and stone. There was a historic Market Square and more colonial architecture around town than you could shake a stick at. Not to mention a couple of photogenic churches. If you were a movie producer looking for a classic New England city to shoot exterior shots in, Amesbury would be pretty high on the list. I might have enjoyed it, too, if I wasn't stuck watching the front doors of the bank.

I was backed into a parking spot across the street from the bank. My wipers occasionally transited across the windshield and the heater was set to defrost. Normally on surveillance I would have kept the car turned off, but the rain and chill in the air meant that I had to have the car on so I could see through the windshield. It was hard to do surveillance through a windshield-sized cataract.

I was waiting for the bank manager, a man named Mark Lintz, to get in his Mercedes coupe. This one was a snazzy, silver Mercedes-Benz 450. Sadly, it wasn't the type with the gull-wing doors that opened upward instead of the way the rest of the world opened their car doors. Even with that minor failing, it was still a pretty sharp-looking car. I couldn't afford one, and unless I was following the country club set around, it would draw too much attention. I sat in my more modest Ford Maverick, wanting a cigarette, having car lust, waiting for my guy to come out of the bank.

A few days earlier in my office near Boston's financial district, I had been sitting at my desk, staring across its expanse at Harry Brock. Brock was the president of the Merrimack Community Bank in Amesbury. He told me so with no small sense of pride when he called to make the appointment.

He had arrived on time, his eyes taking in the cheap furniture in my waiting room. He didn't recoil, at least. In the office he saw my desk, the huge nineteenth-century safe I inherited with the office, and behind me the espresso machine that old man Marconi kept in his pizza joint. I had inherited it when he left for Italy to spend his last, cancer-ridden days in his homeland.

'I don't know anything about embezzling,' I said.

'Well, you don't have to know much. It's basically stealing by someone who has access to someone else's money.' Brock was in his late forties, bald more than balding, brown hair, dark eyes and a slight pot belly. He wore the regulation blue pinstripe suit that bankers were expected to wear and a tie with the crest of an Ivy League school I didn't recognize. In these parts, it was Harvard or nothing.

'I know that much,' I said with mild exasperation.

'Look, we have accountants. They tell me money is missing, and that it looks like a lot of money has been syphoned out of the bank.'

'How much money?'

'A little over two million dollars.'

I whistled. 'That's a lot of money. Where did it go? How do you even move that much money?'

'There are a number of areas in which there is fluctuation in the value of certain assets. If someone had access to accounts and could time it right, they could steal quite a lot of money. But that's why we have accountants.'

'Right, I get that part. Weren't they able to trace where it went?'

'No, they weren't. Whoever took the money was pretty smart about it. There's no trail – or no trail that we can follow. What I need you to do is check around. Follow the people who have access to the money. See if they're living above their means. We know the money is missing. We need to know who took it.'

'I presume it is a short list?'

'Yes, exactly three people long. Though I can't believe any of them would do it.'

'No, but it has to be someone. Money doesn't just embezzle itself. Do you have anyone who is more likely than any of the others?' I didn't point out that he probably wouldn't have hired them if he thought they weren't trustworthy.

'Mark Lintz.'

'Why does he stand out?'

'On the face of it, he doesn't.' Brock furrowed his brow. 'He's married, in his thirties, they have a son . . . but he's the most likely. I don't know, maybe he's having an affair or it's a gambling problem. That's why I need you. Mr Roark, I need to resolve this as quickly as possible.'

'Sure, but why not go to the authorities?'

'We're a small bank and the board of directors would blame me. I hired Lintz and promoted him. He's a little young but he seemed – seems – very capable,' he corrected himself. 'I am responsible for the operations of the bank. In short, I could lose my job.'

'We can't have that.'

'Please, Mr Roark, I need a detective who is discreet and gets results.'

'I'm your guy.' I almost believed it too.

'Good. Their details.' He handed me a manila envelope.

'Who are the other two you suspect?'

'Karen Marti, she's my secretary. I might be the president but she runs the bank. I just sign the papers.' He had told the joke often enough that it had the feel of old denim.

'But you don't think it's her?'

'No, I've known Karen forever. It's just impossible.'

'Then why is she on the list?'

'Access. She has access to everything in the bank.'

'OK, I will take a look at her, if only to rule her out.' That was a bit of a lie. If it was Marti, it wouldn't be the first time that someone got sick of taking orders and watching everyone else get ahead. Brock wouldn't be the first guy to make a mistake because he believed the fairer sex wasn't capable of doing all the nasty things men did. Recently I had been getting a lot of lessons in women's capabilities.

'The other is Frank Cosgrove.'

'Who's he?'

'The assistant manager. He answers to Lintz, but he has access to everything too.'

'What's his deal?'

'He's in his late twenties. Good-looking guy. The women at the bank love him, and he's great at convincing a lot of our female customers to open Christmas Club accounts.'

'But he's not your first choice?'

He laughed. 'No, Frank's just not the type. I think he's pretty religious or something.'

'OK, are their details in here too?' I asked, holding up the manila envelope.

'Yes. I also included pictures of them.'

'That'll help.'

'I really wish it isn't any of them. We're like a family.'

'Sure, sure.' I didn't bother offering him my opinion that it wasn't betrayal if you weren't close to them.

We talked about money and agreed to a fee. It was good to know that I wouldn't have to contemplate drinking cheap whiskey for another few months. He took one of those zippered canvas bags that people use for cash deposits out of his inner pocket. He unzipped it, pulled a small stack of bills out and slid it across the desk to me. Like that, I was hired and a few days later ended up here, parked outside of bank in northern Massachusetts in my battered car.

It rained hard enough to remind me of monsoon season in Vietnam. At least the only threat I was facing in Amesbury was being bored to death. Watching a bank manager was a lot less scary than conducting reconnaissance on the Ho Chi Minh trail, which I had spent three years doing. I had grown up enough to appreciate the pleasure of being bored versus the excitement of being shot at.

Lunchtime came around, and I was waiting to see if Lintz was going to go out. My stomach rumbled, reminding me that breakfast was a long-distant memory. I tried to satisfy my hunger with a cup of warm coffee from my thermos, but it wasn't falling for it. I was pretty sure that Lintz wouldn't be going to lunch in this rain. I didn't know who would venture out if they didn't have to. Even in the car with the heat going, a raw chill managed to find its way down the back of my neck. I wanted a cigarette, but that would mean cracking the window, which meant even more raw chilliness. I could wait a little while longer.

I was on my third or fourth day of surveillance. Surveillance was boring at the best of times, and this stakeout was especially so. The days had started to run together. If it weren't for the need to account for my time for billing purposes, I would have lost track. The problem with this type of job was that I was one man. A good surveillance operation would have a minimum of three people watching one subject instead of one guy trying to watch three people. I could spend weeks on the job, so I had to try and split my time between the potential suspects.

The other two people that Brock had identified as potential suspects weren't that exciting as suspects go. Neither one showed any signs of living above or, frankly, below their means. Both seemed pretty solidly middle class, you know, the white picket fence, two kids and a dog type of people. It struck me that I had more in common with the North Vietnamese Army soldiers who spent three years trying to kill me than I did with the average American family man.

It was not that I was critical of them, or families for that matter. I just didn't understand it. Getting up and battling traffic to go to some job at the office, the mill, the plant, etc. Coming home to a wife or having to go to dance recitals, Cub Scouts or parent-teacher conferences. That was all a foreign language to me. Maybe in part because my own childhood had been a bit different, being raised by my father on his own. He'd done the best he could after my mother had left. He met her while on occupation duty in Germany. He had jumped in on D-Day, fought his way into Germany and stayed longer than he should have.

He ended up with a war bride and, eventually, a son. His job at the mill was there for him when he came home, and one day his wife wasn't. He had wanted to be a poet and had a taste of the world beyond South Boston (Southie). Then he was saddled with responsibility and disappointment. He was a good father and did his best to raise me well. Some of it took, but that didn't stop him from drinking himself to death shortly after I came home from Vietnam. Maybe I had been trying to live up to him or make him proud, or maybe I was bitten by the urge that made me want to leave Southie and see the world. Who knows?

That was the downside of surveillance, you had all the time in the world to sit and think. Fighting off boredom any way you could. In the end, my mind wandered back to my dad. I snapped myself back to the present and was relieved to see the silver Mercedes was still parked in its spot. My stomach rumbled again, and I sipped the coffee, which was still a bit warm.

There was a deli a few doors down, and hunger won out over my desire to stay dry. I pulled my Red Sox ballcap down on my head, opened the door and stepped out into the rain. If it was all of twenty yards to the deli, I would be shocked. In the short few moments it took me to walk there, my coat from L.L. Bean's started to soak through. In its defense, it wasn't really a raincoat but some sort of wool-lined, nylon shell that was a sportier version of an army field jacket.

I opened the door to the deli and stepped inside just in time for the downpour to switch to a light drizzle. I contemplated the offerings and settled on a Reuben. They are a love or hate type of sandwich, but I love them – corned beef, Swiss cheese, sauerkraut and Russian dressing on grilled rye. If you thought about it, it should be disgusting, but the combination of unlikely ingredients worked well together. It was just what I needed to help me power through another few hours of boring surveillance.

I put my order in and waited, sitting, watching the bank parking lot across the street. Surveillance is ninety-nine percent boredom and one percent excitement when your subject does something.

So far, after a few days, none of the bank people had done anything exciting. None of them ever seemed to do anything particularly interesting. They did regular life stuff – grocery shopping, putting a kid on the bus, waiting to get the kid off the bus in the case of the Lintzs. They went to work and went home. The closest thing that I saw to high living or gambling was Karen Marti going to Bingo at the local Knights of Columbus Hall. Not exactly an indicator of someone embezzling to pay for their gambling losses.

When I was a young cop, one of the senior guys told me, 'Kid, the three Ws get guys on the job jammed up. Stay away from them and you'll be OK.'

'The three Ws?' I asked.

'Whiskey, women and wagerin'. Guys who have drinking problems, guys who screw around on their wives, and guys who gamble. Those are the guys who get jammed up at work.'

'Gotcha.'

'Mind you, those things are a lot of fun, so try not to miss out.' I heard his booming laugh as he walked away from me at the end of the shift.

If any of the bank employees Brock singled out were struggling with the three Ws, I hadn't seen any sign of it. Not yet, at least. I might die of boredom before I found any sign of it. Amesbury was a nice town and all, but I was spending a lot of time sitting on my ass and I didn't like that.

The guy behind the counter called my number, and I paid him for the sandwich, some chips from Cape Cod and a bottle of seltzer that was allegedly from New York. He took my cash, slid some bills and coins back to me, most of which ended up in the tip jar. I took the brown paper bag carrying my portable feast back to the Maverick. It wasn't exactly like being on a picnic, but it was better than nothing. The rain started beating down on the car like someone remembering they had a grudge. At least I was mostly dry.

I ate my sandwich, watching the parking lot and a whole lot of nothing going on. Cars drove by and I amused myself by watching how much water they splashed on the sidewalk when they plowed through puddles. I enjoyed the complexity of the

Reuben's flavors and hoped that someone would try to rob the bank. That would at least be a break in the monotony.

When the sandwich was gone, I put the lunch trash in the paper bag it all came in. That went on the floor and, like all the other accumulated surveillance trash, would get cleaned out when I got home. Boston was only an hour away, and it was just as easy to drive up and back each day. Maybe on the weekend I would spring for a hotel if it looked like any of the bankers were going on a wild coke binge or gambling spree.

It wasn't that Amesbury wasn't pretty, it just wasn't pretty interesting. I was sure that the good people of Amesbury liked it well enough. There wasn't anything wrong with the town, I was just sick of being bored, sitting in my car waiting for something to happen. I knew that was more about me being dissatisfied. I usually didn't take cases that I didn't have the first idea about. I was good at blackmail or missing persons cases. Embezzlement was a case for an accountant, not a PI like me. But Brock's stack of cash on my office desk had been a pretty convincing argument. I liked whiskey, and, Sir Leominster, the cat, liked his fancy cat food. I had been seeing Angela Estrella for a few months now, and she didn't mind being taken out on the town now and then. I was a PI with expenses. What was a fella to do?

We were close enough to New Hampshire that I started to notice the occasional snowflake mixed in with the rain. I pushed the sliding lever on the car's heater a little more into the red, hoping to take the chill out of the air. It didn't do much to help, but it made me feel a little better. Snow in April wasn't unheard of this far north. I just hoped it wasn't one of those freak storms that would trash my drive home to Boston.

The bank closed at three in the afternoon. I watched them lock up from a distance. I waited another ninety minutes until the employees all filed out and got into their cars. Lintz got into his silver marvel of German automotive engineering and turned out of the parking lot. I followed him, at a safe distance, out of town to a white clapboard colonial with black shutters on Friend Street. He pulled into the driveway, parking in front of the wooden garage that had been a homeowner's afterthought in the 1920s.

Lintz got out with his briefcase and wore a trench coat against the rain that was coming down lightly now. He started down the driveway, and I had a moment of panic thinking that he had made me. He didn't charge into the street to confront me but instead stopped at the mailbox by the end of the driveway to collect the contents. I exhaled slowly as he turned back up the driveway.

I would have had to consider giving my license back if I had done such a bad job of tailing him that he confronted me. I didn't want to give Brock back any of the crisp bills he had slid across the desk. I stayed on Friend Street long enough for the windows to light up in the Lintz home. I got out of my car and walked down the opposite side of the street for a block and then back. What I glimpsed inside seemed like a warm family scene out of a Norman Rockwell painting.

I got back in my car. Amesbury wasn't the type of place where I could go peeping in windows without a conscientious neighbor calling the local cops. I was pretty certain that Brock wouldn't be pleased. I sat in my car listening to the radio. The radio station out of New Hampshire was playing a slow, mournful song by The Band. After the streetlights came on, I decided to risk one more walk and a peek in the Lintz home. After my pass, it looked like the Lintz family was settling in for dinner. I decided it was time to head home. If Lintz was embezzling, he probably wasn't doing it during family dinner.

It was after rush hour, and the drive into the city wasn't bad. I bombed down I-95 and then took Route 1 into the city. A few months ago, I was driving to Marblehead a lot for a case. This wasn't as bad, and that had been a lot closer. Driving into the city, it occurred to me that I didn't know a lot about embezzlement or banking but maybe my friend Special Agent Brenda Watts might? If she didn't, I was sure she might know an agent who did. Plus, it would give me an excuse to see Brenda. I liked Brenda – she was tough and drank bourbon and generally had no use for my bullshit. Sadly, she had been smart enough to turn down all of my romantic overtures. Fortunately, Angela hadn't.

By the time I parked in the spot in front of my building, I was glad to be off the road. I was hungry, the Reuben a distant memory, and I was in fear that the level of whiskey my body required daily had dropped perilously low. I collected the mail from the box in the foyer and made my way up the stairs to my apartment, anticipating the plaintive yowling from the cat.

I let myself in and Sir Leominster walked over with studied nonchalance. He rubbed up against my ankles once and then proceeded to yowl at me. I wanted to believe that he genuinely missed me, but the reality was that he missed his dinner being on time. I ignored his angry meowing long enough to shut and lock the door behind me and hang my coat on the rack.

He followed me into the kitchen, tail standing straight up and shivering slightly as his meowing grew more insistent. He grew more plaintive as I got a can of his food and opened it. He didn't calm down until his nose was buried in the stinky stuff. I have had girlfriends that were less trouble than my cat.

I poured myself a whiskey and checked the machine for messages. My old friend Danny Sullivan wanted to see about getting a drink soon. We had been estranged for a few years, but recently he had helped me out with a case, and we had fallen into our old habits like a drunk going back to the bottle. There was another from Angela, wanting to see if I was going to be around this weekend.

The last was from my friend Chris. We had met at Fort Bragg going through the Q Course, trying to earn our green berets and later served in Vietnam together.

'Hey, man. I'm coming east and was hoping I could crash with you. I'll be in Boston in a few days. I'll call when I know the details.'

Chris had patched me up a year ago after I had been shot and fallen into Suisun Bay. He nursed me back to health and kept me away from a hospital, which would have meant the police. He'd been a Special Forces medic in Vietnam and knew what he was doing. He also ran with some outlaw biker types, and if he was coming East, he was either one jump ahead of the law or had run afoul of someone he didn't want to go up against. That was hard to picture, because Chris was big and tough and had spent his time after Vietnam as a mercenary in some African country that doesn't exist anymore. It took a lot to convince him to walk away from a fight.

I took a big sip of whiskey and called Angela. I didn't know if she was my girlfriend exactly, but we were involved, and lately I wasn't looking to dance with anyone else. She seemed pretty content to spend weekends and the occasional weeknight in my bed. I was pretty all right with it too. She didn't seem to have much interest in trying to civilize me or convince me to grow up. In my romantic world, that was something of a rarity.

'How'd it go today?' she asked after telling me about her day clerking for Judge Ambrose Messer, a former client of mine, which was how I met Angela Estrella.

'Not bad. I parked and watched a bank parking lot all day. Then followed one of the potential embezzlers home and watched him eat a perfectly normal dinner with his family.'

'And they pay you for this?'

'Hard to believe, isn't it?' I said with a laugh.

'Are you going back tomorrow?'

'Yeah, I have to try and figure out if one of them is living a little too high on the hog.'

'Why don't I come by tomorrow night. We can have a late dinner and get to bed early.'

'That sounds like something to look forward to.' We spent the next few minutes talking about exactly what we could look forward to and then said our goodbyes.

I went into the kitchen to scrounge something to eat. In the end, it was macaroni and cheese, the kind where the box is blue and the cheese is bright orange. I added a cup of frozen peas to the boiling water a minute before I poured the whole mess into the colander in the sink. By adding a green vegetable, I could almost convince myself that I was eating something healthy. Then it all went back in the pot with some butter, milk and orange powder from the packet. I stirred it all up into an orange, sticky mass of pasta with green polka dots. Old man Marconi would have been horrified, but I was a casualty in the ongoing war between hunger and laziness.

I took the pot, a fork and my glass of whiskey to the couch. I should have turned on the radio to the local jazz station and read a book, but instead I opted for the TV. The Movie Loft was playing *Kramer vs. Kramer*, and not having any desire to feel depressed, I changed the channel. Fortunately, TV 56 was playing *Mad Max*, so I watched the leather-clad hero chasing bikers around some dystopian version of Australia. It was a lot better than watching a movie about a contentious divorce.

When the movie ended, I went to bed with a book by Bernard Fall that I wish the generals had read before they started running amok in Vietnam. Fall had been there earlier with the French and knew what was what. I read until my eyelids grew heavy, set the alarm and turned off the light.

The next morning, I woke up earlier than usual. I wanted to go for a run before I would spend the day sitting in the Maverick. Surveillance was tough on my fitness, with all the sitting and eating. The Reuben probably didn't help. I did some push-ups and sit-ups with Sir Leominster watching me. He probably didn't know what to make of my doing all the activities that had nothing to do with feeding him.

Outside, it was cool but not cold, and the rain had stopped recently enough that there weren't large puddles everywhere. I headed out, working my way to Commonwealth Avenue and down to Massachusetts Avenue. It was early enough that traffic was light, and I didn't have to worry about getting splashed by passing cars or run over by anxious commuters. I followed Massachusetts Avenue on to the Harvard Bridge, over the Charles River and into Cambridge. I am partial to Cambridge – it is home to MIT and Harvard, it has some good bookstores and my favorite German restaurant, the Asa Wurst Haus.

I ran along the path next to Memorial Drive and crossed back into Boston over the more affordable but less prestigious Boston University Bridge. I made my way back to my apartment, feeling the way you do after a good run: stretched out, loose, warm and happy to be done.

In the kitchen, I made a pot of coffee to go in the thermos, threw a couple of apples in a paper bag, and, after an unexciting breakfast of yogurt, took a shower. By seven, I was sitting in my car driving north with my .38 snubnose revolver holstered on my hip, a folding lock-blade Buck knife in my right pocket and a speedloader of hollow point bullets in my left. I never left the house without those three things. Over the last few years, it seemed like someone or another was always trying to take a shot at me.

I made it to Amesbury a little before eight and parked outside of Mark Lintz's house. I sipped coffee from the thermos cup and watched the front of the Lintz house from a few houses back, on the opposite side of the street. Al Green was on the radio station, singing a song suggesting something about relationship status. A school bus made its way down the street, and further along, there was a gaggle of elementary school kids waiting to be picked up. The bus stopped, and after a minute or two, moved on. The kids were no longer on the sidewalk like some low-rent magic trick.

A few minutes later, a second school bus came. This one was stubbier and stopped either in front of the Lintz house or the neighbor's. A pretty woman in blue jeans and a flannel shirt walked a smallish kid, maybe a kindergartner, around the front of the bus and helped him or her laboriously climb the steps. The bus moved on, and the traffic backed up behind it began to move too. At twenty-five past eight by the Seiko diver's watch on my wrist, Lintz's silver Mercedes coupe edged out of the driveway and down the street.

I followed him at a distance to the bank and took up my spot across the street. I parked as he was at the front door and the guard was unlocking it to let him in. The guard seemed to be older, probably a retired cop. He had a uniform on that I assumed was made of polyester and a black leather gun belt with a revolver holstered on his hip. I didn't think Amesbury was the wild west, but apparently the Merrimack Community Bank felt the need for an armed guard. Maybe there was more to this town than met the eye.

I watched the bank and sipped coffee. I listened to Elvis Costello on the radio and yawned occasionally. The sun was out today, and I sat low in the car with my sunglasses on, trying not to look like a guy watching a bank. That tends to get police attention. I had called the local police department and let them know that I was here working on a divorce case. It wasn't the truth, but I wasn't obligated to tell them that. My letting the local cops know I was here wouldn't prevent some local nosy neighbor from calling the police, but it would at least keep me from being hassled.

After about an hour, I couldn't take it anymore and had to stretch my legs. I went to the convenience store on the corner. I bought a pack of Lucky Strikes and a copy of the Boston Globe. If Lintz went anywhere, I was pretty sure there was nothing so absorbing in the news that I would miss him. Customers came and went from the bank, and I caught up on the news of the day.

At noon, Karen Marti came out and got into her car. It was a three-year-old Chevy Chevette, black with a red interior. It looked sporty, but I wasn't worried about losing her in Amesbury.

I followed her at a distance to a local pizza place. She went in and a few minutes later came out with two large boxes and a brown paper shopping bag. Soda? Were they having a pizza party at the bank? I might have reached a new low in my investigative career by contemplating the lunch habits of bank employees. Picking up the pizza, even if she paid for it herself, was hardly an indicator of living beyond her means.

Watching Karen Marti pick up lunch was the most exciting thing that happened for the rest of the day. Lintz came out after the bank closed, and I tailed him home. He went inside his well-lit house to what, from a distance through the windows, seemed like a loving family. I had been working on this case for almost a week now, and it was like watching an assembly line go by.

If I thought the weekend would bring any more excitement, I was wrong. Mark Lintz, the bank manager, seemed to spend his weekend doing yard work or chores. He kicked a soccer ball with his young son. The boy was small and ran clumsily but happily after the ball. Saturday night, the Lintz family mixed it up by having pizza from the same pizzeria Karen Marti had bought lunch. By the end of the weekend, I was convinced that the most egregious thing that Mark Lintz was guilty of was being a wholesome family man.

It took me another week and a lot of Brock's money to learn that his secretary, Karen Marti, played Bingo and visited a local nursing home almost daily to spend time with her elderly mother. Frank Cosgrove, the assistant manager, was the closest one to having expensive tastes. He had a girlfriend who he went to dinner or the movies with when they went on dates. Dinner was usually at a Dairy Queen or the local pub. Nothing crazy.

By the end of two weeks, I'd had enough. I wrote a report that basically said that they were all seemingly living normal lives, well within their means. If any of them were embezzling money from the Merrimack Community Bank, there were no external signs of it. I put it in an envelope along with a bill for the time that wasn't covered by the advance Brock had given me. I found myself whistling as I put it in the mailbox. Some jobs are more work than others.

I called Brock as a courtesy to let him know that I would stop work on the case.

'You can't,' he said after I told him.

'Mr Brock, I spent two weeks watching the three of them. There is nothing suspicious about their lifestyles that I can see.'

'There has to be. One of them has to be embezzling the money.'

'They might be, but I can't find any external sign of it. I think you need to get a forensic accountant, someone who is better suited to this line of inquiry.'

'Is it the money, Roark? I can pay you more.'

'No.' I laughed. 'I feel bad about taking your money and not delivering results. I just don't see me being able to get them for you.'

I didn't bother mentioning that I was bored to death with the case and couldn't wait to move on. No sense adding insult to the injury of no results.

Eventually, Brock stopped trying to convince me. He seemed really worried about his job, and I got the feeling that he at least wanted to show his board of directors that he had done everything possible to find the embezzler.

When we hung up, I was in such a good mood that I called Angela Estrella.

'Where do you stand on martinis and watching a movie on my couch or yours?'

'Tonight?'

'Yes.'

'I feel very good about the martinis, but something tells me if this is like every other time I come over that we won't watch much of the movie.'

'That's a distinct possibility.'

TWO

April gave way to May as it usually does, rain and chilly weather giving way to sun and budding plants. Leaves began to poke out of the trees on Commonwealth Avenue, and the flowers in the Public Garden hinted at the riot of colors yet to come. On TV and in the bars and homes in the Greater Boston area, there was excited talk of the Red Sox. The true religion of Boston is baseball, and Opening Day is like Easter for Red Sox fans. It was a glimmer of hope after having our collective spirits so badly dashed by the New England Patriots losing to the Chicago Bears in the Super Bowl.

I was sitting in my office with my feet up on my desk, reading the Boston Globe, enjoying a pipe and an espresso. In the past few weeks, I had wrapped up not one but two divorce cases and an insurance fraud case. I was putting off writing the report about the guy who claimed to have been hit by a moving van while crossing Massachusetts Avenue. He was claiming severe neck and back injury, but I managed to get photos of him chopping wood at a cabin in the Berkshires. He took his neck brace off when splitting cord wood.

I sipped my espresso and then puffed on the pipe, filling the office with the rich smell of a blend of Virginia and Latakia from Peretti's. L.J. Peretti had been supplying the good people of Boston with their tobacco needs since 1870. Like the Union Oyster House and Jake Wirth's, it was a Boston institution. I alternated between sipping my tiny, bitter coffee and puffing on the pipe. The office window was open to let some of the smoke out and the sounds of traffic in.

I hadn't thought much about Amesbury or about the Merrimack Community Bank, but it was right there on page three. Yesterday morning the bank was robbed. Two men had gone in, cold-cocked the guard and, like proper villains, threatened to shoot the place up. Frank Cosgrove, the assistant manager, stood up from his desk for some reason and was rewarded for his bravery with a bullet between his eyes. He was probably dead before he hit the ground. The robbers fled south, presumably toward Boston, in a late model sedan. There was no sign of them anywhere.

I sat back in my chair wondering about the funny way the universe works. I had been watching the bank and Cosgrove, among others, only a few weeks ago. I was so bored during my time there I would have welcomed a robbery just to shake things up. Now one had happened and a nice guy, by all accounts, was dead. I thought about his girlfriend and their dinner-and-movie dates. It left me feeling a little hollow and then angry. Cosgrove didn't seem like the type who deserved to get killed. Not like that. He should have married his girl, started a family and lived to a ripe old age.

It was a hell of a coincidence, though, the bank getting robbed and Cosgrove murdered shortly after I had been hired to investigate embezzlement there. Except they were two different types of crimes. Why rob a bank if you can steal the money from the inside, cleanly, with no violence? That and Brock said that two million dollars was missing as a result of the embezzlement. A robber might get five or ten thousand from the cash drawers, maybe twenty or thirty thousand from a bigger bank. It hardly seemed worth the effort or the heat it would bring.

I picked up the phone and dialed Special Agent Brenda Watts's number. I listened to it ring and pictured her sitting at her desk working on some important government investigation.

She picked up on the third ring, and after we got through our greetings, she said, 'What do you want, Andy?'

'Who says I want anything?'

'Because you don't call unless you do.'

'That's not true, sometimes I call to make a pass at you.'

'That is technically wanting something.'

'True,' I agreed. Brenda had honey-colored hair which she wore in a simple ponytail and pretty eyes that flashed whenever she was angry with me, which was most of the time.

'What do you want?' she repeated.

'I was hoping to take you to lunch and pick your brain?' I

said. Brenda had a soft spot for me, but it wasn't enough for her to have taken me up on any of my earlier romantic efforts.

'About what?'

'Banks.'

'Banks?' she asked.

'Yes, banks.'

'What specifically?'

'Stealing from them.'

'As in robbery or embezzlement?'

'Yes,' I said definitively. I wasn't exactly sure how much I wanted to tell Brenda and figured having a little time to chew it over might not be a bad idea.

'OK. What did you have in mind?'

'Fancy a trip to Chinatown?'

'I'm surprised you didn't suggest Durgin Park or some other old Boston institution.'

'No point trying to have a conversation in Durgin Park at lunch. Besides, the place I am thinking of is an old Boston institution, just in Chinatown.'

'Sure, where?'

'Ee Yong Goey's. It's not far from the Combat Zone.' The Combat Zone was Boston's ever-shrinking patch of sin. When Scollay Square was razed to build the architectural atrocity known as Government Center, it displaced a lot of small businesses. Those businesses happened to be porno theaters, dirty bookstores, burlesque joints and all the ancillary businesses associated with them, like drugs and prostitution. Nothing in Chinatown was actually far from the Combat Zone, which was part of the problem that the Chinatown Business Owners Association had.

'Give me the address.'

I did as I was told, and we agreed to meet at one p.m. and then rang off.

I spent the next few hours typing up my report on the insurance fraud matter. When it was done, I went downstairs to the video rental place, which for reasons I would never understand had a coin-operated Xerox machine. I guess the owner was trying to diversify. When I had fed enough coins into the machine and got my copies, I went back upstairs. The report and the photos I had taken all went into a manila envelope along with my bill. I would stop and mail it along the way to lunch.

I walked through the narrow and winding streets from my office, which isn't too far from the courts and the financial district. The weather was nice, and walking was easier than finding parking in this town. After a brief stop at the post office, I slipped into Chinatown on a street that tourists would have avoided like the plague. It always felt a little like crossing into East Germany from the West.

Chinatown was still in Boston, still in America, but for a few short square blocks it might as well have been a different country. Every now and then, my dad and I would go to see the Red Sox at Fenway. If we didn't feast on ballpark franks, and soda for me, beer for him, he would suggest a hike to Chinatown. When I was a kid, this was only for the early games.

Chinatown was my first hint outside of the library that there was a world outside of South Boston. The first thing that struck me about Chinatown was the smell. It just smelled different, the mix of fish, rotting vegetables, exotic spices, and fried food that overwhelmed the other smells, making me instantly hungry. The next thing that I noticed was the writing on the signs on the buildings. Some were in English with what I would later learn was either Mandarin or Cantonese letters below, but as a kid I just thought of as Chinese. On others, the English was the minority alphabet, and on a few, the phone number on the sign was only written in English.

Many of the plate glass windows had roast chickens or ducks. Some had whole roasted piglets and others still had strips of pork, red on the outside, bright pink on the inside blending to a grayish brown. Being raised in an Irish Catholic neighborhood, my understanding of pork was that it was not properly cooked unless it was a uniform, defeated gray color. At some point it occurred to me that most of the people around us didn't look like we did and weren't speaking English. It was a tiny hint of what Vietnam would be like when I was out on the local economy.

I loved it. I loved how exotic it was and yet how close. The place moved with a bustle, an energy that made my neighborhood feel like it was already in the funeral parlor. Chinatown was like traveling without a passport or a lot of money. The only place that offered as much for so little was the library, but there were no eggrolls there.

Ee Yong Goey's wasn't much to look at from the outside. Plain brick façade, plate glass windows that were so cluttered by plants they blocked daylight from getting in, and three steps up. Above the door was a flat sign with a red background and yellow writing in English made to look like Mandarin spelling out the name of the joint. The phone number below it, an afterthought in plain black script.

Inside, there was the usual smattering of tables with the Formica tops that were supposed to look like wood. The red paper placemats had water glasses and tea cups sitting rim down, paper napkins, paper-sleeved chopsticks and metal flatware on each table. Black metal chairs with red vinyl seats were like clubs on a playing card. The carpet had been new once, but that might have been when John Kennedy was a presidential hopeful. Here and there were a few ficus trees to liven the place up.

A waiter hustled over and bowed. It was a little much, but maybe he mistook me for a tourist. I held up two fingers in a V for victory symbol and he nodded. I followed him to a table and sat down with an eye on the door. For once I was early and I had beaten Watts to lunch.

He came back with two menus under his arm and a small metal pitcher in his hand. He turned over two of the glasses and poured ice water into them. It was Boston's finest tap water.

I made eye contact with him before he moved away. 'Tea, please.'

He nodded and, in a minute, came back with a small metal pot.

I turned over the small teacup – really a glorified white, ceramic shot glass – with a red ring around it and poured some tea into it. Watts walked through the door and stopped briefly, scanning the two-thirds empty dining room. Her eyes settled on me, and she walked over.

'Well, Andy, you do know how to impress a girl,' she said, nose wrinkled as she looked around.

'The place is modest, but the food is out of this world.' I wasn't exactly sure where Watts was from, but I had the feeling it was a part of the country where pizza is considered 'ethnic' cuisine.

'Modest or seedy?'

'No one comes to Chinatown for the décor.'

'Well, let's hope the food is as good as you say it is.'

'Watts, this place is a diamond in the rough. You'll love it.'

'Ha, let's hope your judgment in restaurants is better than your judgment in all other things.'

'Are you saying I have bad judgment?'

'You? Only in just about everything you do.'

'See, it's not all bad.' I smiled my second-most charming smile at her. Using my most charming smile didn't seem right while I was spending time with Angela.

'Only you would see it that way.'

The waiter came and we ordered chicken lo mein, beef with broccoli and eggrolls. There were far more complicated dishes on the menu, but neither of us was willing to invest the time in peking duck or moo shu pork. There was nothing wrong with them, but they weren't chat-about-crime-over-lunch types of dishes.

We sipped our tea out of the hot ceramic shot glasses, and finally Watts asked, 'So, what did you want to know about crime related to banks?'

'I was wondering what you could tell me about embezzling from banks?'

'Why, are you working on a case?'

'I was three weeks ago, but it's over.'

'Someone hired *you* to investigate embezzlement?' She snorted, she actually snorted at the thought.

'Hey! Is that so surprising?'

'Well, Jesus, Andy . . . in the few short years I've known you, you haven't actually impressed me as someone who is subtle or investigates nuanced crimes.'

'That's not fair.'

'And since I've known you, you've shot or beat up half of Boston.'

'That's not true. I beat up some guys in Fairhaven that time.' Fairhaven was a tough little town butted up against the dying textile city of Fall River, Massachusetts.

'And shot a couple of people in Vermont,' she added quietly. There were others but she was too polite to get into specifics.

'It's a crime, how hard can it be?' I asked.

'You aren't exactly a forensic accountant. There's a reason why the Bureau hires a lot of lawyers and accountants. Crimes like embezzlement require something more than your state-of-the-art nineteen-thirties gumshoe approach.' She actually had a point, as insulting as it was.

'I was hired to follow three bank employees and see if they were living beyond their means.'

'Well, that's a little more your speed.' She at least smiled when she said it. Watts had a great smile; it went with her great cheekbones, which highlighted her great eyes. It made the lack of confidence in my investigative skills go down a little easier.

'Yeah, thanks.'

'Was any of them an embezzler?'

'Not that I could see. It was the most godawful boring two weeks of my life. If any of them were up to anything, they didn't show it.'

'Nothing?'

'No, between the three of them, a night of living it up was either pizza for family dinner, going out to dinner and a movie, or the weekly Bingo game at church.'

'You had to watch them for two weeks to come up with that?'

The food came and the waiter put the platters between us and a bowl of rice for the beef with broccoli. We agreed to share the food, and Watts opted for a fork while I went for chopsticks. When we had both helped ourselves to the food and had a bite, the conversation started again.

'Here's the funny thing,' I said.

'What's that?'

'Yesterday, someone robbed that very bank. One of the three people I was watching got shot in the head.'

'Dead?'

'You know any other way that usually works out?'

'You were watching the bank that's almost in New Hampshire?'

'Yeah. Place was so boring that I hoped it would get robbed.'

'You think it's connected?'

'It's an awful coincidence, but I don't know how. The amount of money taken from the robbery wouldn't be enough to hide the money that was embezzled. Also, assuming it is connected, why kill the assistant branch manager?'

'Maybe he's involved and got shot to keep him quiet?' she suggested.

'That doesn't make sense. Why bother setting up a robbery and killing a guy? That brings a lot of heat. It brings the Feds into and the State Police. That seems like a shitty way to cover up a white-collar crime like embezzlement.'

'So, you think that the bank robbery is just a bank robbery then?'

'I don't know. What are the odds? Especially in a town like Amesbury which probably doesn't have a lot of crime to begin with, let alone a fatal one. Boston, Worcester, Providence, sure, but Amesbury?'

'And you are buying me this luxurious meal, which is a lot better than the look of the place would lead you to believe, so that I will get you the skinny on the bank robbery?'

'I would appreciate it,' I said.

'If I know you, you aren't going to let this go, are you.' It wasn't a question.

'I don't know. It's too soon to tell, but I want to know more about it.'

'There's no point in telling you to leave it alone, is there? You know, to leave it to us and the Staties.'

'Well, certainly not after I've spent a fortune on lunch.'

What I couldn't tell Watts was that I couldn't reconcile Cosgrove's murder with the young guy who I had watched for a few days, the guy who held the car door open for his girl or went on nice, all-American kind of dates. There had been a wholesomeness to all of it that I wasn't used to. Maybe that's why the whole thing was bothering me so much.

'Yeah, that's it. I'll just pretend you don't have that look,' she said.

'What look?'

'The same look you always get before you go off and do something stupid.'

'And piss you off in the process?'

'Yep, that look.' She smiled when she said it.

Watts's feelings for me were wholly platonic and ran the gamut from irked with to worried about me. It wasn't much emotional range, but at least she cared. She had been in my corner often enough despite my best efforts to annoy her.

'It's probably just a coincidence.'

'Probably,' she said, clearly not convinced.

We finished lunch and I left some bills on the table. Out in the street, May sunshine wasn't shining on Chinatown.

'I don't suppose you'll let me know if you come up with anything criminal going on?' she asked.

'Hey, I'm a duly licensed private investigator, obligated to report crimes if I come across them.'

'Yeah, but somehow your circa nineteen forties sensibilities get in the way sometimes. Plus, you have some very shady friends.'

'Well, that's true.'

'Which part?'

'All of it.'

What could I say, she was right.

I watched Watts walk to where she had parked her non-government issue Saab. It was red and nifty-looking. It seemed too early to go home, so I walked back to the office.

I kept going over my conversation with her in my head. Other than coincidence, there was nothing connecting Cosgrove's murder to my being hired. I had spent weeks watching all three of them, and none of them were living above their means. None of them had a secret life that I could see. The only option if one of them had been embezzling was that they were very disciplined. Saving the money, not touching a penny of it until one day they could get out of Amesbury and spend it on the high life. The problem was that I had no way of getting into any of their financial records. None of them struck me as the type to bury that much money in their backyards.

The spring weather made for a pleasant walk back to the office and, except for what I was thinking about, it was enjoyable. There were no messages on the machine. An espresso and pipe were just things that would help me clear my head.

I set up the espresso machine and then packed tobacco into the pipe while waiting for it to brew. I was able to light the pipe with a single match, and it was drawing nicely by the time the tiny cup was filled with the dark, bitter brew. I opened the office window, letting the smoke out and the street noises in. I decided to call Brock. I was sure he was up to his eyeballs in cops right now, but I was getting squirrelly.

I dug my address book out of the desk drawer. When I found Brock's number, I pulled the phone closer and dialed. I listened to his office number ring and ring. Finally, it went to an answering machine that stated that the bank was closed due to an emergency. That made sense, it wouldn't do to have the bank open the day after an employee was murdered in it. I hung up and, after consulting my address book, called Brock's home number.

This time he answered after a few rings. 'Hello.'

'Brock, it's Andy Roark. I saw the news in the Globe.'

'Oh. You don't think it's connected to why I hired you?'

'No. At least I don't think so. It seems very unlikely, but . . .'

'But what?'

'It's just a bit of a coincidence, happening so soon after.'

'Mr Roark, I was with the police going over this all day. I can't see how any of this would be connected. Banks get robbed all the time. That's why we have an armed guard.'

'What happened to him?'

'Two men came in, and before Chet could do anything, they hit him over the head. Knocked him out cold. Chet isn't a spring chicken, and I am not surprised they got the better of him. He's been retired from the local police department for almost twenty years now.'

'I see.' I knew plenty of guys who had traded a cop's uniform for the pale imitation of a security guard's. The pay usually wasn't great, but it was a nice way to augment a pension.

'They were waving their guns around. Yelling at the tellers to empty the drawers and that if anyone tripped the alarm, they'd start shooting.'

'How did Cosgrove get in the mix?'

'He stood up, started to say something. I think he was trying to calm them down. One of them just shot him. No warning. No nothing.'

'Didn't say anything at all?'

'No. He just fired once and Frank was dead. Just like that.' Brock's voice sounded a little detached, and I started to wonder if he had a drink or three when he got home from the cops. I couldn't blame him. Seeing someone you know and work with every day cut down in front of you was tough.

'That's tough. How's everyone taking it?'

'Taking it? How do you think we're taking it?' he snapped.

'Easy, Brock.'

'Sorry, it's just upsetting seeing someone shot in front of you. I'm just a banker, for Christ's sake, I've never seen anyone killed before.'

'It's hard to take in. I get that. I was just wondering if there was anyone in the bank who didn't act shocked?'

'Not that I can think of. I mean, it happened so fast.'

'What about afterwards?'

'After, I think we were all in shock, and then the police were there in no time.'

'OK.'

'Why are you asking? I thought you had closed the investigation?'

'Well, I didn't see any indication that anyone was living above their means, which was what you hired me to do.'

'I hired you to find an embezzler.'

'You don't think this recent string of crimes, like your bank getting robbed, is a little odd. You know, timing-wise?'

'I don't know, Mr Roark. Like I said, banks get robbed all the time. All that cash attracts a lot of felons with guns. Some of them think that a smaller branch in a smaller town is an easier target. Small town cops and not a lot of security, that type of thing.'

'They do, but . . .'

'Look, Mr Roark, I hired you to find an embezzler and you came up short. If you think I'm going to pay to keep looking into it when you left after a couple of weeks because it was boring, you're mistaken.'

'Listen, Brock, you hired me to—'

'I know what I hired you to do, and you didn't do a good job of it. Now one of my employees is dead and you're looking for more money.'

'Brock . . .'

'Good day, sir,' he said and he hung up.

I sat in my chair with the handset in my hand, the dial tone unpleasant and a bit harsh, not unlike how Brock had been. I put the handset in the cradle and couldn't decide if I wanted another espresso. It didn't seem particularly appealing, or maybe my mood had just gone sour. I decided against more coffee.

'He actually said, "Good day, sir,"' I said to the empty office in mild disbelief. I pulled one of the many yellow legal pads I have on my desk over to me. I took out a felt-tip pen and started writing down the names of everyone involved in the Amesbury Community Bank, starting with Brock, the three names he put forward for being potential embezzlers, and lastly, Chet, the unfortunate security guard.

The smoke from the pipe filled the office, and I tapped my blue felt-tip pen against my desk. Then I added 'Bank Robber 1' and 'Bank Robber 2' to the sheet. I decided since one of them had to be it to add, 'shooter' next to 'Bank Robber 1.' I thought about it some more and added, 'Getaway Driver?' to the page. If repeated viewings of Charley Varrick had taught me anything, it was that any bank robbery team required a getaway driver.

I tapped my pen and doodled on the pad trying to think of more relevant things to add to the legal pad. It was frustrating to have so little to show for a couple weeks of surveillance work. Or maybe I was annoyed with myself. Brock wasn't wrong, I had been bored with the case and I wasn't sure that I could say that I did the best job on it. That had nothing to do with Cosgrove's murder, but it still irked me.

What if I had still been on the case? Would I have realized a robbery was going down? Rushed over to stop it with my .38 or called the cops? Getting in a shootout in a strip mall in the afternoon didn't seem like the smartest idea. Too many people around to catch a stray bullet. It wasn't worth playing hero with those odds.

I stood up and pushed the legal pad away from the desk. I tapped my pipe bowl down against the bottom of the ashtray, knocking out the ash and a small wad of unburnt but useless tobacco. There wasn't much point in staying at the office anymore. I grabbed my jacket off the hook on the coat tree, let myself out of the office and locked the door behind me.

It was late afternoon and nearing the point when a certain type of person slips out of the office early to go to a bar for the first much needed drink of the day. I wanted to join them, and my old friend Danny Sullivan would be sure to be in a bar not far from my office, but I was meeting Angela for dinner at my place. Needless to say, that was a much cheerier prospect than a drink or five with Danny.

Danny was a defense attorney. A good one and, like all the good ones, expensive. His clients tended to be mafia types who didn't like the idea of going to federal prison, or any prison for that matter. I couldn't blame them for that. Danny had once sent a case my way and then was indiscreet about it, which almost got me killed. I was angry about that, and in the Grille at the Ritz Carlton, I had told him I would kill him if he crossed my path again. It was the anger talking.

The walk home helped ease some of the annoyance I was feeling. I had half-assed the case because it bored me. But that didn't mean that I was wrong in not finding signs that Cosgrove, Marti or Lintz were spending lavishly. The case was a dog that didn't hunt. Maybe I had missed something with Cosgrove? That's what was nagging me.

I kept going over it in my head. If he had been embezzling, robbing the bank and murdering him just seemed like too much effort. There were a lot easier ways to kill someone that would draw a lot less attention from the law. If anything, now that the Feds and the State Police were involved, it might lead to the embezzlement being uncovered that much sooner.

I let myself into the apartment and was greeted by Sir Leominster's plaintive wails. It didn't matter how long I had been out, the minute I walked through the door he demanded food. Attention was a secondary concern, but he was very pragmatic and associated food with love. I didn't bother petting him until after he had eaten. At least he was up front about it.

After I hung up my jacket, checked the machine for messages and couldn't bear his wailing anymore, I went to the kitchen. He followed me at a trot, increasing the frequency of his wailing in anticipation of my opening a can of his foul-smelling cat food. He stomped back and forth while I twisted the handle on the can opener and almost had a stroke while I dumped the whole fishy-smelling mess into his dish. He finally stopped wailing at me when I put the dish down on the floor and he buried his snout in it. He ate like he hadn't eaten since winter.

Once that cat was appeased, I went to wash my face and make myself presentable for a dinner with Angela. We'd been seeing each other since the new year and were at the point where we were comfortable around each other but not too comfortable. No one was leaving a toothbrush in anyone else's apartment yet, but neither of us was seeing anyone else either.

I wasn't rushing anything. My last few relationships hadn't worked out well and a couple had almost been the death of me. Most of them ended with me in an empty apartment with a surly cat and a drink in my hand. At least with Angela, things seemed to be going well.

The intercom buzzed at six thirty, and after hearing the tinny version of Angela's voice say, 'It's me,' I buzzed her in, and shortly after, there was a knock on my door. I opened the door and Angela stepped in. She put her arms around my neck, and after a longish kiss, she stepped back and said, 'Hello, Roark.'

'Nice to see you.' It was. She had changed from her usual clothes for work as clerk in District Court into clingy blue jeans, a cream-colored silk blouse and light sweater over it. Even with the low heels she was wearing, she had to stand on her tiptoes to kiss me.

'You too. I have had a day. I'm hungry and in need of a drink. Provide me both and you will be handsomely rewarded.'

'I was pretty sure that was the plan?'

'What gave me away?'

'Besides the passionate greeting, the overnight bag was what we call in the trade, a clue.' I didn't bother to point out the expertly applied make-up or the perfume that smelled mildly intoxicating. No point in being a showoff.

'Very observant of you.'

'I am a trained detective.'

'True. How about you tell me all about that after you get me a drink.'

'Martini or something else?' I asked, confident what the answer would be.

'Martini.'

She went to drop her overnight bag in the bedroom while I went to fix her drink. We had already established on previous visits that she preferred her drink being made over my taking her bag. I think both were equally hospitable. By the time she joined me in the kitchen, I was shaking the martini shaker for all it was worth until the outside of it was covered in frost and my hands felt like I was outside in Vermont during winter.

'How was your day?' I asked while pouring the contents of the shaker into two martini glasses.

'Ugh, I had to listen to lawyers argue back and forth about nonsense. Some days I think they get paid by the argument. How was yours?'

'Do you remember that surveillance job I had up in Amesbury a few weeks back?'

'Yes, the really boring one.'

'That's the one. Well, today I found out the bank was robbed yesterday, and one of the people I was looking at was killed in the robbery.' I handed her a martini.

'What?'

'Shot in the robbery. Cheers.' We clinked glasses, which I managed to do without spilling more than a few drops of mine. There wasn't much sense in wasting valuable space in the glass with air.

'Cheers. Just like that?'

'Yeah, just like that. Dead.'

'Do you think it's related?'

'Probably not, but something about it bothers me.'

'What?' She took a sip which was a pleasure to watch, something about the delicate way she held the glass, and her lips just grazed the surface of the drink. Martini glasses made me feel afraid that I would snap the delicate stem in my hand.

'I don't know. Timing is odd. Plus, Amesbury doesn't strike me as a hotbed of crime.'

'Banks get robbed all the time.'

'True. I also called Brock, my old client.'

'How'd that go?'

'Not well. He accused me of half-assing the case initially and sucking around for more money now.'

'Ouch.'

'I know. But you know, he is only half wrong. I was bored with the surveillance and couldn't wait for it to be done. Maybe I should have dug into it more.'

'You were hired to watch them and see if anyone was living larger than they could afford.'

'Yep.'

'And did you see any sign of it?'

'No.'

'Did you write a report?'

'Yes.'

'So, in short you did your job?'

'Yes.'

'OK, stop worrying about it and tell me about dinner.'

'How does steak sound?'

'It sounds good,' she said with enthusiasm.

'Baked potato and salad to go with.'

'Perfect.'

'How is the Judge doing?' Angela clerked for the Honorable Ambrose Messer, who had been my client on a thorny blackmail case a few months before.

'He's doing OK. He wasn't himself after the case wrapped up. I think he felt bad about how it turned out.'

'I can see that.'

'The trial is going and that is keeping him busy.'

I checked the two potatoes that I had put in the oven forty-five minutes earlier. Then I took two petite filet mignons out of the refrigerator and liberally sprinkled both sides of them with salt and pepper. I put those aside for a minute while I put a pan on the stove to heat up.

When the pan was hot, I dropped in a big pat of butter, and when it foamed, the steaks went in. I listened to Angela and the sounds of the steaks sizzling. I flipped them after three minutes, by which time the kitchen was smoky and the smoke detector was making a racket. When the steaks had a nice crust on each side, I put the pan in the oven with the potatoes.

I pulled the pan out of the oven and took the steaks out, letting them rest on a plate. Resting the steaks is the key. I took the potatoes out of the oven and put one on each of two plates. After the steaks had rested enough, I put one on each plate. Then I put some butter in the pan, added the juices from the steaks and plenty of ground black pepper. The result was a decent black pepper sauce that went over our steaks.

'Do you want to stick with martinis, or do you want to switch to red wine?'

'Martinis,' she said definitively.

We ate slowly, enjoying the meal and each other's company.

Later, lying in bed, Angela said, 'You're going up there, aren't you?'

'That obvious?'

'With the exception of recent activities, you've been a little distracted.'

'Distracted?'

'When we were on the couch, allegedly watching TV.'

'Well, maybe the TV part, not the rest of it.'

'No, of course not. But instead of watching one of your movies on the Movie Loft, you were OK with watching *Falcon Crest.*'

'Well, I was just being a good host. I knew you didn't want to sit through *The Conversation.*' I love Gene Hackman's quiet, meditative essay on paranoia and surveillance. I loved that it proved the point that just because you're paranoid doesn't mean you're wrong.

'You hardly said five words to me until we came in here.'

'Oh, that bad. I'm sorry.'

'It's OK. You were paying attention when you should have been.'

'It would have been hard not to.' It wasn't just that Angela was pretty. There was something about her I noticed when she first walked into Jakie Wirth's last December with her boss, the judge, to hire me.

'Good. My feelings would have been hurt.'

'Would never happen. Plus, if I am going to be distracted, during *Falcon Crest* is the perfect time to do it.'

'Good point.' It was fair to say that I was about as interested in the Ewing clan as she was in watching Gene Hackman play his saxophone in his destroyed apartment. Thankfully before *Dallas* came on, we met in a mutually satisfactory middle ground. Bed.

THREE

The next day was Saturday. We spent a lazy morning in bed and then a leisurely breakfast with the paper. The afternoon was spent checking out the shops on Newbury Street. I resisted the urge to drag Angela over to the Brattle Book Shop. If she thought I had been distracted thinking about the goings-on in Amesbury, then she would have been shocked by how distracted I can get in a good bookstore. That night we went out to a new restaurant that Angela wanted to try, and Sunday at noon we kissed goodbye on my landing as she headed home to get ready for the workweek ahead.

I went back into my apartment which both felt lonelier and also more like itself again after she had gone. Outside it was raining, not the unrelenting rain of November but the steady drizzle of spring that helps wash the pollen off the cars. I sat on the couch, smoking a Lucky and thinking about what my plan of attack was going to be. I didn't have a client; I didn't have a case. I was just going to go up to Amesbury and watch people. Maybe poke around and ask some questions. It wasn't much of a plan, but more often than not, that was how I operated.

Monday morning found me parked up the street from the Lintz house. If I was expecting a change in the routine that had bored me so much a few weeks ago, I was to be disappointed. The kids were in front of the same houses. The same school buses came and went. Lintz pulled out of his driveway at the same time with the same consistency of a Swiss watch.

Tailing Lintz wasn't very challenging. He drove from his home to the bank and back again. There were no sudden turns, no doubling back, no indication that he was looking for a tail. It has been my experience that people doing criminal stuff tend to be suspicious people. Suspicious people drive like everyone behind them is a potential tail. Not Lintz. Nope, he drove like a man with no worries. He mostly obeyed the rules of the road and didn't seem overly cautious.

Lintz pulled into the bank's parking lot and into his spot. I drove by and noticed that Karen Marti's car was there too. Also conspicuously parked in front was an Amesbury police car. In case anyone in the Commonwealth didn't realize the bank had recently had some excitement.

It looked like the bank was going to be open. The police must have taken all the crime scene photos they needed, and Brock probably had the place cleaned up over the weekend. After all, it was highly unlikely that anyone was going to try and rob the joint just a few days after it had been robbed. Which made the police car parked in front seem all the more a waste, but I wasn't paying taxes in this town, so it wasn't any of my business.

Figuring the local police might be a touch more on guard than usual, especially about cars parked outside of banks for long periods of time, I decided it was a good idea to check in with them again. Better to be proactive than try to explain myself at gunpoint to a jumpy, small-town cop. It was just too easy to get shot these days.

The police station was a pleasant two-story building. It was on School Street in front of a traffic circle with a flagpole in the middle of it. It was the type of town that would have had a Veterans Day parade, and it was easy to picture it going right by the police station. I parked in the lot, which was flanked by the police station on one side and City Hall on the other.

It was a short walk to the main entrance of the station, and I was pleased to see there was a blue light above the door. It was a nice touch that a lot of the more modern steel and glass stations seem to lack. Inside, there was a counter, and behind that was heavy-set man in his fifties. His sandy-colored hair was closely cropped, and he looked up at me with watery blue eyes. He was wearing the requisite blue uniform and badge.

'Can I help you, sir?' The politeness was a bit different from what I was used to in Boston where my old neighbor Detective Sergeant Billy Devaney peppered every third word he said to me with an insult.

'Yes, I'm a private investigator on a case and I wanted to just check in.' I slid my license across the counter to him.

'From Boston?'

'Yes.'

'What brings you up here?'

'I am working a case that requires me to follow a couple of people who work at the Amesbury Community Bank.'

'Oh,' he said slowly.

'Yeah, I read about what happened last week and figured I'd better check in in case anyone got nervous seeing a strange car out front.'

'Hang on a second.' He stood up with my license still in hand. He had the thick build that most cops over forty had. It was a product of too many fast food meals and not enough sleep layered over a younger, fitter man's muscles. He was gone for a minute or two, and then a door by the side of the counter opened and he poked his head out.

'Come with me.'

'Sure.' I followed him through an office area, down a nonde- script corridor to an office that had a nameplate on the wall next to it that proclaimed, 'Paul Dixon, Chief of Police.' You would think in a department for a town this size everyone would know who he was. The cop knocked on the frame of the open door and a gruff voice inside told us to come in. We went in.

'This is the private eye from Boston, Chief.' The chief in question was sitting behind a green institutional metal desk. He looked to be in his early fifties. He was thickly built through the shoulders and neck with dark hair greying at the temples and cut just a little longer than most men his age wore it. The office smelled faintly of Vitalis and menthol cigarettes.

'Come in.' He stood up and I noticed that, while the cop from the desk had been carrying a plain Jane .38 special revolver, the chief seemed to favor a larger .357 Magnum with a stainless-steel finish.

'Paul Dixon,' he said, sticking his hand out across the desk.

'Andy Roark,' I said as we shook hands. It was the usual thing where he tried to crush my hand, and I just ignored it. After a few seconds, he let my hand go.

'Please sit down.'

'Thanks.'

'What brings you to my town, Roark?'

'Business.'

'What type of business?'

'I'm here to conduct surveillance on two employees of the Amesbury Community Bank.'

'What for?'

'It's a delicate matter, Chief,' I said in my best, 'we're both men of the world' tone.

'Divorce?'

'Something like that.'

'Who are they?'

'Again, I can't say. This is a small town.'

'Not that small. Who are you working for?'

'Chief, again, I can't say.'

'Can't or won't?' At least he stuck to the script, which tended to make things easier.

'Same thing. I was hired in part because my client wanted things done discreetly.' Which had been true back in April when Brock had actually hired me.

'If you don't tell me what I want to know, you won't be doing anything in this town unless it's leaving it.'

'Chief, all I can tell you is that I was hired to watch a man and a woman and see if they're doing anything.' It was the biggest, vaguest, most suggestive hint I could stick under his nose.

'Oh . . . well, how do I know this isn't related to the bank robbery?' I was starting to wonder if the mayor was his brother or something.

'Well, there wouldn't be much use in surveilling a bank that's already been robbed. Also, if I was up to no good, coming into the station to let you know I'm here seems like a pretty bad idea.'

'Or maybe you're trying to convince me you're on the level.'

'Chief, you can call Boston PD. Detective Captain Johnson or Detective Sergeant Billy Devaney will vouch for me.'

He looked at me the way cops look at anyone who isn't their mother or their kid, hard and suspicious, and then he flicked my license across the desk at me. It skittered across and landed in my lap.

'OK, Roark. Just watch your step while you're in my town. This is a nice little town, and we don't need any trouble . . . not any more trouble. If you're up to any funny business, I throw you in jail so fast your head will spin. If that isn't enough, I'll see that your license gets yanked. Got it?'

'Yes sir. You won't have any trouble from me, Chief.' I was sincere. I wasn't looking to cause any trouble. I wasn't a big fan of trouble, but then again, trouble seems to find me whether I am looking for it or not. I didn't feel the need to share that tidbit with the chief.

'All right, Roark, see yourself out. Tell the front desk what you're driving and the plate.' He didn't bother to get up or shake my hand again. I followed his advice, pausing only to slip my PI license back in my wallet. I stopped at the front desk and told the bored looking cop the details about my slightly battered Ford Maverick. He wrote them down and then I stepped out into the pleasant May morning. There are few places finer than New England in May or June, but I am not exactly objective about it.

Back in the Maverick, I started it and listened to the healthy rumble coming from under the hood. The radio came on to The Guess Who, who sang to me about the trials of being a bus rider. The drive from the police station to the bank wasn't a long one, and I found a parking spot that allowed me a good view of the parking lot.

I poured myself a cup of coffee from my thermos and settled in to wait. If I had been expecting anything to have changed in the last month, I would have been disappointed. Fortunately, I had a good idea of what to expect. The only real changes were the police car out front and seemingly fewer customers using the bank. Also, it wasn't raining and I was able to have my window open, which was a nice change.

I spent the day doing the crossword puzzle in the Globe, drinking coffee, and listening to the radio. I tried to ration my cigarettes by playing little games like only having one Lucky Strike every half an hour. At lunch time, no one left the bank to head home or go get pizza for everyone. It was quiet, and when I couldn't stand it any longer, I went to the deli I had frequented before to get a sandwich.

When the bank closed for the day and everyone headed home, I followed Lintz back to the homestead. I sat up the street from his house, watching as the afternoon slid into early evening. The bugs started to come out and I decided I had enough. It's not like I was getting paid to put up with the bugs. Even in Vietnam, I had gotten paid to deal with it. Tomorrow, I decided, I would mix it up and follow Karen Marti.

The next morning, I was parked outside Karen Marti's. She lived in a brick row house that at the beginning of the century had housed workers for one of the many local mills. Somewhere along the line, after the mills had closed, someone had the bright idea of turning them into condominiums. I was struck by how much the mill houses reminded me of post housing on Army bases like Fort Devens, brick and uniform and with no individuality expressed nor welcome.

Marti's front door opened, and she came outside dressed for work in black slacks and a dark green blouse, with a cream jacket over it. She got in her car and started it up. If Lintz was a boring driver to follow, Marti wasn't. Her driving style seemed to involve mashing down on the gas or brakes as necessary. She drove fast but well, and I had to pay a little more attention to the road tailing her compared to Lintz. I was starting to think that there was no way Lintz could do anything as exciting as embezzle from the Merrimack Community Bank. I wondered, idly, if his lunch was peanut butter and jelly with the crusts cut off.

I spent the day as I had spent so many other days, watching the bank. Bored. Bored and hungry, doing the crossword puzzle in the Globe and rationing my cigarettes just to have something to do. The bank closed at three thirty p.m., and an hour later Karen Marti came out. She got into her black Chevette, and I followed her back to her brick row house.

I parked a few doors down so that I could see her front door and parked car. I sat listening to the engine tick slowly in the mild air as late afternoon started to slide into evening. Dylan strummed his guitar and sang softly about buckets of rain on the radio. The song complimented the bugs that were flying around doing their aerial mating ritual that they do every spring. I lit a cigarette to encourage the bugs to bug off and smoked it with a hand cupped around the ember. It was a trick that every soldier learned.

I watched the lights in her condo go on with a pleasant glow. I considered wrapping it up when the front door opened and Marti came out. She was moving like she had someplace to be five minutes ago. She wore tight jeans and the same blouse. Her low work heels had been replaced with ones that were considerably higher, and in the light from her condo, I could see she had put on lipstick.

She started her car and backed out of her spot with a mild screeching of tires. I tossed my cigarette butt out the window and turned over the Maverick's engine. I followed her, turning on my lights only when I was on the main road behind her for a few seconds so it wouldn't be obvious I had followed her out of her parking lot. This was shaping up to be the most exciting thing that had happened to me in all my time in Amesbury.

I followed her through the surface streets on to Route 110. She drove fast, faster than was advisable, and, while the Maverick could easily keep up, I had to juggle my speed so as not to get too close. A little way out of town, she abruptly turned off of Route 110 into the parking lot of what could loosely be described as a roadhouse. It was actually a joint that had a sign of a dancing pig holding two mugs of beer in its front hooves.

I drove past it, not because I was trying to act like a super suave private detective, but she had turned off the road so fast I wasn't sure I could do the same without drawing too much attention to myself. A hundred yards down the road, I banged a U-ey or if you're not from Boston, I made a U-turn. I doubled back, pulled into the parking lot and found a spot well away from Marti's car.

I eased out of my car, locking the door behind me. There was the unmistakable smell of wood smoke and grilled meat in the air as I crossed the parking lot to the door. My stomach rumbled, reminding me that a thermos of coffee, a tuna sandwich and an apple were not going to cut it. I pulled the front door open and stepped inside. I was enveloped in a cloud of cigarette smoke. The jukebox was playing George Thorogood, and I was pleased to see that they had Lowenbrau beer.

The roadhouse was exactly what you'd expect, nothing fancy but the food coming out of the kitchen looked good and the price of beer posted over the bar wasn't going to bankrupt me. There was a small dance floor that no one was dancing on. The tables were black Formica topped with the matching metal and vinyl chairs. The bar was long with tall, wooden, hardbacked chairs. The whole place was just like every other barbecue joint/road-house I had ever been in. They had their own type of uniformity, like McDonald's, just with better food and booze.

Karen Marti was sitting at one of the tables in the middle of the room, and she wasn't alone. Sitting across from her was a blond man in his thirties. He was wearing a light-colored polo shirt with blue horizontal stripes. His neck and shoulders were thick, and his forearms had veins that were prominent. My guess was that Captain Muscles spent a lot of time in the gym, falling in love with himself in a mirror while he pumped iron.

I moved across the room to the bar which had half a dozen people sitting at it – a couple clearly on a date, a few guys watching sports on TV, and one lone woman. The bartender was my age, pretty and brunette.

'What can I getcha?'

'Lowenbrau.'

'Only got it in a bottle.'

'That's fine.'

'You need a menu?'

'Please.'

'OK.' She handed me a menu from her side of the bar and stepped over to a cooler and pulled out my beer. She popped it with an opener affixed to a pole that supported a load-bearing beam in the ceiling. She put it down in front of me, all of it done with the fluid motions of long practice.

'Need a minute?'

'Is there anything you recommend?'

'The brisket is good, but the pulled pork sandwich is the thing to get. It comes with coleslaw on it. Not everyone cares for it, but I think it's good.'

'Pulled pork it is.'

'Fries?'

'Yes, please.'

'Back in a bit.' She moved off and I turned my attention to the mirror behind the bar which afforded me a good view of Karen Marti and Captain Muscles. They seemed to be having some sort of animated discussion. I couldn't tell if it was animated as in they were having a good time or something else. There was no chance of hearing them over the jukebox, which seemed to be at max volume.

I sipped my beer, casually looked around at my fellow bar patrons, then acted like I was watching the TV while trying to watch Marti and Captain Muscles. I couldn't see his pants or shoes under their table, but I would bet anything he was wearing boat shoes and no socks. At this time of year, at night it might have been a little cold for that. Also, Amesbury was a little too far from the ocean for the Yacht Club look.

The bartender brought my sandwich and fries, and there were also a few slices of pickles on the plate. They looked to be reasonably fresh, and, though not half-sours, they weren't the almost neon green things that have been sitting in a jar on a supermarket shelf for months if not years. I have nothing against storks, but I didn't associate them with good pickles.

'Getcha anything else?'

'No, thanks. Not yet.'

'Enjoy.' She drifted down the bar to check on the other patrons. I picked up the sandwich and managed to take a bite without wearing any of it. It was good, but you have to get up pretty early in the morning to screw up a pulled pork sandwich. I tried a French fry, dipping it in the paper cup of ketchup on the plate. Having firmly established that quality control was being taken seriously at the Dancing Pig, I tucked into the meal in earnest.

I also watched Karen Marti and Captain Muscles. They were having a pretty serious discussion. Based on the number of times she touched his veiny arm or he took her hand in his, I had to believe that they were a little more than just casual acquaintances. How had I missed this last time I was tailing her? Or was this a new relationship? They stopped touching every time the waitress went over. If they were there for a romantic dinner, it was a liquid one. They never ordered any food.

I had finished my sandwich and was on my second Lowenbrau. There was nothing exciting happening on the TV when I heard raised voices. I couldn't make out what they were saying. In the mirror, I could see Captain Muscles scowling at Karen Marti, and then he stood up suddenly. She stood up and reached out to touch his gym-bloated forearm, but he shook her off and stormed away. Karen looked after him as he pushed the door open with considerable force, slamming it behind him. I didn't have to be some sort of relationship expert to see that she was unhappy about this turn of events.

I started to reach for my wallet to pay the bill. I figured that she would be leaving now that their date or whatever it was had ended so badly. Instead, she stood up and walked over to the bar, sitting a couple of seats away from me. She flagged down the bartender, and I heard her order another beer and a shot of tequila. It looked like I wasn't going anywhere yet.

I caught the bartender's eye and pointed to my empty bottle of Lowenbrau. She nodded, went to the cooler and in no time, there was a cold bottle of beer in front of me. She poured Marti's tequila and poured a beer then brought them over to Marti. I took a sip of beer and watched Marti down her tequila shot in one gulp. She grimaced and her face flushed. She placed the shot glass down on the bar instead of slamming down.

I sipped my beer and Marti raised her own glass of beer. She drank a third of it in one go. I was starting to think that maybe she had more hobbies than just the occasional weekend Bingo tournament. She caught my eye in the mirror, and I nodded. She didn't seem to be in the mood to be smiled at by some random guy in a bar. She nodded back. We made eye contact a couple more times. I was breaking every rule in the book where conducting surveillance was concerned.

'You gonna stare at me all night, or do you wanna have a drink?' She wasn't quite slurring her words.

'When you put it like that . . . I'll take the drink.' I slid over next to her.

'Two tequilas and get us each another beer,' she said to the bartender with familiarity that I would need a few more years in the place to develop.

'What are we drinking to?'

'We aren't celebrating, that's for sure.'

'Tough week?'

'Mister, you don't know the half of it.'

'Try me.'

'A friend of mine died . . . unexpectedly.'

'Oh . . . that's rough. I'm sorry.'

'Yeah . . . he was . . . he was a nice guy. Decent, you know?'

'Sure. I know the type.' I wasn't trying to sound like a cheap imitation of Sam Spade but sometimes I couldn't help myself. Fortunately, the shots of tequila came, and the bartender put a fresh Lowenbrau down next my three-quarter full Lowenbrau. I was going to have to pace myself if I was going to keep drinking with Marti.

'Cheers.' She held up her shot glass and I clinked mine against it.

'Cheers.' I drank the stuff. It went down the way tequila always does, like medicine but with a less pleasant taste.

'You ever lose anyone?'

'Sure. You get to a certain age . . . you know how it is.'

'Yeah . . .' She trailed off and I was afraid she'd clam up.

'Who was that guy who stormed out? The one you were talking to?'

'Why, what's it to you?'

'He's kind of big. The last thing I need is some jealous boyfriend coming back in here looking for a fight.'

'Stan . . . he's not my boyfriend.'

'Oh, he looked . . . you guys looked like you were together.'

'No, I know him from work.'

'Where do you work?'

'At a bank.'

'You're both bankers. That sounds interesting.' It didn't. Actually it sounded godawfully boring, but I wasn't the first guy to lie to a woman in a bar.

'No. I work in a bank. He's a real estate appraiser. He does business with my bank.'

'Oh, so is that part of your rough week too?'

'Yep. What do you do?'

'I work in Boston. Sales.'

'What do you sell?'

'Kitchen and bath fixtures.'

'Like toilets?'

'Sure, those too. Sinks, faucets, vanities. Whatever you need.'

'You don't look like a salesman.'

'I'm not working now.'

'You're not trying to sell me a toilet?' she said and giggled.

'Nope. Just having a drink in bar with a lady who looks a little down.'

'You're a good egg. I'm gonna buy you a drink.' She waved at the bartender and circled her index finger above her head in the universal signal for 'another round.' The bartender nodded, and I put my half-full beer down toward the back edge of the bar and started in on the untouched one.

'What do you do at the bank?' I asked.

'I'm Mr Smarty-pants's secretary.'

'Who's Mr Smarty-pants?'

'Mr Brock, he's the bank president.'

'Is he smart?'

'Not as smart as he thinks he is,' she said with a sneer.

I had to stop myself from agreeing with her. I wasn't supposed to know Brock. 'How so?'

'Well, he thinks . . .' She trailed off as the bartender put two more shots and beers down in front of us.

'You might want to slow down after these, Karen,' the bartender said with all the authority of one who controls the taps.

'Wha . . .' Karen started to ask, but the bartender had already moved away. 'Well, who the hell does she think she is?' Her mood switched with the speed that too much tequila too quickly can bring.

'You were telling me about your smarty-pants boss.'

'Yeah, yeah, cheers.' She held up her shot glass and we clinked. The tequila didn't taste any better than it did before, but it didn't taste any worse. That was tequila's strength, it couldn't taste worse than it did. I had drunk worse stuff, Montagnard rice wine for sure.

'You were saying?' I prompted.

'He was such a nice guy.'

'Your boss?'

'Frank. Frank Cosgrove. He was a gentleman. Why'd they have to kill him? He didn't do anything to anyone.'

'Who killed Frank?'

'They did. Those sonofabitches! They shot him for no good goddamned reason.'

'Who did?' But there was no point. She was sobbing at the bar, tequila and grief rendering her incoherent.

'What'd you say to her, mister?' The bartender was back and decidedly not friendly.

'Nothing, we were talking, and she started in about a friend of hers who was shot.'

'Yeah. Sure.'

'Listen, I didn't do anything.'

'Save it. Why don't you pay your tab and be on your way. She's got enough problems without someone like you hanging around while she's too drunk to think straight.'

'Hey, lady, I told you I didn't do anything.'

'Good. Settle up and go. I'll make sure she gets home OK. It won't be the first time.'

'Sure. Fine.' There was no point in arguing, and despite what the bartender might think of me, there was no point in hanging around. I dropped some bills on the bar to cover my tab and, in spite of the bum's rush, leave a tip. I walked outside into the evening air of mid-May. I lit a cigarette and got into the Maverick, which started up with its usual throaty roar.

I started back to Boston thinking about Karen Marti. I had thought the most exciting thing in her life was Bingo. Instead, I found out that she had something going on with Captain Muscles, and

she had a fondness for tequila, which showed only marginally
better judgment than having something going with Captain
Muscles.

If I had missed so much stuff about Karen Marti, what had I
missed about Mark Lintz? He was the first name on Brock's list.
Brock had thought Lintz the most likely one to be embezzling,
and maybe his first instinct had been right. That made me wonder
about Frank Cosgrove. Had I missed something about him? Was
there more to his murder than met the eye? The other thing that
kept going through my head was her saying, 'They didn't have
to shoot him.' Was she lamenting Cosgrove's bad luck or was
she saying he had been shot on purpose? And if she was, did
that mean she had an idea why? Or was I just trying to create a
case where there wasn't one?

I wasn't on the highway yet, and I wasn't far from Cosgrove's
apartment. I pulled over into a parking lot and wheeled the
Maverick around, bumping back up on the road and moving in
the direction of Cosgrove's place. Cosgrove lived in a small two-
story apartment building on the edge of town.

While most of Amesbury favored either colonial architecture
or the red brick uniformity of mill housing, Cosgrove's building
looked like it was designed by the same firm of architects who
designed Dairy Queens or McDonald's restaurants. The big difference, other than the lack of a bright red or yellow sign out front,
was that his building was two stories. It had a stairwell that went
up the middle of the building with large windows so you could
see anyone walking on it from outside. There were six units in
all, each on either side of the stairs. Cosgrove had rented one of
the basement apartments.

I pulled into one of the visitor spots in the parking lot. I was
just a regular guy who was here to visit a friend. I certainly
wasn't going to act like someone looking to break into a
murdered man's apartment. Nope, nothing to see here. I opened
the glovebox and took out the penlight that I kept in there in
case I had an unexpected B&E come up. I got out of the Maverick
and gently closed the door but didn't lock it. If I had to beat a
hasty retreat, I didn't want to have to fumble with my keys in
the lock.

I walked to the back door of the building with all the confidence of a man going to meet his girlfriend after a late-night phone call. It's been my experience that while the front door in an apartment building is usually locked, people get lazy about the back door. The handle turned easily, and I let myself into the common stairwell. Downstairs, the hallway was a little more dimly lit and maybe just a little shabbier.

Cosgrove's apartment door had a doorbell on the door frame and a helpful little placard with his name written in blue ink. There was nothing so dramatic as police tape on the door, but that probably had to do with the fact that his apartment wasn't the scene of the murder. I stood outside the door listening to the building and then pressed my ear against the door, listening intently.

When I was satisfied that nothing was moving inside, I gently tried the handle. It was locked but when I pressed against the door, there was a little give. There was a chance that the deadbolt wasn't locked. I took an old Diners Club card out of my wallet, pressed my weight against the door and ran the card up against the frame. It ran smoothly past where the deadbolt should have been. It wasn't locked. I then went to work on the jam and the handle lock. It didn't take long to spring the lock, and the door started to open.

I paused, standing as still as possible, listening for any noise coming from inside the apartment or any sign that someone in the building was stirring. My breathing, in my ears, sounded like the cannonade in the 1812 Overture. Finally, satisfied that no one was onto me, I stepped into the apartment. I gently pushed the door closed behind me while turning the handle so the latch wouldn't click.

I flicked the penlight on and played it over the apartment in front of me. I heard the rustle of cloth behind me, and something connected with the back of my head. I heard it as much as felt it, and fireworks went off inside my skull. Then the floor opened up and I fell right in. The lights went out.

I woke up, or more accurately, came to, on the cold tile floor. It was still dark, and my penlight had rolled under the couch. It was throwing light off in an odd direction, giving me the momentary impression that I was in a Salvador Dali painting. I had drooled, and my cheek, where it pressed into the tile, was in a puddle.

I gingerly touched the back of my head. He had hit me off to the side and fortunately not squarely in the back. That might have killed me. I have blackjacked a few people in my time, and you would have to be careful to avoid the temple or the back of the head. I couldn't tell if he had been good, or I was just lucky. Probably both.

I felt a lump where he had connected, and my hair was tacky with blood, but it was starting to congeal. I slowly sat up and then managed to pull myself upright to a standing position using the back of the couch that was currently hosting the lightshow from my penlight. Once I was standing, I took a couple of deep breaths. My head hurt, and it took me a few minutes of leaning on the back of the couch for the dazed feeling to go away. I wasn't in any rush to test out my legs, which felt about as steady as those of a newborn deer.

I didn't feel dizzy or nauseous, I just needed the world's biggest Anacin. A check of my Seiko diver watch showed that I had been in the apartment for all of about fifteen minutes. I felt a breeze and realized that the apartment door was open a couple of inches. I pushed it closed with my foot. When I felt like I could bend over without my head falling off I retrieved my penlight from under the couch.

The apartment was small, a typical bachelor pad. One bedroom, one bathroom, a small living room and a kitchenette with a counter to eat at instead of a table. Cosgrove wasn't making a fortune at the bank, but he should have been able to afford something a little better. Or maybe he was sending all his money home to ma and pa on the farm. Or saving up to buy something big like an engagement ring or a house.

Cosgrove's apartment might have been neat, before someone had gone through it like a tornado. Books had been pulled off the bookshelves, and pages of them had been ripped out and were scattered everywhere. The couch cushions had been slashed open. The kitchen looked like someone had spent a lot of time dumping out every jar or box of food, powder or sauce. The bathroom hadn't faired any better.

I went into the small bedroom, which looked like one of the winter scenes from a department store window at Christmas, but instead of fake snow, it was all feathers from slashed pillows and down comforters. Here and there were more destroyed books and general carnage. Someone had torn through the place in a hurry and with a fair bit of anger, by the look of it. Then when I showed up, they took some of that anger out on my poor but thankfully thick skull.

Someone had already gone through it pretty thoroughly. They either found what they were looking for or they had made enough of a mess to hide anything of value. Either way, I wasn't in much shape to dig through the wreckage of Cosgrove's apartment. I found a dishtowel in the rubble that wasn't in bad shape. There was no sense in leaving any of my fingerprints behind so that the local cops could pin the wreckage on me.

I noticed on the floor by the phone there was an address book. It was blue vinyl and was the type that had a calendar in it and clear slots to hold business cards. I slipped it in my back pocket and then, as an afterthought, checked to make sure I still had my .38 and my wallet. They were where I had left them.

I should have done that right away, but I had been distracted by the aftereffects of being hit in the head. It wasn't the worst sapping I'd had, but even the light ones are still unpleasant. I was just thankful that I didn't seem to have a concussion.

I listened at the door for a long, slow minute before I opened it and stepped into the hallway. I pulled the door shut quietly behind me, wiping the handle with my purloined dishrag. The building was quiet as it should be with everyone having to get up and go to work in the morning. Outside, the night had turned chilly the way spring nights do. I got into the Maverick and started it up and turned the heat on.

By the time I was on the highway, heat was easing its way out of the vents, and the Kinks were on the radio singing about their budgetary problems. My headache had receded to a mild throbbing that I was pretty sure could be negated by a healthy-sized whiskey. It was just shy of midnight when I pulled into the parking spot in front of my building.

I had made good time from Amesbury to home. Driving had given me some time to mull it over. Cosgrove getting shot in the robbery might have been a coincidence. Cosgrove having his apartment broken into and tossed, that might have been a co-incidence, but the two things happening days apart . . . that was no coincidence. You didn't even have to be a good detective to see that.

FOUR

'Well, I've said it since I first met you, but you are hardheaded.'

'Ouch.' I winced as Angela probed the bump on my head with one lacquered fingernail. We were in my office, and I was, at Angela's insistence, sitting in one of the client chairs while she stood behind me examining my thick skull.

'I think you'll live.'

'Thanks, doctor. I figured that out last night.'

'What'd he hit you with?'

'It might have been a blackjack, but he didn't split my skin open, so I am thinking it was something else. Something hard, wrapped up in a pillowcase or a sock.'

'But, specifically, not a blackjack?'

'The leather tends to split the skin where it comes into contact.'

'I don't even want to know how you know these things. You have longish hair, it might have cushioned the blow from a blackjack.'

'Sure, it could have. They just aren't the type of thing that most people carry around with them.'

'You carry one.'

'Only sometimes, and I am not exactly normal.'

'True.'

'If the place hadn't been torn apart so much, I might have thought it was a professional job, but the apartment was trashed.'

'Professionals can't be messy?'

'No rule about it, but in general, the whole point of searching a place is to find something. The level of destruction and mess at Cosgrove's would make finding anything hard.'

'You found something.'

'I'm a professional.'

'Hmmph.'

'You disagree?'

'I think you're a bull in a china shop, banging into everything until you find something.'

'Ouch, my pride,' I said in mock protest. Angela wasn't wrong about my investigative technique.

'Don't get me wrong, you're a good detective, but you're kind of a mess.'

'Those are some of my finer qualities.'

'Haha . . . that and you can cook.'

'Reasons enough to keep me around.'

'Sure . . . so you think the bank robbery, Cosgrove's murder and the guy in the apartment are connected?'

'It sure seems like an awful lot of coincidences for a place where most of the crime involves teenagers or bar fights.'

'OK, so what's next?'

'I'm not sure. I am curious about Karen Marti's date, Captain Muscles. I might like to talk to Brock if he's cooled down.'

'Are you gonna follow that other guy, Lint, around?'

'Lintz, funny lady, his name is Lintz. There's nothing that rules him out as the guy who sapped me at Cosgrove's.'

'So, that's a yes then.'

'Yes, I think I should look at him a little more closely, and I would also like to talk to Karen Marti when she isn't crying in her beer.'

'As long as you don't look at her too closely,' she said probing the lump again with her nail.

'Ouch, she's not my type.'

'Oh, you don't get involved with women you meet on cases?'

'Other than you?'

'Yes.'

'Not since we met.' Which was true, but I had also learned the hard way that meeting women in the course of cases didn't always work out.

'Good, I'm not sure I want the competition.' She slid round to sit on my lap and reminded me why she had nothing to worry about by kissing me. After a while she stood up. 'I have to go back to work.'

'The trial must go on.'

'Exactly.'

'It was nice of you to stop by.'

'I wanted to make sure you were OK. You seem like the type to not go to the hospital when you should.'

'Depends on what's wrong with me.'

'Probably a lot, but I am glad that none of it is serious.'

We walked to the office door and stopped.

'You might try taking better care of yourself.' She said it gently and kissed me, leaving me no room to argue. Then she walked out, making me wonder if our relationship had shifted from casual to kind of serious. I'm usually the last to know.

I went back to my desk and pulled out my old case notes from the original time spent in Amesbury, along with a fresh legal pad and a couple of felt tip pens. I had slept late this morning. I'd stayed up last night watching *The Thin Man* on TV 38, holding an ice pack on my head and drinking whiskey. The whiskey was purely medicinal for the pain caused by my bruised ego. I got caught worse than a gang of cartoon teenage investigators.

I pulled out my pipe and packed it with one of Peretti's special blends of pipe tobacco. This one had a nice balance of Latakia and Virginia. It was more mellow than strong but still had plenty of flavor. It lit easily, and when I had it drawing nicely, I opened the office window a few more inches to let out the smoke. The day had started with plenty of May sunshine and mild breezes, but now the sky had turned the color of pewter. The rain would be along shortly.

I sat and wrote down the names of everyone involved, now adding Captain Muscles. I jotted down all the recent events starting with Cosgrove's murder and the bank robbery. It might have seemed like I was going over old ground doing all this, but writing it out helped me see it more clearly. Written out, it was a series of events on a timeline. I could make connections or see where events stood out.

The problem was that Cosgrove's murder overshadowed everything else. The original embezzlement case was obscured by the murder. The bank robbery itself was just so much noise compared to the murder. The fact that someone had broken into Cosgrove's apartment and torn it apart looking for something, that was also obscured by the murder. Even getting cold-cocked somehow didn't seem to rate in comparison.

I sat hunched over my desk, puffing away and writing on the legal pad, drawing lines, connecting ideas and feeling more and more frustrated for the better part of two hours. By the time I sat up straight, my back hurt, the pipe had gone out and the rain had arrived in big, heavy drops beating against the window. I stood up and closed the window in an effort to keep the place from getting flooded.

The sky lit up in bright jagged flashes, and I watched as the cars in the street plowed through the sudden torrents of water. Only the most desperate of people were moving around on the sidewalks. Most people had taken shelter in stores or doorways in a vain effort not to get drenched.

I watched the storm until the lightning flashes and downpour faded into a mild drizzle. Then I went back over my notes hoping that something would leap out at me. Nothing did. By the time I locked the office up to head home, the rain had given way to sunshine. That was New England for you.

I stepped out of the doorway of my building with the intention of walking. That had been the idea but the big man who stood up from the car he was leaning against had other ideas. My hand was already snaking for the .38 holstered under my shirt. I didn't like it when people are waiting for me unexpectedly. History has taught me that they usually have ill intent.

'Say, pal, sport a brother a smoke?'

'Jesus, you gave me a start.'

Chris was one of my few surviving friends from Vietnam. He looked a lot different than when I had seen him last. Last spring, he had long hair and dressed like a biker. Now he was dressed in loafers, khaki pants, a blue polo shirt and a denim jacket. His hair was cut shorter so that he looked like he belonged on *Miami Vice*. That and his hair was dyed almost black.

'Hey, Red.' He wrapped me in his customary bear hug.

Chris and I had gone through Special Forces selection and training together with our friend Tony. Tony had been killed in Vietnam when NVA sappers had attacked our base at Nha Trang. Chris and I had survived the attack, the war and a whole lot of other violence since.

'Hey, man, what are you doing here?' I asked.

'I told you I was coming to town.'

'Shit, let's get a drink.'

'That sounds like a plan.'

'Do you have any bags?' I asked.

'They're in a locker at the bus station.'

'Cool, let's go get that drink. You hungry?'

'I could eat. What happened to your ear?' he asked.

'When I came home from San Francisco, I was in a gunfight with some Vietnamese gangsters in a Chinese restaurant. One of them, a former ARVN colonel, clipped my ear.'

Chris grimaced. 'Ouch.'

'It could have been worse.'

'Sure, he could have had better aim.'

'At least he didn't try to talk me to death. You'd be surprised at how many villains love to brag.'

'I can see that,' Chris said.

We walked and talked, catching up, as we did, about guys we knew from Special Forces in general and especially those from Vietnam. It was the same unwritten ritual that all veterans fell into when seeing each other again. By the time we were sitting in a booth in a dimly-lit pub I knew, we had not only caught up with our informal roll call but had ordered a couple of Reubens and beers.

'Chris, why are you in town and dressed like the New England version of *Miami Vice*?'

'I had to leave San Francisco in a hurry.' Chris used his training as a Special Forces medic patching up biker gang types who couldn't go to the hospital or a doctor for legal reasons. He wasn't affiliated with any one gang, but he hung around.

'What happened?'

'Guy I knew was the head of a crew that was part of a larger

MC. He thought it was a good idea to offer an opinion about Vietnam.'

'I take it was negative.'

'It was. He opined that we lost because GIs didn't have any balls. He then opined that Green Berets were nothing more than overrated pussies.'

'Ohhhh. That couldn't have gone well for him.' There were some things that couldn't be tolerated.

'No, it didn't. I'm told that in a few months he'll be able to move from eating with a straw to Jell-O.'

'You broke his jaw?' I asked, surprised.

'And a few other bits and bobs.'

'How'd his guys react?'

'That was the problem.'

'Oh?'

'A few of them felt they had to get involved. I didn't mind when we were all throwing hands, but someone pulled a piece. And naturally I pulled mine.'

'Dead?'

'Not sure. I wasn't going to stick around and find out. Between the bikers and the cops, it seemed like a good time to visit Boston.' Chris was smart and tough. He also didn't scare easily, so if he felt he had to leave town that meant someone had put a contract out on him.

'Well, you can crash with me until you figure out what you want to do.'

'Thank you, bro.'

'Least I can do.' Chris had saved my life when I was in San Francisco, but I would have put him up even if I didn't owe him. There weren't a lot of guys left who had been in SOG. We were part of a small, tight-knit brotherhood within a small, tight-knit group of elite soldiers. There was almost nothing I wouldn't do for him and vice versa.

After we finished our sandwiches and beer, we made our way to the Greyhound Station on St James Avenue. I spent some time there last summer looking for the missing daughter of an old Army buddy. Chris went to one of the lockers. Opening it, he took out an Army issue duffle bag and gym bag. I took the duffle, and we made our way back to my apartment by way of my local package store. I had a sneaking suspicion that with Chris around, my supplies of Irish Whiskey wouldn't last long.

The effects of the beers had worn off by the time we made it upstairs to my apartment, and I resolved to reverse that unpleasant turn of events as soon as possible. I unlocked the door and Sir Leominster ran over, mewing loudly to remind me that he was on the brink of starvation even though he had a can of food this morning. He stopped for a second when he caught sight of Chris. He edged over and sniffed the hem of Chris's pants.

'You've got a cat?'

'Yeah, he's all right. Pretty decent company but not much of a conversationalist.'

'Haha, I just never pictured you with a cat.'

'What's wrong with cats?'

'Nothing, nothing at all.'

We dropped Chris's bags by the couch, and I set about opening up a can of Sir Leominster's foul-smelling food and plating it up for him. His urgent cries increased in pitch until I put the dish in front of him and he buried his snout in it. While Chris was freshening up and Sir Leominster was gorging himself, I went over to check the blinking light on the answering machine.

'It's Watts. Your guy at the bank was shot with a .357 Magnum, one round in the forehead and it made a very messy exit wound, according to the coroner's report.'

.357 Magnum rounds were the same diameter as a .38, which is actually .36 inches in diameter, but the early days of bullet development weren't known for exacting standards. The .357 Magnum had a longer cartridge case, which meant more powder, which meant more velocity, or, in layman's terms, more power. The entrance wounds would be similar in size, but the .357's exit wound would be a lot bigger. Hence the messy exit wound comment.

'They found a car matching the description of one seen leaving the bank parking lot in a rest area off Route 95. That's the good news. The bad news is that it was stolen from the parking lot of

the Braintree mall and wiped clean. Call me if anything turns up
at your end.'

'Working on a case?' Chris asked.

'Sort of.'

'Tell me about it over a drink. I heard the lady on the machine
mention someone getting shot with a .357.'

'I was hired to follow some bank employees around. The bank
is up north near the New Hampshire border. The client thinks
that one of his employees was embezzling from the bank.'

'He hired you to solve the case?'

'Not exactly. He hired me to see if any of them were living
above their means.'

'Oh, that makes sense. I'm pretty sure you're no accountant.'

'Not by a long shot.'

'So, did you find the guy?'

'No, that was just it. I spent two weeks following people
around and none of them seemed to be living above their means.
Then the bank got robbed and one of the three caught a round
in the head.'

'Coincidence?' He took the glass of whiskey I had poured
him. 'Thanks.'

We clinked glasses. 'I was starting to think it was a coincidence,' I said.

'What changed your mind?'

'I let myself into the dead guy's apartment last night. Someone
sapped me, and when I came to, the place had been ransacked.'

'So not a coincidence, then.'

'Doesn't seem like it. No.'

'No, it doesn't. So, what are you going to do?'

'That's the sixty-four thousand dollar question, isn't it?'

'I can't see you just letting this go.'

'No, me neither. I'll probably keep digging into it. What are
you going to do?'

'I'll start looking for work and a place to stay. I can't go back
west anytime soon.'

'OK, can I help?'

'Yeah, you know that I am not looking for an office job or a
nine-to-five. You know what I was doing in San Francisco.'

I knew what he had done, and, while it was illegal, it wasn't exactly immoral. Chris had fought in our part of the secret war in Vietnam and then instead of settling down, he had ended up as soldier of fortune in Africa and then South America. His resume wasn't the type that would get him a job in the normal world.

'Sure, I know a guy. He's a former paratrooper, Korean War vintage. He runs a garage, and he is on the fringe of the type of people you're looking for. I'll introduce you.'

Carney ran a garage and sold guns, clean cars and anything else someone might need for breaking the law. He had his rules and his own sense of honor, and it wasn't my place to judge him. I had helped him out a few years before when his daughter got hooked on smack and he wanted help getting her out of the life. I had helped him find her and get her away from the asshole boyfriend who got her hooked so he could pimp her. He was later found floating in the harbor. The imprint from a craftsman's wrench on his forehead was the type of clue that pointed to Carney, but no one was looking to arrest him. I was sure he was at a poker game with his ten best friends when it happened.

'Thanks. I appreciate it.'

'I'll take you by tomorrow to meet the guy.'

'Cool.'

We spent most of the night drinking whiskey and talking about our time in Vietnam. The downside of having been in SOG was that it was still classified. There weren't a lot of people who we could talk to about it and fewer still who would understand our part of the war. When SOG guys ended up hanging out, we tended to talk about it, our missions, funny stories, reminiscing about friends who didn't make it home or talking about legends like Bob Howard or Mad Dog Shriver.

At a certain point, my apartment was thick with cigarette smoke. The hour had grown late, and my brain was as fogged by whiskey as the apartment was by smoke. I dug my .45 Lightweight Commander out of the gun locker and slipped a magazine in it without chambering a round. I handed it to Chris.

'Here, I know you won't sleep well otherwise.'

'Thanks . . . Jesus, did you buy this from a pimp?' The gun was stainless steel with stag horn grips. It had been reworked by a smith after I had come back from the Colonel's school out west. The Colonel had very specific thoughts about how to employ a pistol and what pistol that should be. He would be mortified to know I preferred my customized Browning Hi-Power in 9mm to the Commander. No one is perfect.

'I had a friend who used to say the same thing.'

'What happened to him?'

'He didn't make it out of the gunfight that I lost my earlobe in.'

He didn't say anything because there wasn't anything to say. It wasn't that we were used to it, losing friends. We had lost so many that there just wasn't a lot left in the well of emotions.

The next morning, I woke up feeling a lot better than I had any right to feel. When he got up, Chris handed the pistol back to me and I locked it up. He wasn't licensed in Massachusetts and didn't want to jam me up if he got caught with a pistol registered in my name. I didn't have anything off the books for him to walk around with. I, mostly, try to play by the rules.

We had breakfast at greasy spoon to help soak up some of the whiskey from last night. Chris tended to spend a lot of time in the gym pumping iron and he ate like it – whole wheat toast, a double order of scrambled eggs and a side of Canadian bacon. I opted for a cheese omelet, bacon and an English muffin. We both opted for black coffee.

'Do you like it?' Chris asked.

'What, the omelet? It's pretty good.'

'No, being a PI. You were once part of the most elite fighting force our nation ever fielded.'

'Don't tell the Marines it wasn't them,' I said in a conspiratorial stage whisper.

'Seriously.'

'OK, do you like patching up bikers and criminal types?'

'I like the freedom it affords me. No office. No suit and tie.

No commanding officer or sergeant major telling me my shit needs to be Dress Right, Dress all the time.'

'It's the same for me. I'm my own boss. I have clients, and sometimes they're demanding, but I can always tell them to pound sand. Once in a while, I run across someone who really needs my help, and that is a pretty good feeling.'

'So, we're both slumming so we can stay free?'

'That and SOG is gone. Those days, the thing we were, it doesn't exist anymore, and it never will again. I can't imagine being in the Army and doing anything else. It was hard for me to accept that when I first got out. If that isn't an option, being as free as I can is as good as it gets.'

'You were a cop for a while, how was that?'

'Like being in the Army but with worse looking uniforms. It was better and worse at the same time. It lacked the sense of purpose, but the chain of command was loose, and I could pretty much be my own man. I didn't have to worry about a team or getting anyone, other than myself, killed.'

'I can see that.'

We finished our breakfast, and our next stop was the nearby Old Stone Bank. I needed some walking around money now that I had turned into my own client. I drew two-hundred dollars out of my savings account. The teller was able to spread it out over some twenties, tens and fives without actually acting like I was asking her to push a boulder repeatedly up a hill. Chris turned a small stack of Amex traveler's checks into a respectable pile of greenbacks. I was struck by how much better his form of personal freedom paid than mine.

Outside, each armed with our respective amounts of cash, we got into the Maverick. I navigated the car through the narrow one-way streets of Boston's Back Bay as The Doors sang about the streets in New Haven. Carney's garage wasn't far from the Charles River, Mass General Hospital, the Charles Street Jail, and the red line, which by Boston crime standards made it pretty prime real estate.

I parked in front of Carney's garage, and we walked in. Carney was in the office with the handset of a phone pressed against his ear. He was nodding and saying, 'ah-ah' at intervals. Then he hung up. He looked up at me and almost smiled. Carney's face just wasn't built for it, and he looked like a cartoon alligator in the middle of a gas attack.

Carney wasn't a villain; he didn't run a crew or plan jobs. He made his money supplying criminals with the tools they needed. He offered discretion and demanded a premium price for it. He once told me, 'I don't mind selling a professional a gun. You can trust them to act right and not do anything stupid. If they get pinched, they know the deal and keep their mouths shut. But some junkie looking to knock over a liquor store . . . forget it. Nothing but trouble.'

'Andy, good to see you. How's the car treating you?' Carney said after he hung up the phone.

'Good, you do nice work.'

'Thanks.'

'This is my friend, Chris.' Carney's generation didn't call anyone their bro, as was the fashion with my generation of veterans. 'We were in SF together and in Vietnam together.'

Carney stood up and stuck out his hand. 'Any friend of Andy's . . .' Carney had been a paratrooper and, like everyone who voluntarily jumped out of a perfectly good airplane for a living, saw the world as Airborne and everyone else.

'Pleased to meet you,' Chris offered and they shook hands in what I imagined to be an attempt at mutual bone crushing.

'Can I leave Chris with you? He's got some business, and I figured you might be able to help him out.'

'You're not gonna stay?'

'I have my own business to look after. I gotta run up to Amesbury on a case. He'll be OK.'

Chris had the spare key to my place, and I didn't feel like dragging him along while I poked around Amesbury. It wouldn't do to bore a friend to death who had saved my life. Also, whatever 'business' Chris wanted to discuss, I was sure that my knowing about it might make me an accessory. I had enough trouble. I didn't need that too.

I left Chris in good hands and wove my way through the city to the highway. I aimed the Maverick north and enjoyed the spring weather on the way to Amesbury. The radio kept me company, and I tried to think about where the case was going. The problem was that it all kept going back to Cosgrove's death. It was, as I had noticed yesterday when trying to make sense of it all, overshadowing everything else.

I pulled into Amesbury a little after ten in the morning. I found a spot where I could watch the bank parking lot. The Amesbury PD car was still there, as were all the bank employees' cars with the obvious exception of Cosgrove's. Either the cops had towed it away as evidence or, more likely, it was turned over to a family member.

If I had any illusions that surveillance had gotten any more interesting after last night, they quickly evaporated. The weather was mild and I watched the pollen collect on my windshield. I smoked sparingly, something that would have been suicide while watching the Ho Chi Minh trail. The hands on my Seiko crawled slowly around the dial. I drank coffee or seltzer from little glass bottles. When I got hungry, I had a handful of salted peanuts from a little blue can that I had brought with me.

I sat in my car listening to the radio and contemplated all of the wrong turn decisions I had made in life that had brought me to this point. Then it occurred to me that if I hadn't made those decisions, then I might have really screwed up and ended up working a straight job . . . the type of job that goes with living in suburbia, doing all those suburban things until the inevitable heart attack ends the tyranny of middle-class American boredom, once and for all. I was not the type to raise a family, get up early, go to a job in an office or PTO meetings.

I was contemplating all of this when 'Memo From Turner' came on the radio with its twangy slide guitar complementing Mick Jagger's lyrics. I had heard that the song was about Ike Turner, and I had heard the song was about organized crime producing the 1960s London music scene. It was a coin toss, but it was a great song either way that coin landed.

I was still sitting in my car, bored out of my mind, when a silver flash of a car screeched into the bank parking lot. The car was one of those aerodynamic hunks of muscle-bound automotive engineering that Detroit excels in, a Camaro. This one was an '85, and from across the street, I could hear Van Halen's 'Mean Street' pouring from the T-top. The car was all testosterone and flash.

I shouldn't have been surprised when Captain Muscles got out of it. He was dressed in pressed chinos and a blue blazer, no tie with one of those shirts with a white collar and cuffs. I detested those shirts. It was irrational, but for some reason I couldn't stand them and, often, the people who wore them. Muscles stopped long enough to gratuitously tug at his crotch, rearranging it, before heading into the bank. That at least explained the car. Overcompensation.

I dug the small set of binoculars that I kept in the glovebox out and took a look at his license plate. I trained the binoculars on the front plate of the Camaro. It was a New Hampshire plate, which wasn't odd considering that Amesbury was on the state border. I wrote the plate number down in the notebook I carried in the car. It would be neat to find out more about Captain Muscles. I was pretty sure that he wasn't someone I would like. That wasn't just the irrational dislike of his shirt talking.

Captain Muscles came out of the bank half an hour later. Even from across the street, it looked as though his neck disappeared into his shoulders. He got into his Camaro and for a second, I thought he was going to peel out of the parking lot. I didn't know if it was the presence of the Amesbury cop in the lot or the fact that in the midday traffic it would have been an instant accident. Captain Muscles eased his Camaro into traffic, and after a short pause, I eased in behind him.

He headed through town, picking up Interstate 95 North, and I dutifully followed at a safe distance. Muscles drove the way I expected him to, fast and impatiently. He kept it at ninety miles per hour and would weave around cars rather than wait for them to give way. I did my best to keep up with him without making it too obvious. I wasn't sure who he was, and while I believe that honest people didn't worry about being followed, I had nothing to indicate he was an honest man.

We drove north past the collection of New Hampshire towns on the state's tiny sliver of coast. Most of New Hampshire is inland, known for good skiing, mountains that the Europeans think are foothills, and famous for Mount Washington. But now I was driving on the scant, fifteen miles, of the Granite State that touched the Atlantic Ocean. The only downside of the drive was that there was no scenic view of the ocean. Instead, I was driving through a tunnel of trees, lots of which seemed to be pine trees. Just when I was sure we were going all the way to Maine, Captain Muscles veered his car to the off-ramp for Portsmouth.

Portsmouth, like its English namesake, was a Navy town. What was funny was that all of the Navy stuff was next door in Kittery, Maine. In this case, home to the Naval Shipyard and the Naval Prison, which I had to imagine was cold and damp from October to May. Portsmouth built ships and tended to the submarine fleet. It was a small, tough town that was benefiting from Ronald Reagan's 600-ship Navy and wasn't being hurt by tourism either.

Portsmouth hosted the conference and the signing of the peace treaty that ended the Russo-Japanese war. It also had a museum and park built around the USS Albacore, which was a Navy test submarine. Portsmouth, it turned out, was also home to Stanley Clark, Real Estate Appraising, Inc. I found a spot to park a few doors down from Clark's business. After feeding a few quarters into the parking meter, I crossed the street and walked back up the street on the uneven brick sidewalks that are a hallmark of most old New England cities. The trees that were planted when this country was still part of England grew and grew, their roots playing hell with the work that the brick-layers did centuries ago.

I learned this because Captain Muscles or Stan as a very drunk Karen Marti had called him, parked his Camaro on a nice scenic street in the downtown area. It wasn't in Market Square, but the building was definitely vintage eighteenth century. The real estate appraisal office was in a small storefront wedged conveniently between a real estate agency and a gift shop. You could find a home to buy, have it appraised and buy tacky kitsch to fill it with, all within three doors of each other. Portsmouth was a pretty convenient town. I also noted that if the gold paint on the window of Stanley Clark's business was to be believed, he was licensed in New Hampshire, Maine, and Massachusetts. That

might have something to do with his trip to the Merrimack
Community Bank earlier.

I smoked a Lucky and tried to get a good look at Captain
Muscles, aka Stanley Clark, in his natural environment. His office
was small and seemed to consist of him and a secretary. When
he wasn't on the phone, Clark seemed to spend a lot of time
perched on the corner of the secretary's desk or trying to subtly
flex for her. It was an entertaining type of theater, even if I
couldn't hear what he was saying. Though I think he thought he
was like some French romantic lead, but he was more Jerry Lewis
than Alain Delon.

It didn't make sense to waste the rest of the day watching
Clark perform for an uninterested audience. I had his name,
business and his license plate. That meant that I could find him
again if I needed him. It also meant that I was going to have to
listen to my old childhood nemesis and friend Boston Police
Detective Sergeant Billy Devaney insult me almost good-
naturedly. If having Billy call me 'shanty Irish' and hurl insults
at me was the price for having him check Stanley Clark's record,
it was a pretty cheap price to pay.

I went back to the Maverick, and leaving the next lucky person
to use that parking spot a free forty-five minutes, I headed south.
The nice restaurants, the historic town and the submarine museum
would have to wait. Maybe I could convince Angela to take a
weekend trip to Portsmouth. It was a much more romantic destination now that the tourist council and the historical society had
teamed up. They seemed to be winning in their goal to save the
town's reputation from the best efforts of the sailors who were
stationed there.

The ride back to Amesbury took about twenty-five minutes. It
wasn't a long drive, but getting on and off the highway always
took longer than you think. Once on the highway, I floored the
gas pedal down and listened to Faces cover 'I'm Losing You.' I
didn't know if it was as good as the original version by The
Temptations, but Rod Stewart's gravelly voice did the song justice.
It was impossible to resist drumming on the steering wheel with
the song. Heading back to Amesbury, I was trying to figure out

who I wanted to talk to more, Brock or Karen Marti. Figuring that Brock was still under a lot of pressure and still pissed off at me, I opted for Karen Marti.

I parked in the lot by the bank and settled in to wait. It was a little after noon, and there wasn't much traffic in or out of the bank. I think the good people of Amesbury were a little skittish after a bank robbery gone wrong. They were probably statistically a lot safer in the Merrimack Community Bank because, like lightning not striking twice, the bank was unlikely to be held up so soon after a recent robbery. The Amesbury cop parked out front would certainly be a deterrent.

For once my stomach wasn't rumbling to let me know it too had needs. That had been the benefit of the big breakfast from the greasy spoon. My usual breakfast of faux French yogurt and wheat toast usually left me feeling hungry sooner than a meal of Chinese food. Sometimes I needed the greasy spoon big breakfast to power my investigative efforts through the day.

My train of thought was interrupted by Karen Marti emerging from the bank. She was wearing a skirt suit combination in blue with a yellow blouse that looked very smart. She had white sneakers on instead of anything with a heel. I wasn't the best detective in the world, but that at least told me that she planned to walk somewhere.

I rolled my window up, and, after locking the car, began to tail her. It wasn't the most challenging tail I had ever done, just the opposite. Innocent people didn't worry about being followed, and she certainly didn't do any of the things to see if she was being followed. There was no stopping to tie a shoelace, abruptly changing direction, looking in store windows or varying her pace. Nope, Karen Marti plowed down the sidewalk without a care.

She went into a deli, not the traditional kosher type that you'd find in a real city, but more of a sandwich joint. Probably the closest that you could find in New Hampshire. She waited in line to order and then sat down at a table, and I figured this was as good a place as any to talk to her.

Inside, I stood in line and ordered a BLT when it was my turn. I like to pretend that because vegetables figure prominently in the name of the sandwich that it is healthy. I got a bag of potato

chips from Cape Cod and a small bottle of blueberry seltzer. My
meal was a real regional melting pot. When I had ordered, I
walked over to Karen's table and stopped.

'Karen?'

'Yes,' she said, looking up from a *Reader's Digest* that she
was reading while waiting for her order.

'Andy, we met last night at the barbecue place.'

'Oh . . . Andy . . . of course. Hi,' she said, clearly trying to
sift through tequila-hazed memories.

'Can I sit down?' I asked as I sat down.

'Um . . . well, sure.'

'Thanks. Karen how much do you remember talking to me
last night?'

'Um, not that much, to be honest. I was kind of sad and had
too much to drink.'

'You were drinking a lot.'

'Was I making a fool of myself?'

'No, you were sad about Frank Cosgrove, which is
understandable.'

'Did you know Frank?'

'No, not exactly. Karen, I'm a private investigator from Boston.'
I didn't see any point in telling her that I had lied to her about
my job. I was pretty sure that wasn't the best way to go about
trying to gain her trust.

'You are?'

'Yep.'

'Like Magnum, PI?'

'Well, not as tall and I certainly don't drive a Ferrari.'

'Why are you interested in Frank?'

'I was hired to investigate him by a company that was thinking
of hiring him. I can't tell you who, but they are a big name in
banking, and they wanted to be sure he was trustworthy. Then
you were robbed and now he's gone, and I can't quite figure out
how a guy like him gets murdered.' It was only two-thirds a lie.

'Jeez. Frank was thinking of leaving? He never said anything
to me. He always seemed happy at the bank.'

'The position pays quite well, and he was engaged . . .' I
trailed off, letting her fill in the blanks.

'Yeah, I guess. I just, well, we were close. He would have said something.'

'Maybe, maybe not. We don't really know the people we work with, do we?'

'No, I guess not.'

'Karen, can you tell me what Frank was working on? Was there anything unusual or anything, I don't know . . .'

'Say, mister, that's a crummy question to ask about a guy, a nice guy, who was killed.'

'I'm just trying to make sense of this, too. Guys like Frank Cosgrove don't get murdered. That just doesn't make sense to me.'

'No, me either.'

'Was he working on anything in particular?'

'He did some real estate stuff. He also did some commercial bank stuff and investment services. He was kind of a jack of all trades.'

'Does anything stick out in your mind?'

'No. Why does any of this matter? He's dead now. What difference does it make?'

'I honestly don't know. Frank's death seems incongruous. It makes me want to find out more about him, maybe explain things.'

'Why? Who was he to you? You didn't know him.'

'No, I didn't. I guess I am just trying to make sense of why a seemingly decent man was killed.' I was laying it on thick, but her drunken comments last night made me think that there was something more going on. That was the problem with my approach to work – I would get an idea, it would turn into a theory and, until I figured the case out, it was like an itch that was impossible to scratch.

'He was killed by the bank robbers. There's no great mystery. People get killed in bank robberies. Frank wasn't involved in anything!' She got up and stormed out without her lunch.

'Only if they go really wrong,' I said to a room of people who weren't listening to me.

My number was called, and I went to the counter and collected my lunch. There was no point in trying to talk to her again today, so I took my lunch to the car and ate it on the way back to

Boston. I drove back to the city wondering if she was too upset
or not upset enough with my line of questioning.

I got back to the office, checked my messages and went through
the pile of bills and junk mail that had accumulated over the past
couple of days. When I was done with that, I called Detective
Sergeant Billy Devaney of the Boston Police Department.

'Roark, you shanty Irish piece of trash, you've got some nerve
calling me after the mess you made for me last winter.' The mess
had involved calling Billy about a couple of dead bodies that
turned up while I was involved in a blackmail investigation. Billy
was a robbery/larceny detective and didn't appreciate my gener-
osity in trying to help him broaden his professional horizons.

'Jeez, Billy, I made you look like a superstar. And if I'm shanty
Irish, you are, too. We were neighbors in Southie.' Billy and I
had grown up on the same block. While he now lived in the
suburbs with a wife and growing family and I lived in Back Bay,
we both started in the same place.

'Don't remind me. Best thing that ever happened to my family
was that my screwy kid sister got over dating you in high school.'
Billy was a few years older than me and had come home from
the Marine Corps deciding that I wasn't good enough for his
sister. He had expressed this by bruising his calloused, large-
knuckled fists on my face.

'Ha! You didn't do much better.' Billy wasn't fond of his
brother-in-law.

'Still better than you, you piece of trash.' This was about as
nice as Billy was, and the conversation was downright nostalgic
as conversations go with him.

'Whaddaya want this time, you mooch. You never call me
unless you want something.'

'Can you run a plate and the BCI on the guy associated with
it?'

'Sure, give me the information and call back in ten years when
I've hopefully forgotten you.'

'Come on, Billy, help me out? Think of how miserable I've
been since you convinced your kid sister to dump me in high
school.'

'Why, so you can dump more homicides on my plate? I think the Lieutenant's still pissed off at me.'

'Naw, no way. It's been a few months. Somebody has to have fucked up worse than you by now. You know what they say, "If you screw up, wait a couple weeks. The next guy will screw up and in no time, no one will remember what you did."' I quoted the old advice I had been given when I was a cop.

'My only mistake was getting all sentimental and helping you out.'

'Aw, come on, Billy.'

'I'll call you back in half an hour.'

I sat back in my office chair contemplating the case. I still couldn't see where killing Frank Cosgrove would or could be tied to embezzling. Killing him wouldn't get any of the money back. Robbing the bank wouldn't hide the embezzlement. Killing him only made sense if he was involved in it and someone was trying to protect themselves. Maybe Karen Marti knew more than she was letting on. Or maybe Frank Cosgrove was just murdered by some bank robbers. That was the problem with this case, there was just too much that I didn't know.

FIVE

'So there Red was, running around in the middle of a fire fight, just wearing Jungle boots, skivvies and bandolier of CAR-15 magazines, his ass hanging out. He was throwing grenades and shooting at the enemy sappers. If I wasn't so scared, it would have been funny as hell,' Chris said with a big grin.

'He must have looked ridiculous,' Angela said, smiling at me. I shrugged. I had too much on my mind during the attack on the Special Forces headquarters in Da Nang to worry about it.

'No, actually, just the opposite. He was like some ancient warrior, but instead of a spear, he had a CAR-15,' Chris said with a quiet, sincere tone. It had been a bloody attack on the camp, the worst single loss of Special Forces soldiers in the war, including our friend Tony.

'CAR-15?' Angela asked, smiling at me.

'A shortened M-16. Much handier for using in the jungle.' It had been my preferred weapon, and in SOG we had our pick of the litter of exotic weapons. Some guys liked to carry AK-47s because of their rock-solid reliability, but they were heavy and slow to reload. The CAR-15 was handier, I could carry more rounds for it, and it was faster to reload. I liked the little carbine and carried it along with a Browning Hi-Power pistol, a lot of grenades and as many magazines as I could carry for the CAR-15.

'Red was one tough hombre,' Chris said in his best imitation of John Wayne, which almost every Special Forces veteran I knew did after the Green Berets came out. 'He fought his way in and out of the bars and brothels in Saigon more than once.'

'Hey, hey now . . .' I was blushing and not exactly sure that the first woman who I had dated for any length of time in a long time needed to hear about my exploits in the fleshpots of Saigon. Or anywhere else, for that matter. Chris laughed at my obvious discomfort.

'Oh, I'm sure.' She laughed. 'But why do you call him Red?'

'He hates the heat.'

'I do, I do.' I took a sip of wine. We were drinking a bottle of Dao, Portuguese red wine, and sitting around the remnants of dinner we had just finished in my kitchen.

'I met Red in Special Forces training at Fort Bragg. It was warm. I'm from Alabama and was used to it. Not my Yankee friend from *Bahstin*,' he said, imitating my accent.

'It was summer and hotter than Hades . . . humid, too.'

'Well, there was this poor Yankee slob,' Chris jerked his thumb at me, 'who every time we ran or did any PT, his face would get bright red. Even in-country, his face was bright red in the heat.'

'Only the first few months. I acclimated after a while.'

'Sure, sure, keep telling yourself that.'

'I got better,' I said, mock defensively. 'I was there for three years.'

'That's true, you were there long enough.'

'What did you guys do?' Angela asked.

'I was a weapons sergeant and Chris was a medic. We worked with the locals who were fighting against the North Vietnamese.'

That was a broad brushstroke and, in the strictest interpretation, true. Ours had been a secret war, the facts of which were still classified. We had been keeping the government's secrets for so long, it was second nature. It was easier to minimize what we did rather than say we couldn't talk about it. That would have guaranteed Angela hounding me about it.

'And you saw a lot of action . . . not in the brothels of Saigon?'

'Sure, we saw some,' I said casually.

'Andy . . . you've got a lot more scars than someone who just saw *some* combat.'

'Plenty of other guys saw a lot more.' Not many outside of SOG.

'I doubt that,' she said tersely. Angela had spent enough time in court to tell when someone said something that didn't ring true.

'Ange . . . it's not something I love talking about.' Which was true. Even if I hadn't signed a lot of non-disclosure agreements, all of which had threatening language to the effect that I could go to federal prison for a long time, I still wouldn't want to talk about it. I had lost a lot of friends, not just Tony. There were guys on my teams, American and Montagnard, and there had been friends on other teams. It was a small community.

'Andy, you've nightmares almost every night I've shared your bed. You talk, sometimes you scream, sometimes you just shake next to me.'

'Ange . . . I saw some shit, but there were a lot of guys who had it a lot worse than me.'

'Hey, hey, kids. Let's not ruin a nice dinner with all of this talk about America's involvement in the Pearl of Southeast Asia,' Chris said, trying to lighten the mood.

'You too?' Angela said to Chris.

'I shouldn't have brought it up. It isn't polite dinner conversation. There should be a new rule, don't discuss politics, religion and war service at dinner.'

'It's OK. It gets frustrating, you know. Every time Vietnam comes up, he clams up. Or he tells some funny story that doesn't tell me anything at all, like a little kid trying to trick you by pointing and saying, "look over there."'

'Ange, there's a lot of stuff from over there . . . a lot of it that I just don't want to talk about, much less talk about with my girlfriend.'

'Girlfriend?' she asked. It had slipped out of my mouth unconsciously, and now I didn't know what to say.

'Um, well, we spend almost every weekend . . .'

'Relax, Andy. I'm just giving you a hard time.' She smiled and put her hand on top of mine.

'Sweet Jesus, Red, you shoulda seen the look on your face just now. She got you good.'

Later, Angela and I were lying in bed. Chris had ducked out under some pretense or another. He had a key, and after his visit to Carney, he acquired a Smith & Wesson Model 27 with a four-inch barrel. It was a .357 Magnum. The barrel wasn't too long to carry and made the most of the hi velocity round. He also had picked up a Spanish Star BM 9mm. It was a smaller copy of the 1911 but with a couple of differences.

'Chris is a character.'

'You have no idea.'

'How long have you known him?'

'Fifteen or sixteen years . . . a lifetime.'

'Because you were in Vietnam together?'

'Yes. It's hard to explain, but yes.'

'Sort of a brotherhood?'

'Sure, but also, we shared this wild, intense experience that damn few people did or would understand. It brings guys close together. We can go months or years not seeing each other and when we are around each other, it's like no time has passed.'

'And you're there for each other. A guy fleeing bad things on the west coast can crash on your couch, buy guns and you don't ask any questions?'

'I did ask a couple, and he was up front about it all.'

'But it doesn't matter that he was on the wrong side of the law?'

'No, it doesn't. It doesn't figure into it. He could have shown up at three in the morning covered in blood, and I would have taken him in.'

'Really?'

'Sure, he's saved my life in Vietnam more than once. I've returned the favor. He didn't ask questions last spring when he brought some heavy hitters to bail me out of trouble when I had been shot. He cleaned me up and treated me and never once thought of how it could jam him up. That's just how it is.'

'You know that you guys aren't normal, right? Normal people don't give each guns or patch up each other's bullet wounds.'

'True, but I've never pretended to be normal.'

'No, thank god. What will he do now?'

'That's up to him, but I suspect that he will go into business here the way he did in San Francisco.'

For the second time that night, I wasn't being exactly honest with her. Chris hadn't just gone to see Carney because he wanted a big revolver to tote around.

'Aren't you guys on opposite sides of the law?'

'You know better than anybody that the law isn't always right.'

'I do,' she said quietly.

Angela had shot a man. It had been sort of justifiable but, in the end, I found a way to keep her out of it. It wasn't something we talked about. At times, I wasn't entirely sure if she was still with me out of an overwhelming sense of obligation.

'Billy Devaney called me today,' I said, changing the subject.

'What did Devaney say?'

'Captain Muscles has a couple of arrests for simple assault, all misdemeanors, the type of guy who gets in a fight at bar or at Fenway after a few too many. Nothing serious.'

'That's it?'

'Speeding tickets and a DUI, but nothing crazy.'

'Something tells me you weren't satisfied.'

'You're right, I wasn't. So I called Brenda Watts over at the FBI.'

'The pretty lady agent you have a crush on.'

'No, I only have eyes for you.' That earned me a jab in the ribs.

'It's not your eyes I'm worried about.'

'Hey!'

'What did the lady Fed say?'

'She said that there were a few times when Captain Muscles had been close to people that were being investigated. He was never one of the players, never the focus, but he just kept turning up with shady people a little too often. He wasn't on the radar, but she seemed to think that was only a matter of time.'

'What type of people? Mob guys?'

'No, even worse. White collar types. Fraud guys.'

'Haha, he doesn't sound like the brains of the operation.'

'Don't joke, he graduated from Brown.'

'Ivy Leagues turn out their share of criminals too.'

'I've met some but he had to have some brains to get in and to graduate. Not like me eking out my degree at night school.'

'I've seen plenty of Ivy Leaguers in the courtroom who I am sure the only way they graduated was because of mommy and daddy's deep pockets.'

'No doubt. That being said, just because he's built like a pale version of the Hulk doesn't mean it's a good idea to underestimate him.'

'Good point.'

I was drifting off when she rubbed her leg against mine.

'Andy.'

'Um-huh.' I was almost asleep.

'You said I was your girlfriend.'

'Uh-uh.' I drifted off to sleep with the distinct impression that she might be gloating a little.

The next morning the sun streamed into the bedroom. I woke up when Angela came over to the bed to kiss me.

'I'm off to work, sleepyhead.'

'Oh, have a good day,' was the best that my tired self could manage.

'You too. Stay out of trouble.'

'Will do.'

I watched her back as she walked away. It occurred to me that I was a pretty lucky guy.

I should have gotten up and gone for a run. Instead, I lazed in bed. I read a chapter of Truman Capote's beautifully written *In Cold Blood*. Somehow he had managed to write about a horrific murder in Kansas and turn out a piece of fantastic literature. I didn't love how he humanized the murderers, but maybe that was what made it great writing. Eventually Sir Leominster got tired of ignoring my sworn duty to feed him and hopped up on the bed, meowing loudly. He came around the side of the book and started to butt up against my chin with his tiny, hard forehead. I got the point.

Chris was snoring on the couch, under the blanket and bedding. His right hand was under the pillow, no doubt resting on the walnut grips of his .357. I went into the kitchen and started the coffee brewing. I opened the can of fish parts the cat thought of as a delicacy. I put his plate down on the floor to the chorus of his insistent meowing.

I rummaged in the refrigerator for a package of bacon that I had picked up at the market yesterday. I dug out eggs and a block of cheddar cheese. I also pulled out the whole wheat bread and some leftover broccoli that I had made recently. I put the frying pan on the stove and added strips of bacon.

Soon the apartment was filled with the smell of fried bacon and freshly brewed coffee. I heard Chris stirring. The smell of fried bacon is one of life's best alarm clocks. I made toast for the two of us and put another pan on the stove. I cut a square of butter that was about a tablespoon and a half, which went into the pan.

Four eggs went into a big bowl with a pinch of salt. I beat the eggs with a fork until there was no sign of white left in them. When it was done I buttered the toast and then tipped the eggs into the pan of melted butter. I took the block of cheese, cut the packaging off and put the block of cheese on the cutting board. I cut it into long, thin slices, enough to cover each piece of toast.

I went to the pan and started to slowly make circles in the egg with the fork mixing them until they started to stiffen and form curds. I kept stirring the egg mixture, watching them slowly set and eventually ended up with a soft but not wet scramble.

I put two pieces of toast down on the two plates I pulled from the dish rack placing thin slices of cheese on them. Then I took the slices of bacon from the pan, shaking the fat off them and put two per each slice of bread. I picked up the pan of eggs and slid them out of the pan on to the toast, the heat from the bacon and eggs melting the cheese underneath. Lastly, I sprinkled chopped chives over the top.

'You're going to make someone a wonderful wife someday,' Chris said from the doorway.

'If it's worth doing, it's worth doing right.'

'Sure. Coffee?'

'Yeah, grab a mug from the cabinet to the left of the sink.'

'Gotcha.'

'Grab me one, too.'

When the coffee had been poured, we sat and ate in companionable silence.

'So, *are* you going to make someone a wonderful wife?' Chris asked.

'Angela, you mean?'

'Yeah.'

'Haven't thought that far ahead, pilgrim.' I said the last word in best imitation of John Wayne, which, like most of them, wasn't that good.

'But you like her, and she clearly likes you.'

'You know, I don't have a great track record with relationships. I'm just trying to take it easy and see where this is going. I've only known her for a few months. How about you? Did you break any hearts in San Francisco when you left?' I said, desperate to change the subject.

'No, no one steady. My life . . . the guys I meet . . . it doesn't really work that well. How is your case going?' I wasn't the only one who liked to change subjects abruptly.

'I think there is something going on at that bank. I am just not sure what it is.'

'Something other than embezzling?'

'I dunno. I am great at leading a recon patrol. I'm pretty good with a gun and make a decent breakfast, but white-collar crime isn't exactly my forte.'

'What will you do now?'

'Drive up to Amesbury and see if Karen Marti or Harry Brock will talk to me.'

'What if they don't?'

'Then I will start talking to my friend in the FBI and my shady mob lawyer friend. If there is something going on in this state, between the two of them, someone should have an idea of what it is.'

'Well, that seems like a plan.'

'What about you? What's going on?' I asked.

'Carney and I talked. He can arrange work and, more importantly, some wheels. I was going to look for a place of my own.'

'You're welcome to stay as long as you want to.'

'No, I don't want to cramp your style.'

'It's no problem.'

'I appreciate that, but I also don't want you to cramp *my* style,' he said with emphasis. I had known Chris for a long time, but he only told me that he was gay a year ago when I was crashing at his place in San Francisco while on a case. I could see where sleeping on my couch might not help his love life.

'Fair enough.'

'I appreciate the hospitality, bro, I do but I can't crash on your couch forever. I can't imagine that Angela would be cool with it either. Don't want to cramp her style, either.'

He had a good point.

I went to the office. I told myself that I was there to check my messages but in reality, I was just trying to figure out the next step. I listened to my messages but, other than a couple of prospective clients, there wasn't anything worth noting.

I picked up the phone and dialed Watts at the FBI over in the brick monstrosity known as Government Center. Her phone kept ringing, and eventually I was dumped back to the switchboard. I declined the nice lady's offer to take a message for me.

I thought about calling Danny Sullivan, my childhood friend and mob lawyer, but talking to him was best done in a bar after he'd had his first expensive scotch and pointless after his third. It was too early to meet with him anyway, as I was sure his clients were keeping him busy keeping them out of prison. What could I say, he was a good defense attorney.

I killed some time flipping through the pages of *Soldier of Fortune* magazine. The articles were the usual mix of stories about Communism in South/Central America, finding work as a mercenary, survival tips and gun reviews. I wasn't that interested in any of it, not even the review of the South African 'Street Sweeper' shotgun.

I tossed SoF down and picked up a copy of *Guns and Ammo* magazine. They reviewed new guns that I couldn't afford, and continued the revolver versus automatic debate that had raged for the last seventy years. Jan Libourel offered an opinion piece that the 9mm was the cartridge of the future. The Germans had figured that out in 1908. Colonel Jeff Cooper penned an editorial that could be summed up as, 'liberals are fools and the .45 ACP was god's chosen bullet for serious-minded pistol shooters.' The debate about which cartridge was better had only been exacerbated by the Army's decision to replace the venerable 1911 .45 caliber pistol with the 9mm Beretta. People were oddly passionate about it. Either way, I was staying out of it. They were both just tools in the toolbox.

I broke for lunch from the local deli. It was much more convenient when old man Marconi had his pizzeria downstairs. I could pop in for a couple of slices. But he sold the place last year to move back to Italy when he found out he had cancer. He did leave me his espresso machine, the one he special ordered from Italy. I was getting to be a fair hand at turning out cups of the bitter stuff. I brought my turkey sandwich on pumpernickel back to the office and went back to reading magazines while I ate.

When I had caught up on my professional development reading and there was no more procrastinating to be done, it was time to go to Amesbury. I locked the office and headed north again. I tuned the radio to the local classical station to counter the best efforts of early afternoon traffic to frustrate me as I negotiated my way out of town. Once I was on the Mystic River Bridge, which they now insist on calling the Tobin Bridge, I switched to the rock and roll station.

I rolled northward watching the sky darken and listening to The Who complain about being misunderstood. The sky was threatening rain, and the humidity was offering a hint of what summer in Boston had to offer. When the skies finally did open up as I was on Interstate 95, I rolled up my window until it was cracked just enough to let the smoke from my Lucky out and not too much rain in. The windshield wipers kept time to Creedence Clearwater Revival's 'Fortunate Son.'

I formulated my strategy as to how to approach both Brock and Marti. Brock was simple. I was just going to wait for him in the parking lot of the bank. He might be more willing to talk to me in person, preferably away from the bank crowd. I wanted to see if he thought that Lintz had anything to do with Cosgrove's murder. If Lintz was embezzling, maybe the young Cosgrove had something to do with it. Weddings are expensive. Or maybe Cosgrove stumbled on to Lintz's activities and Lintz had him whacked? Maybe he could also shed some light on Captain Muscles and his connection to the bank.

A bank robbery seemed like a good way to hide the targeted killing of a bank employee. Brock had said that the embezzlement was to the tune of a couple million dollars. People had been murdered for a lot less. Lintz seemed boring, a regular man, family and all, not the type to murder anyone. On top of that I hadn't even found evidence of him embezzling either. But who knows? Plenty of decent family men had done horrible things.

I was on thinner ice with Karen Marti. Our last meeting didn't go well and now I was bordering on harassment. I was convinced she knew more than she was letting on. I wasn't sure where she fit in, but as Brock's secretary, she had to know everything that was going on in the bank. Maybe she was just trying to protect Cosgrove's memory, his good name? Or maybe she was scared to talk to me.

By the time I pulled into the parking lot of the Merrimack Community Bank, I had decided that it was all as clear as mud. It might help if I had some idea of the financial end of it. Brock had told me to focus on his employees living above their means. What I didn't understand was the mechanics of the embezzlement. If all three of them had access to the bank's money, how did the embezzler siphon it off? Not only that, but where did it go? Brock had said that it was over two million dollars. It had to go somewhere. What I didn't know about banking and finance in general could fill volumes.

The rain stopped a little after three thirty. I rolled my window down a little more and let in the smell of rain on warm pavement. It wasn't as pronounced as it would be in a couple of months, but it was there. It was a smell that I always associated with childhood, running out of the apartment to play stickball with the gang. Or the smell that offered the hope of a break in an oppressive August heatwave. It always held the promise of good things to come and occasionally delivered.

At four, people started coming out of the bank in ones and twos. The doors had been locked since three, and the first to leave were women who I assumed to be tellers. Karen Marti came out at four twenty-five and got into her Chevette. She drove off without so much as glancing at me. Lintz came out at four thirty, got into his Mercedes and headed back to his home. By then, the only three cars in the lot were mine, the Amesbury PD car and Brock's.

He came out the front door at quarter to five and waved at the Amesbury cop. His smile faded when he saw me get out of the Maverick. I walked over to him.

'Roark, what are you doing here? I thought you weren't interested in this case.'

'Mr Brock, I was hoping to talk to you.' I had decided to follow John Wayne's advice about apologizing.

'I told you that you'd had your crack at the case. Now Frank's dead. Maybe if you'd taken this more seriously the first time, you wouldn't be here now.'

'Everything all right, Mr Brock?' The Amesbury cop was in his twenties, and, other than his hand on the butt of his revolver, there wasn't anything I found interesting about him.

'Yes, thank you. Everything is fine. I know this man.'

'OK, sir. You have a good day.' The cop made a half-assed attempt at a salute, and I couldn't tell if it was a mark of respect or satirical act. Either way it didn't make a difference. He went back to his patrol car and drove off.

'I can't stop thinking your man Cosgrove's murder. The timing is just too coincidental.'

'So what? Now you think there is a case. Now you're interested. Or do you see another chance to make some easy money? Whatever you're selling Roark, I'm not interested.'

'Brock, a man is dead. A man who everyone tells me was decent and upright. By all accounts, a man who didn't deserve to die. If I missed something or made a mistake that led to his death, then I owe it to him to try and make it right.' I hadn't actually intended to say all that, but it came over me suddenly. I had been dancing around it in my mind for so long but until now, I hadn't fully come to grips with what was bothering me about Cosgrove's murder.

'OK, Roark. Take it easy.' He smiled. 'All right, maybe I got it all wrong about you.'

'Thanks.'

'Listen, your profession, you know, it isn't the most reputable.'

'Sure, sure.' It isn't that I agreed with him, but I wasn't going to get into a debate about ethics with a banker, especially when he was starting to warm up to me.

'Plus, I was rattled by Frank's murder . . . we all were.'

'I get it. Who could blame you. Listen, is there some place we can talk?'

'About what?'

'You hired me to look at the angle of people living above their means, but I don't know anything about how the money was actually taken.'

'Sure, there's a bar in Market Square. Why don't we go over there and talk about it over a beer?'

'That's the best idea I've heard all day.'

'Good. I know I could use a cold one. I've been under a lot of pressure.'

'That sounds like a plan.'

We got back into our cars and drove the few blocks to Amesbury's rather attractive collection of red brick buildings that surround Market Square. I parked the Maverick and walked over to where Brock was waiting for me on the pavement in front of a place unoriginally called The Market Square Tap Room.

'This place is pretty good. I come here a lot after work,' he said.

'I am sure it is,' I said blandly.

I followed him and we found seats at the bar where I ordered a Lowenbrau, and he ordered a scotch on the rocks. I had been under the impression that tap rooms were supposed serve mostly beer and very limited food, but looking at the menu, it seemed like they weren't sticking too closely to that convention.

'So, how does it work?' I asked.

'Embezzling?'

'Yes. How does someone like Lintz steal from the bank? I have to imagine that you guys have all sorts of checks and safeguards.'

'We do. Sure.' Brock took a sip of his drink. 'The first thing is access. You have to be able to get to the money in order to steal it.'

'Sure, that makes sense.'

'So, there are a few ways of embezzling. One is to find an account or accounts where there is a large amount of money and someone who is not very attentive, say, like an elderly person or someone who has taken ill. Then the embezzler syphons money out of the account, not so much that raises anyone's interest.'

'What would he do with it?'

'Move some into another account, multiple accounts, until he eventually puts it in one he controls. Then take the cash out.'

'That doesn't sound super complex.'

'No, it isn't, but it leaves a trail.'

'Doesn't everything leave a trail?'

'Sure, but there're some trails that are harder to follow than others.'

'Like what?'

'Let's say you have access to the computer systems that calculate things like interest. Different types of accounts accrue different interest rates. The depositors open accounts thinking they're getting, say, three percent, but our embezzler recodes the account so it is getting three point one percent interest. Then he moves the zero point one percent interest into another account that he controls.'

'That doesn't sound like a lot of money.'

'No, not for one account, but let's say that the bank has accounts worth ten million dollars that he has reconfigured like that. That would work out to a hundred thousand dollars.'

'That's a lot, but it doesn't seem like it's worth the risk.'

'Well, that depends on when the interest is earned. It might be monthly or semi-annually etc. Then it starts to add up. We aren't even talking about the financial products that are based on interest rate fluctuations.'

'So, then what does he do with it?'

'Sits on it. Leaves it in an account, gathering interest until it is time to cash out or take a nibble at it now and then as he needs to pay for things, say, groceries or anything that can be paid for in cash with the embezzled money.'

'Is that it?'

'No, there are probably a couple hundred other schemes. Moving currency through various banks and markets, shaving a tiny percentage off and bundling it with the associated fees and then moving it back into your account. At the end of the day, it is still about access to the money and how the money is spent.'

'I have to assume that you looked at your employees' accounts.'

'Sure, I personally looked over private accounts and accounts that they had access to. I couldn't find a damn thing. Whoever the embezzler is, they're damned smart. They've covered their tracks well.'

'Well, there's no point in being a sloppy embezzler is there? That would just lead to a prison cell.'

'Exactly.'

'The thing of it is that I looked at all three of them. None of them are leading what you'd call extravagant lifestyles. Lintz is Mr Family Man who drives a nice but older car. I am thinking he bought it before they had a kid. Karen Marti doesn't seem to have any vices other than Bingo.' I didn't point out that I recently learned of her appreciation for tequila.

'And Cosgrove?'

'Cosgrove seemed like a nice kid who took his fiancée on dates to bowling alleys, movie theaters or McDonald's. A big night out for them would be dinner and drinks at Bennigan's. He wasn't living the high life.'

'But you still think his murder has something to do with the embezzling?'

'I don't know if it does or doesn't. I just know that I won't be able to get any peace until I know for sure.'

'OK, if you want it, you're back on the case.'

'I'm going to look into it whether I have a client or not. He seemed like a nice kid.'

'Let's make it official. Here's . . . five hundred as a retainer.' He took the bills out of one of the long wallets that was meant to ride inside a suit jacket inner pocket. His was made of pigskin, and my guess was English. They are classy with their animal hide accessories.

'What are you hiring me to do, exactly?'

'Do what you're going to do anyway. See if there's a link between Frank's killing and the embezzling. Then who's my embezzler? I am still betting on Lintz.'

'Is it possible that Frank found something in the course of his work? Something that would have tipped him off to the embezzler's identity?' I didn't feel like telling Brock about the episode in Cosgrove's apartment. That might have been as much from embarrassment about getting caught wrong-footed as my policy of not admitting to committing felonies.

'It's possible. But robbing a bank and murdering him seems like a lot of risk. Wouldn't there be easier ways to silence him?'

'Sure, there would. But no one would question a bank employee murdered during a robbery. No one would look too closely at that.'

'But this is Amesbury, not Detroit or LA.'

'That's true, but how many bank robberies have there been in Amesbury?'

'Until mine . . . none since I've been in banking.'

'That might be an indicator.'

'It might, or our luck ran out. Every bank is at risk of getting robbed. That's just one of the risks involved. OK. I gotta run. Keep me posted on your progress.'

'Sure, will do.'

And like that, I was gainfully employed again. Maybe all of my efforts at self-improvement were paying off – the cat hadn't died, I had a girlfriend, and I had a paying client again. Or maybe it was just that nothing had gone wrong yet.

It occurred to me that I wanted to talk to Cosgrove's fiancée. I wasn't sure that I wanted to show up on her doorstep smelling of beer and asking uncomfortable questions about her late fiancé. That might be something better left for tomorrow. Plus, I was already sick of sitting in my car watching that damned bank. Tomorrow I could talk to Cosgrove's fiancée and then try to talk to Karen Marti again. That would at least be a break from boring myself to death.

I got back in my Maverick and headed back to Boston. I did some of my best thinking on the road. While on the face of it, the family man Lintz didn't seem like an obvious choice for an embezzler and criminal mastermind, but he did have a lot to lose. If he got pinched for embezzling, goodbye family, goodbye nice home, goodbye freedom. That could be motive enough to set up an elaborate murder plan. Just because I had parked outside of his house and job didn't mean I actually knew anything about the guy.

I got back to the apartment to find Sir Leominster as demanding as ever and Chris sitting at my kitchen table cleaning his newly acquired hardware with my gun cleaning kit. There was a bottle of Lowenbrau next to him.

'Hey, how'd the sleuthing go today?'

'Good, I have a client again.'

'New one?'

'No, oddly enough, the bank president rehired me.'

'That's good. Did you find anything out?'

'Not much, except there is a lot more and lot less to embezzling than you would think.'

'What do you mean?'

'Well, the embezzler has to have access to the money.'

'That seems pretty obvious,' he said, reaching over to the fridge to pull out another beer, which he handed to me.

'Right, but then there are two major issues, moving the money and hiding the money so he doesn't get caught.'

'Those do seem like important points. So, what's next?'

'Tomorrow I am going to go talk to Cosgrove's fiancée and see if she can offer any insight. Then I will take another run at Karen Marti.'

'You don't sound very hopeful.'

'I'm not. The odds are that Cosgrove's murder was exactly what it was, a robbery gone wrong.'

'So why pursue it then?'

'Because it is the only part of this that stands out, the only part that is inconsistent. Like being out in the field and seeing something, maybe not even knowing what, but knowing it couldn't be ignored because it meant the NVA was out there.'

'OK, Truong Si, I get it.' Chris calling me Sergeant in Vietnamese didn't actually make me feel any better.

The next morning, I woke up and went for a run. Chris's presence was not helping my liver or my attempt to stay in shape. Though frankly, neither was all the time I had spent sitting in my car, watching the bank parking lot. After cleaning up and conferring with Chris about our individual plans for the day, I left for Amesbury.

Cosgrove's fiancée was an elementary school teacher. She hadn't gone back to work yet, and Brock had been good enough to provide me with her address. I dressed reasonably respectably today – sneakers, jeans, a polo shirt, and I had a khaki sport coat so I wouldn't look like a total bum. I had my .38 on my hip under the polo shirt. My Buck knife was in my pocket and a speedloader of hollow points was in the other pocket in case of unforeseen trouble. Chris might want to carry a .357 Magnum hand cannon or need a compact 9mm automatic, but I didn't have his sort of problems. Most of the time, a humble .38 snub-nose was enough for my needs.

I had made the trip to Amesbury so many times that I basically drove on autopilot. The radio favored me with good music the whole way up. The spring weather was fine, and May was the gateway to summer and baseball. For those of us from Boston, baseball is a passion, and the Red Sox are a religion.

This year the squad was showing promise, and while it was too early to tell, this might be a World Series year. It might have even been the year that the boys reverse the curse of the Bambino.

Brock had called earlier and gave me Cosgrove's fiancée's information. Her name was Sheila Gardner, and she was twenty-three years old. She seemed too young to be, for all intents and purposes, a widow. Not that there was ever a good age for that sort of thing. Her house was outside of town on the type of road that was more country than suburban.

I parked on the shoulder, just down from her house a bit. I got out, put on my jacket, and made one last pointless effort to make my hair presentable. I had at least shaved this morning, and my moustache wasn't accompanied by a rash of stubble. I walked up the path from the road to the door of a home that had started life as a farmhouse a hundred and fifty years before.

I knocked on the old door that had generations of paint on it. Somewhere inside, a dog barked. I stood on the flagstone step wishing I had a cigarette until I heard faint footsteps from some-where inside. The door opened with a creak by a woman that I had only seen from a distance while I was watching her and her late fiancé on dates.

'Miss Gardner, my name is Andy Roark.' I held up my license. 'I'm a private investigator. I was hoping I could talk to you about Frank.'

'What? Talk to me about Frank?'

'Yes, Mr Brock has hired me to investigate.'

'Investigate Frank?'

'No, just the circumstances surrounding his death.'

'OK. Come in, please.' I followed her inside. The house had the look of a place that was normally neat and tidy but the need to maintain had been usurped by grief. I followed her into the living room where the TV was playing *The Price is Right* at very low volume. The furniture was comfortable-looking, if a bit dated. She plopped herself down on the couch opposite the TV, legs folded under her. She pulled the blanket over her legs. I noticed that the area around the couch was dotted by crumpled tissues.

'Sit down, Mr Roark. I'm sorry I am not much of a hostess right now and mom's at the market.'

'Thank you.' I sat in a chair facing her and, mercifully, to the side of the TV. 'That's understandable. I'm sorry for your loss.'

She dabbed her eyes with a tissue. 'Thank you. It just doesn't seem real.'

'I am sorry to intrude. I just have a few questions that are routine.'

'Go ahead. The police have been a couple of times. I can't imagine there are any questions left to answer.'

'I used to be a cop so mine will be more of the same.'

'What do you want to know?'

'What was Frank's mood like in the days before the robbery?'

'He was fine. Normal. We spent most of our time talking about our plans.'

'Plans?'

'We were planning our wedding. Not just that but also things like saving up to buy a house. Frank was very good with money. Frugal but not cheap.' She dabbed at her eyes and wadded up the tissue in her small fist. 'I used to tease him and call him Frugal Frank.'

'Did he talk about work at all?'

'Not too much. If he did, he talked about the people at work but not the work itself. To be honest, I thought his job was boring.'

'What did he have to say about the people at work? Was there anyone he had a problem with?'

'A problem?'

'Or didn't get along with?'

'He seemed to like everyone. Well, almost. He didn't care for Mr Lintz.'

'Any particular reason?'

'I don't know. I just know that he and Mr Lintz had some disagreement at work and that it bothered Frank.'

'When was this?'

'Um, the week or two before he was killed.'

Bingo. I sat still for a second, not daring to move. This was the closest thing I had to a clue, and I was afraid it would slip away like a fish wriggling off the hook.

'You don't know what the disagreement was about, do you?' I asked as casually as I could.

'No, I just know that whatever it was about, it soured him on Mr Lintz. Like he was OK before but suddenly he wasn't.'

'Did Frank seem preoccupied with anything recently or act out of character in any way?'

'No, I mean, he worried a little bit about money. Starting our life together. Frank was hoping for a promotion at work. We talked about starting a family in a few years . . . oh god, I can't believe he's gone.'

She started to sob, and it was pretty obvious it was time for me to go.

'Thank you. I am sorry.' I would have told her that I would show myself out, but there was little point. I walked back the way I had come, listening to her sobbing on the couch. I couldn't blame her.

I let myself out, closing the door softly behind me. I shook a Lucky out of the pack and lit it on the way to my car. Hopefully Karen Marti would be more willing to talk to me now that I was working for Brock again.

I made my way to the bank but noticed that Marti's car wasn't in the lot. I headed over to the deli, but her Chevette wasn't parked there either. I would try her apartment and if I didn't find her there, I would call it a day in Amesbury.

I eased my car into the late morning traffic and a few minutes later pulled up to Marti's apartment. Her little Chevette was in its spot in front of her apartment door.

I found a spot to park a few doors down and walked to her door. I knocked on it and waited, listening. Apart from the sounds of the birds happily tweeting about spring, I couldn't hear anything. I knocked again, a little louder this time. Still no movement from inside. The blinds on the windows were all down. Maybe she was in the shower? Or maybe she just didn't want to talk to me?

I was about to turn and leave, but something wasn't right. I was trying to figure it out in the bright, beautiful May morning. In Vietnam, running recon missions on the Ho Chi Minh trail, we were all very attuned to our environment. We had to be – the slightest hint or something out of place could be enough to tip us off to danger. It often meant the difference between life and death.

I stood back, looking at Karen Marti's front door, the painted door frame, the brick walls and the black cast iron railings on either side of the steps. The sounds of the birds receded into the distance as I stared. A drop of blood stained the brick wall. I only noticed it because it was an oddly smooth patch against the porous brick. I leaned closer and saw a second bloodstain on the wall. Then two more drops on the steps, under the railing where they weren't easily seen.

Avoiding the blood, I went up to the door and tried the handle with just my thumb and index finger. The handle turned, and I carefully pushed the door open. I slipped my hand under my shirt on to the butt of my revolver. I paused, listening. I could hear water dripping from somewhere in the apartment.

I looked around. I was in a small entryway with stairs leading up, and to my right was a living room that was separated from the kitchen by a countertop. The couch, an overstuffed recliner and coffee table all seemed new, except that the glass top of the coffee table had a spiderweb of cracks in it. Some of those cracks were filled in with red where someone had bled into them. The Sears catalogue was on the floor by the couch.

I eased around the couch, avoiding the carpet, and stepped carefully on the vinyl tiles. There was a door on the other side of the kitchen, and the dripping was coming from beyond it. There was blood in small pools and smears on the kitchen floor. It was congealed but hadn't dried. I did my best to avoid stepping in it. I moved gingerly toward the door.

When I got to it, I realized I was holding my revolver in my hand, pointed at the door. I knew what was on the other side. Death had a smell all its own. There was no describing it to the uninitiated. That smell came from the other side of the door. I carefully nudged the door open with the toe of my shoe.

Karen Marti had been a pretty woman in her way when she was alive. In front of me was the broken rag doll version of her. She was sitting up, wedged in the space between the toilet and the sink, her back against the wall. Her skirt was hiked up, showing an expanse of pale thigh. To my left was a clawfoot tub, filled with dirty-colored water. The toilet was at the end of the tub, and I was facing her.

Her blouse and hair were wet but not dripping. Her bruised and battered face told the story of a bad beating. Her fingers were broken, the tips all pointed in the wrong direction. Whoever had done it wasn't satisfied with just beating her to a pulp. He had drowned her in the tub, then dumped her between her own sink and toilet. Her shower curtain had been ripped from its hangers and was on the floor.

There was no point checking her pulse or stepping further into the bathroom. I backed out slowly. I carefully crossed the bloody kitchen floor and stopped by the telephone on the wall. I almost picked it up, but the cord had been ripped out, so there was no point.

It took me a few minutes to find a neighbor that was home in a nearby apartment. After looking at the copy of my license, or maybe the look on my face, they let me use the phone. I called the Amesbury police and told them a woman was dead and that they needed to send a unit over to Karen Marti's apartment. Then I went outside and leaned against the hood of my car. I smoked a Lucky Strike until the distant wailing of the siren became almost deafening as the cop came screeching into the parking lot. For a few minutes before I had gone inside her apartment, it had been a nice day in May.

SIX

If you've never had the pleasure of sitting in a holding cell, I wouldn't recommend it. The cells in the Amesbury police station were cleaner and less used than most. It would have been more comfortable if my jaw wasn't sore, but I was lucky that it was not broken. It was my fault. Sometimes, even when I know better, my mouth gets the better of me.

When the first Amesbury cop showed up on scene, I showed him my identification and told him what was inside Karen Marti's apartment. Like all cops, he couldn't just take my word for it but went to see for himself. He came out a minute later and threw up in the decorative shrubbery outside. Then he had the presence of mind to go to his squad car and get on the radio. It didn't matter. In a town like Amesbury, every car on the road was coming. Which unfortunately included the Chief of Police, Paul Dixon.

By the time he arrived, the town's two detectives were on scene taking pictures and drawing their sketches. Uniforms were combing through the parking lot and the shrubs looking for clues, and I was three Luckies into a fresh pack. The older of the two detectives asked me to hang around because they'd need a statement. So, I was hanging around when Dixon came up to me.

'Mister, what's this that I hear you broke into her apartment?'

'I didn't break in. The door was unlocked.'

'So, you just went in?'

'Yep, I saw drops of blood on the steps, and I was concerned for Ms Marti's well-being.' I was tired, it was warm, and Dixon was starting to annoy me.

'Don't take a smart tone with me, mister. You broke into her apartment, and I can arrest you for that.'

'Chief, why would I break into her apartment?'

'How do I know you didn't kill her?'

'And then call the police to report her death? Then hang around and talk to detectives? Why would I do that?'

I didn't bother to point out the lack of bruising on my knuckles, scratches or other wounds that the killer surely had. I didn't feel like explaining to the chief about basic criminal procedure.

'You could be trying to cover your tracks, playing at being innocent.'

'Chief, in all seriousness, can I ask you a question?' I said in my most sincere, professional voice.

'What?'

'Are you related to the Mayor of Amesbury? Like a brother or cousin or something?'

'No.'

'Then how did you get this job, because you seem too fucking stupid be a meter maid, much less the Chief of Police.'

His face went red and the last thing I saw was his beefy fist coming at me. The first one caught me in the jaw and then I covered up. I weathered the blows that he rained down on me. Dixon was strong, but he wasn't in shape and he quickly tired.

I thought about swinging back, I was certain I could take him, but there was no percentage in fighting with cops in this case. When he got winded, he called one of his guys over to handcuff me and take me downtown. Dixon actually said, 'Take him downtown,' like he was Kojak or something. That was how I ended up in a holding cell in Amesbury, Massachusetts. It wasn't as exciting or lyrical as Alice's Restaurant, but it was my sordid little story.

I waited for an hour or two; they had taken my watch, so it seemed longer. They had also taken my wallet, belt, shoelaces, gun, my pocketknife, my lighter and my cigarettes. No one had asked my name. No one had booked me, no one had printed me, and no one offered me my one phone call. I stretched out on the metal bench in the cell and closed my eyes. There was nothing else to do.

After what could have been fifteen minutes or an hour, I heard a door open and then footsteps coming toward my cell. They stopped in front of my cell and voice said, 'Hey, Roark, wake up.' I opened an eye to see one of the two detectives from earlier. He didn't seem like a bad sort.

'What's up?'

'I need to ask you some questions.'

'Sure, call my lawyer.'

'C'mon, Roark, you don't need your lawyer. You were a cop, you know how it is. We gotta talk.'

'Sure, I was a cop. I was assaulted, arrested, and thrown in a cell without being booked or given a phone call.'

'You pissed the chief off.'

'Sure, that's an arrestable offense in this state.'

'Roark, he's the chief.'

'He's a dimwit and an asshole.'

'C'mon, Roark.'

'Book me and let me call my lawyer or let me out.'

'That's it?'

'Uh-huh. You want me to talk, be happy to but not without my lawyer.'

'Chief's not gonna be happy.'

'Your chief's happiness is pretty low on the list of things I give a shit about.'

'Jeez, Roark, what's the problem, can't you take a punch?'

'Naw, it's not that. I just don't like his style.'

'You're making this harder than it needs to be.'

'I was cooperating, I called you guys. Now I think I am just going to enjoy your lovely accommodations.'

'Roark, don't break my balls.'

'Your chief accused me of murder, hit me and dragged me down here. Pretty sure that means I need a lawyer.'

'C'mon, Roark, talk to me. He just lost his temper,' he pleaded.

'Lawyer.'

'C'mon, man, cop to cop. Help me out.'

'Sure, cop to cop, get my lawyer. Or book me.'

'Shit.' He stormed off. I couldn't blame him, it had to be hard working for an asshole like Dixon, and I had no intention of making his life any easier.

I waited some more, trying not to think about how much I wanted a cigarette. Come to think of it, a whiskey wouldn't be too bad either. I sat there trying to think of the 1975 Red Sox lineup and where they all ended up. Then I tried to recall the lyrics to all of my favorite Van Morrison songs. I even thought about 'Brown Eyed Girl,' which is a fine enough song but way overplayed. By the time I had gotten to 'Crazy Face,' my stomach was rumbling. I was going over the steps to tie a Swiss seat rappelling harness when Dixon walked in.

'Roark. You need to talk to my detectives.'

'That makes sense.'

'So, you'll talk to them.'

'Sure, just as soon as my lawyer's here. I'll give a full statement,' I said as though I was the most reasonable man in the world.

'Jesus, Roark, you are stubborn. Why do you think you need a lawyer? Are you guilty?'

'Well, after you slugging me and throwing me in a cell, I am pretty sure that you'd be more than happy to further trample all over my constitutional rights.'

'Aw, c'mon, Roark.' He said it like we were pals.

'Also, I'm pretty sure you aren't actually smart enough to solve a murder, so pinning one on me seems about your speed.'

I laid back down on the hard steel bunk and closed my eyes while he began to sputter and yell. He stormed off. I closed my eyes and thought about the charred cheeseburgers at Brigham's. It didn't make me feel less hungry, but it gave me something to focus my hunger on.

A uniformed officer came in. He had a phone on a long extension cord. He put the phone on the shelf that food was passed through. I called Danny Sullivan's office and told his secretary where I was and under what circumstances. Compared to Danny's mobster friends, I was pretty low rent, but Gladys was used to having Danny bail guys out of jail. I just hoped that Amesbury PD wasn't too low rent for a guy who was usually in the federal courthouse downtown. I hung up and the cop took the phone, coiling its long cord as he shuffled away.

I'd love to tell you that it wasn't much longer. Eventually two uniforms came to get me. They unlocked the cell door and

motioned me to follow them. They brought me to a small interrogation room where Terry McVicker was waiting for me.

'Hey, Terry, how'd you end up with this?'

'Hey, Andy. Danny called me. He was tied up and figured that
you would rather see a friendly face than one of his associates.'

'Sure. Makes sense.'

'Tell me what happened.'

I told him the short version. I was hired by Brock to investigate
some irregularities at the bank. I hadn't found anything. Then
after the botched robbery Brock hired me to look into it. That
led me to Karen Marti's corpse.

Chief Dixon came in with the detective from earlier in tow.
'All right, Roark. Your lawyer's here now. Talk.'

'Chief, are you charging my client?' Terry asked politely.

'Well, that remains to be seen.'

'What are you charging him with?'

'Well, we found him at the scene of a murder.'

'Which he called you to report. I don't think he would do that
if he was the murderer.'

'He assaulted me.'

'That's funny because there is a very nice, retired lady who
was a neighbor of the deceased. She was so fascinated by the
comings and goings of the police that she was glued to the
window. She told me that you punched and struck my client
numerous times and that he didn't strike you.'

'Bullshit.'

'Acting under the color of authority, assault, false arrest.' Then
to me, 'Andy, did I leave anything out?'

'Being an asshole?' I asked unhelpfully.

'What are you getting at?' Dixon asked.

'Oh, those will be listed as part of the lawsuit.'

'Lawsuit?'

'Sure, I can tell that Andy didn't have anything to do with the
murder. No blood on his clothes, no scrapes on his hands, etc.
Plus, he was a Green Beret in Vietnam. I think he knows a thing
or two about violence. By the time the jury hears about how you
treated him, he'll end up with a significant portion of the
Amesbury's police budget for that year.'

'What?' Dixon said.

'I suspect that the town fathers won't be too happy, and they'll be looking for a new chief.'

'What . . . you can't . . . I didn't do anything wrong,' Dixon started to splutter.

'I want my client released. *Now*!' I had never heard Terry raise his voice before.

'Right. Cut him loose,' Dixon said to the detective.

'And I want his property returned to him right away.'

'We're not giving him his gun back.'

'He's a private detective, licensed by the Commonwealth and licensed to carry a firearm. If you aren't charging him with anything, return it. Or do I have to call the State Police to report the theft of a firearm?' I almost felt bad for Dixon as I watched him deflate, pierced by Terry McVicker's words.

'OK, OK.'

'As a gesture of good faith, my client is prepared to leave a statement, a *brief* statement, about his discovering the deceased while he waits for his property to be returned.'

'OK. Thank you.'

'Andy,' Terry said with a nod in my direction.

I told the detective that I had been hired by Brock to look into some irregularities in the bank, that I was interviewing various employees. I had tried on a few occasions to talk to Marti, but she was too upset about Cosgrove's murder to talk. I was going to her apartment to talk to her when I noticed the blood drops. I tried the door, and it opened. I saw the apartment in disarray, and fearing she was injured, entered into the apartment and found her dead in the bathroom. It was almost that simple.

A uniformed officer brought me my property, to include my gun and knife. I answered a few short questions with Terry's approval while I laced up my sneakers. Then with everything in place, Terry and I left the police station and walked out to his car. I was glad to see that Terry was doing all right for himself, as evidenced by the blue Audi he was driving.

I lit a Lucky and inhaled deeply. It had been a long day and now it was evening. Insects were wheeling around in the fading warmth of the day. It still got chilly at night this far north. Terry drove me back to Marti's where my car was parked. I sat back in the leather seats of his car. Maybe someday I could afford West German automotive perfection.

'Thanks, Terry, you were truly magnificent. You made that asshole jump.'

'Ha. No worries, pal. Listen, stop pissing people off. You know you catch more flies with honey than vinegar.'

'Yeah, so I've been told. But you have to admit that guy Dixon is an asshole.'

'Sure, he is, but he's also the law in that town. I'm surprised you didn't clean his clock when he took a swing at you.'

'Naw, there's no percentage in fighting with cops.'

'You are smarter than you look.'

'Thanks.'

'Sure, sure.'

'Send me your bill.'

'Naw, it's on Danny. He could have come himself and, frankly, he'll throw me something more lucrative on the back end.'

'Lawyers, you guys always have an angle.'

'Yes, we do.'

He nodded and we said goodbye. I made a mental note to drop a nice bottle of something with an unpronounceable Scottish name off at his office.

I got in the Maverick and started my way back to Boston. I had been in Amesbury since midmorning, and now it was almost nine at night. After over eight hours in a jail cell, even a nice, relatively clean jail cell, I needed a shower. I was hungry, and I was long overdue for a very tall whiskey with very little ice. Also, I couldn't get the image of Karen Marti's battered corpse out of my head.

She didn't deserve to die like that. I am not saying that no one deserves to die like that – there is no shortage of rapists and child molesters in the world. Karen Marti wasn't in that league. My first thought was that Captain Muscles was a likely candidate. I was thinking of him storming out of the barbecue joint the other night. He hadn't struck me as the type to control his temper well.

I started cruising through the radio stations and stopped when
Willie Nelson's voice came on singing 'Bloody Mary Morning'.
I couldn't tell if the universe was trying to be ironic or if life
was just that random. I almost changed it, but the song was
up-tempo, and Willie managed to make being left by a girlfriend
into a tune that I found myself tapping my fingers against the
steering wheel to.

The door to the apartment hadn't been forced open, at least
not the front door. I could go back and check the back door. If
it wasn't forced open, then she opened the door for someone or
they had a key. Maybe it was picked. While that was common
on TV and in the movies, it was just pretty rare in real life. Most
burglaries involve jimmied doors or a pushed in air conditioner.
Most criminals aren't locksmith types. If the lock had been picked,
there'd be evidence, usually scratches around the face of the lock.
I didn't have much confidence in the local police after seeing
who was leading them.

By the time I parked the Maverick in front of my building, I
still hadn't figured out what my next step was beyond a shower,
something to eat and a lot of whiskey. Death did that to me. I
took the mail out of the box in the foyer and made my way up
the three flights of stairs to my apartment. I opened the door and
was greeted not by the plaintive meowing of Sir Leominster but
instead by the sound of country music. In this case, Willie Nelson
and Waylon Jennings were offering the mothers of the world
parenting advice.

Now, country music is not really my thing, but the song was
iconic, if a bit twangy. It wouldn't be hard to substitute 'cowboys'
in the lyrics for Green Berets or private eyes.

Chris appeared in the doorway to the kitchen. The Spanish
9mm was in his hand, which was hanging at his side. Having
trained side by side with him, having been in combat with him,
I was glad that the pistol wasn't pointed at me. Chris was good
with a gun, probably better than I was.

'Hey, Red,' he said.

'Hey.'

'Where you been?'

'In a jail cell.'

'That sucks. Here?'

'No, Amesbury.'

'What'd you do? Jaywalking?'

'Naw, my mouth talked me into the cell.'

'Ha! That's not surprising.'

'Yeah. Let me grab a shower real quick and I'll bring you up to speed.'

'Sure. I fed the cat.'

'He wouldn't give you any peace.'

'Nope, and I figured you'd object to my mistreating him, so opening a can of that smelly stuff he calls food was the easiest thing in the world.'

'I am fond of the cat.' I didn't tell Chris about my theory that Sir Leominster stayed awake at night, on guard, in case the VC or NVA attacked. He didn't need any clues that I had an irrational side.

I undressed and turned on the shower. I washed the stink of the jail cell off me. I couldn't wash the smell of Karen Marti's death away. It was in my nostrils the same way the sight of her corpse was lodged behind my eyes. I was starting to think there was someone behind all of this, and I decided that if I was given the chance, I was going to kill the son of a bitch.

When I was done showering, I put on some running shorts and a t-shirt. Lintz was the last one left. Lintz was the person that Brock had thought most likely to be embezzling. Was Lintz behind the murders? Was he some sort of master criminal? If so, we had a date.

The lights on the machine were blinking, but I ignored them. Whiskey was a priority. I went into the kitchen for a glass and ice. Chris didn't say anything as I poured whiskey over the ice until there was almost no freeboard in the highball glass. I took a long pull on the drink. Then I went to the machine with its blinking lights.

'I heard you got arrested again. I'm sure it has nothing to do with your mob or hoodlum friends. Give me a call when you get a second. I can act as a character reference at your trial.' Watts was the queen of sarcasm, and she was usually most sarcastic when she was worried about me. It was no surprise that she of

the FBI didn't care for my more colorful friends. What could I
say? They were fun.

'Terry McVicker let me know that he was going to Amesbury
to bail you out. Give me a call in the morning.' Angela's tone
wasn't much softer than Watts's, but in the few months we'd
been dating, I hadn't done much to convince her that I made
good decisions. It was weird having people in my life, people
who worried about me. I wasn't used to it.

I went back into the kitchen where Chris was sitting at the
table, cigarette burning in one hand and the other absentmind-
edly petting Sir Leominster, whose loyalty I was starting to
question.

'You eat?' he asked.

'No, not for a while.'

'I'll make something in a minute.'

'Yeah, empty stomach and half a glass of whiskey already
gone, something tells me you won't make it long.'

'I'll get to it,' I said irritably.

'Sure, you will.' He got up and rummaged in the fridge. I was
too tired to argue with him.

'I found that woman, Karen Marti.'

'I didn't know she was missing.' He put a pile of things on
the kitchen counter.

'She wasn't. She was dead. Someone beat her to death, tortured
her, too.'

'Jesus.'

'Exactly.'

'How?'

'Broken fingers and then the old drown or talk routine in the
bathtub. You know, I've seen my share of bad things, done some
myself, but this . . . this is different.'

Chris didn't say anything but busied himself at the kitchen
counter. When I stayed with him in San Francisco last year, he
had impressed me with his cooking. Soon, the most comforting
smell in the world filled the kitchen – bacon frying.

'You know, when we were in Vietnam running missions or
later, here, when I have seen people killed or killed them it . . .'
I was struggling to find the right words. I had seen some stuff

in the last year, a pregnant woman shot for no reason, horrible things. I couldn't put words to it. Not tonight.

'We were soldiers in a war, Red. We were volunteers, and we knew what we were getting into . . . I have to imagine that this is different.'

'I didn't know her, not really, but she seemed sad. Vulnerable.'

'Any idea why it happened?'

'It has to do with that damn bank. It has to. Two employees of the same bank, in the same town, killed days apart. That can't be a coincidence.'

'Eat.' He put a plate down in front of me. He had transformed the remains of a loaf of sourdough bread and some bacon into a grilled cheese sandwich. I bit into it hungrily, tasting not just the brilliance of grilled cheese and bacon, but also tomato and pesto from the jar that I had forgotten about in the refrigerator. Even if I hadn't been starving, I would have wolfed it down.

Chris had taken a glass from the cabinet and poured himself a couple of fingers of whiskey. 'So, what's next?'

'Of the three people that Brock thought was possibly embezzling from him, there's only one left.'

'That seems significant.'

'Usually the last guy standing in a case like that is the guy doing the crime.'

'You going to go pay him a visit? Have a discussion?'

'You mean like beat a confession out of him?'

'I meant kill him.'

'Years ago, in Vietnam or shortly after I got home, probably. But now . . .'

'But now, you've evolved?'

'Grown up. I can't just go and off a guy based on the fact that he's the last suspect left. It doesn't . . . it shouldn't work like that. There's a big leap between knowing and proving.'

'And you don't fancy yourself judge, jury and executioner?'

'No, I guess I don't.'

'Good. It has to mean something.'

'Taking a man's life?'

'Sure, that and all the shit we went through. Going through that . . . surviving it, you can't just piss it away on some shit math. He's the last guy left and it is a lot less certain than proving he's responsible. In this town, even the cops have to have proof. You can't just run off half-cocked because you saw another dead body.'

'Yeah, well, for the record, I wasn't going to just off him.'

'I know, but I figured it couldn't hurt to remind you of your better nature and high-minded ideals.'

Then, through the haze brought on by a shitty day spent in a cell, by hunger, by whiskey on an empty stomach and by seeing the aftereffects of a woman brutally killed, I understood what Chris was trying to tell me. He was trying to tell me not to piss away my ethics but also not to piss away the gift of surviving the war. Dead or in prison, either would have been equally a waste.

We sat up drinking whiskey in the kitchen. I should have called Angela, but drinking whiskey and telling war stories got the better of me. We told each other funny stories about friends from Vietnam, both dead and alive. We toasted our friend Tony who had been killed in the attack on the FOB in Nha Trang when both Chris and I had lived. Then, very drunk, I staggered off to bed under the disapproving eye of Sir Leominster. He had hoped that my drinking would lead to an extra can of cat food for him. It was my newly formed opinion that since he and Chris were so chummy, he could take it up with the big Alabaman sleeping on the couch.

SEVEN

I woke up the next morning and came to the realization, not for the first time, that if Chris and I insisted on drinking like we were still in our twenties, then I wasn't likely to make it to my forties. I got out of bed and drank a glass of water. Against my better judgment, I decided to go for a run to sweat out some of the toxins and clear my head.

The morning was warm and yellow pollen was drifting on puddles as I ran by them. It must have rained sometime in the night. I ran down Commonwealth Avenue, and spring was in the air. The warm, wet, flowery smells combined with the slight scent of decaying leaves left over from the fall. My run took me on my usual route across the Charles River via the Harvard Bridge.

As I ran, I gradually stopped thinking about being sick and thought about the case. I was going to have to go back up to Amesbury and take a closer look at Lintz. I was also curious to see what Brock could tell me or show me about his banking activities. Or maybe it was just time to go up and talk to Lintz? I was pretty sure that he wasn't just going to break down and confess to being an embezzler and murderer. Probably wouldn't even confess to one of those things.

It was hard to picture Lintz, the family man, beating Karen Marti to death. It just didn't fit with the image. I could see Stanley 'Captain Muscles' Clark doing it. I had suspicions that his muscles weren't just from picking up all the time he spent at the gym. He was a customer of the bank. He more than likely knew Lintz. Maybe they were partners in some sort of scheme, the type of thing that the family man would want to keep quiet. It was hard to watch your kids grow up from inside prison. Things were starting to make a little more sense. I could ask Brock about Captain Muscles's business and if he worked closely with Lintz.

By the time I reached the steps of my building, I had the vague outlines of what I thought was going on. There were still a lot more questions than answers, but I had a bearing to follow. That was a hell of a lot more than I had yesterday. Now I needed something to eat before I went to the office to make some phone calls.

Chris snored on the couch with Sir Leominster curled up by his head. I was going to have to have a talk with that cat about loyalty and how it relates to feedings. I called Angela from the phone in the bedroom.

'How was your stay in jail?' she asked after we had exchanged greetings.

'Not bad. If you have to spend time in a jail cell you could do a lot worse than Amesbury.'

'You didn't meet any new friends?'

'In jail? No.'

'So, I don't have to be jealous?'

'Nope, no cellmate, no prison romance. I was able to stay faithful.'

'Did you at least miss me?'

'Of course, time passes slowly in jail. I had a lot of it to think about you.'

'Tell me what you thought about.'

I did. In some detail. I was fairly confident that she was blushing by the time I finished my account. We both agreed that we should get together soon. If Chris was still on my couch, I would go to her place. Then we said our goodbyes.

I needed breakfast and a shower. I made my way into the kitchen to start the coffee. I ate a yogurt, one of the fake French ones, and headed for the shower. By the time I was out of the shower and dressed, the coffee was done and Chris was stirring.

'You're up already?' he asked.

'Yeah, I went for a run to clear my head.'

'Ugh, my head hurts.'

'You aren't on a case. I needed to think clearly about the whole thing with the bank.'

'And you came up with something?'

'That I need to ask more questions.'

'People actually pay you?'

'Shocking, isn't it?'

'Naw, you were always a good poker player.'

'Thanks.' I took his backward compliment or insult in stride. He was the only person other than me who had figured out that I didn't know what I was doing in my chosen career. 'I figured maybe I need to start asking the relevant questions of the right people.'

'Jesus, you sound like one of those Irish poets.'

'This whole time I've been following people around or asking about the murders. Instead, I should be asking about embezzlement. That's what kicked this whole thing off. Someone stole a couple of million from the bank. That's worth killing a couple of people for.'

'People have been murdered for a lot less than that.'

'I need to talk to Brock.'

'The bank president?'

'Yeah, I need to talk to him and have him show me the trail. If I can pick up the thread, that will take me to Lintz and then I can brace him.'

'Brace him?'

'Question him. I don't know enough about embezzlement to know what to ask him. Right now, all I know is that he lives in a nice house, drives a nice car and seems to have a nice family. He doesn't look like a criminal mastermind or a murderer, but maybe he has a partner.'

'Or maybe he's real good at not looking like what he really is?' Chris's Alabama twang came out more pronounced than he realized.

'Maybe that too.'

I had left Chris to fend for himself for breakfast. He was certainly more than capable. The office smelled of stale smoke and coffee grounds when I opened the door. I went in and opened the window to let in the warm spring air. The weather was shaping the day up nicely. If only the Red Sox season would shape up nicely too. They were half a game out from first place behind Cleveland and the Yankees.

The weather was nice, and like all true New Englanders, I was waiting for the other shoe to drop. The weather here tended to be famously fickle, and that bred suspicion in all of us when it was sunny for more than three days in a row. Regardless, I had the windows open in the car and Boz Scaggs' smooth sounds were coming out of the speakers, singing 'Gone Baby Gone'. On top of that, the traffic through town on the way to the office wasn't even bad. It was enough to make me worry that something bad was going to happen in the face of so many good things.

When I got to the office, I opened the window wide to let out the smell of stale pipe smoke. I started the espresso machine as had become my habit. Ignoring the blinking lights on the office answering machine, I picked up the phone and dialed Watts.

When I finally got through to her, she said, 'How did you get yourself arrested?'

'I might have told the Chief of Police in Amesbury that he was so stupid that he had to be related to the mayor to have his job.'

'Oh yeah, your stellar personality again. It tends to get you in trouble.'

'Funny, I thought it was my mouth that got me in trouble this time.'

'Even you have to know that there is no percentage in insulting a cop, much less the chief in a small town.'

'Maybe so, but he is too stupid to be believed.'

'Why do you say that?' Watts asked.

'A woman was murdered. I found her body in her apartment hours after the fact. Rather than just asking me questions, he tried to pressure me, told me he'd arrest me for the murder.'

'Oh, so he's a special sort of stupid.'

'That was my conclusion too. He didn't appreciate my candid assessment of his intellect,' I said.

'Hence the time well spent in a jail cell.'

'Exactly.'

'You seem to have survived.'

'I did. It was hardly the Hanoi Hilton,' I said.

'Who was murdered?'

'Karen Marti; she worked at the Merrimack Community Bank.'

'Doing what?' Watts asked.

'The president's secretary.'

'A secretary who didn't type?'

'No, I didn't get the feeling that they were having an affair. Actually, Brock described her as knowing everything that went on in the bank. He spoke highly of her,' I said.

'Do you think she was killed because of her job?'

'Whoever did it spent some time torturing her.'

'How's that?'

'Broken fingers, she was badly beaten, and it looked like someone used her bathtub as a dunk tank.'

'Jesus!'

'Exactly.'

'You think someone wanted to know what she knew about the embezzlement?'

'Sure, like the embezzler is getting worried about who knows, who's onto him.'

'Or she took the wrong guy home, or her boyfriend liked to use her as a punching bag and it went too far.' Watts was always one to dash cold water on my theories.

'Yep, also very real possibilities.'

'So, what's next?'

'I'm going to go to Amesbury and have a talk with Brock.'

'Just Brock?' Watts asked skeptically.

'No, there is one person left alive who he thought might be embezzling.'

'That seems like a good start.'

'Yeah, he just doesn't look the type.'

'Well, we all know that you're always right.'

'No need for the sarcasm.' She had a point though.

'OK, try to stay out of jail this time.'

'Sure, sure,' I said.

I meant to go to Amesbury. I did, but plans go awry. My phone rang. Not that that should have derailed my plans. Phones ring all the time. I picked up the receiver and the voice of my childhood friend, Danny Sullivan, came down the line to me.

'Andy.'

'Hey, Danny, what's up?'

'You busy?'

'Not especially. I was just gonna take a drive up to occupied New Hampshire.'

'Quit clowning around. A guy needs to see you.'

'Right now?'

'In ten minutes.'

'Who's the guy?'

'The guy who you talked to a few months ago about certain familial investments.'

I worked a blackmail case three months ago, the one where I met Angela. It looked like there might be a mob connection, and there had been, but it didn't have anything to do with the blackmail. But it did have to do with money laundering, and Danny had introduced me to a man that I thought of as The Banker. His job was to take dirty money and make it clean for his family and various associates. Suddenly a trip to Amesbury didn't seem as pressing.

'Where?' I asked.

'Faneuil Hall. Go in on the Government Center side.'

'OK.'

'He said that you guys can talk in there.'

'Sure, makes sense.'

It did, especially if you were someone who was careful about being overheard. The tourists and the lunch rush would mean that any type of parabolic directional mic would be useless. For that matter, so would a wire. I had to give The Banker credit – it was a solid choice.

'OK. I'll be there.'

'Good. Thanks. He's important.'

'I get it.'

Danny was important in his world. The criminals he represented and advised trusted him. If Danny thought The Banker was important, then that said a lot. Danny had done me a considerable favor introducing me to him, and now that debt had come due. They always do.

I hung up the phone, grabbed my keys and locked the office up. My office isn't far from Government Center, and given the parking situation in this town, it made more sense to walk. It didn't hurt that the weather was nice. May was doing its best not to disappoint.

I made my way to Government Center; fortunately I was in too much of a hurry to have to take in its brutalist architecture. I went down the steps to the brick-covered plaza where the kids ditching school careened around on skateboards like landlocked surfers. A few minutes later, I walked through the entrance of Faneuil Hall and into a maelstrom of hungry tourists. Like all true Bostonians, I regarded the place as a tourist trap and avoided it like the plague.

I only made it ten feet in when I noticed that there was a very large man walking in front of me. Not fat, but tall, broad across the back and with a very thick neck. He was one half of the bookended muscle that The Banker always had with him. The other half was following behind me, and both had guns in shoulder holsters under their armpits. Probably the new 9mm Berettas that were all the rage.

Another man fell in beside me on my left. He was tall, intelligent and handsome, if you liked them with dark hair and money. He was dressed in a blue suit that was cut so simply it had to cost a fortune. The Banker had the type of money to spend on elegant clothes. Me, most of the time I dressed like I got my clothes from the Salvation Army.

'Mr Roark, thank you for coming.'

'You're welcome, Mister . . .?'

'Angel, Michael Angel.'

'Pleased to meet you. Was it always Angel?'

'No, it was Angelotti. It would appear that this time I am the one asking for a favor.'

'Do tell.'

'You have been making inquiries about the Merrimack Community Bank?'

'I have.'

'May I ask what sort?'

'You can, but I don't usually discuss my client's business with anyone else.'

'I could point out that I did you a favor a few months ago.'

'You did, but you being here having questions worries me. Makes me want to ask a few questions of my own.'

'I see. A quid pro quo?' His voice and mannerisms were cultured, but he wasn't that far removed from the jungle.

'Sort of. An understanding that we both have questions, and we are both limited in our ability offer answers.'

'That seems fair.'

'I was hired by the bank president because he thinks that someone is embezzling money.'

'Who did he suspect?' he asked.

'Well, the two leading candidates seem to have had a sudden onset of being murdered. Your people?'

'No. Why do you ask?'

'Um, well, you are involved with people willing and able to do that sort of thing. One of them was, for lack of a better term, questioned prior to her untimely end.'

'Questioned?'

'Tortured.'

'And you think is related to one of my clients?' he asked.

'You're wanting to talk might be, what we call in my line of work, a clue,' I said.

'Ah, of course.'

'Is it one of your banks?'

'No. We have some money invested in it, but it isn't one of ours.'

'So, the people who currently own it might resent someone stealing from them.'

'Definitely. But I would have heard about it.'

'Even the messy part?'

'We deal with a great deal of money. My clients would want to ensure it was safe. Splashy murders that draw the attention of the police and the FBI wouldn't be done lightly. If nothing else, they would want me to move their money . . . which cannot be done easily or quickly.'

'How does it work?'

'My end of it?'

'Yes.'

'Are you going to share this with the pretty FBI agent you sometimes have drinks with?' he asked.

'No.' He knew I was friends with Watts. I wasn't thrilled that he felt the need to let me know that he knew it.

'I would imagine that if someone wanted to launder large amounts of money, they would buy a bank.'

'Buy a bank?' I asked incredulously.

'Sure, they aren't that expensive.'

'What do you mean?'

'Do you remember inflation under the Carter administration.'

'Sure, who doesn't?'

'When Reagan got elected, his administration saw easing of banking regulations and offering incentives to bankers as a way to counter inflation.'

'OK.'

'So, there are different types of banks. There are the big banks, like Old Stone or Citibank. Those are insured by the Federal Deposit Insurance Corporation which was created during the Depression to restore people's faith in our banking system. FDIC is great, but it also comes with rules and federal regulators.'

'Which probably isn't ideal if you are laundering money.'

'Correct.'

'So, what about the Merrimack Community Bank?' I asked.

'It's a type of bank called a Savings and Loan. Four years ago, President Reagan eliminated certain regulations concerning interest rates and changed the loan-to-value ratio.'

'What's that?'

'Prior to 1982, banks had to ensure that they had enough capital to cover their loans. It was higher for S&Ls. Also, the 1982 changes allowed them to hold up to seventy percent of their assets in consumer or commercial loans. You see S&Ls were originally about providing loans to people who wanted to build or buy a house.'

'Like in the movie, *It's a Wonderful Life*.'

'Exactly.'

'So how did you get involved?'

'With these changes some smart investors who saw an opportunity, specifically the opportunity to buy banks.'

'Buy banks?'

'Sure. No one can afford to buy Citibank or Old Stone, for

example, but a smaller bank, an S&L or a community bank as we call them in New England, absolutely. They're not as expensive as you think.'

'What does a bank go for these days?'

'It costs about three percent of the value of the bank's assets. So, let's say a bank has a one hundred million dollars' worth of assets, then all you have to do is find a bank that is in trouble and come up with three million dollars.'

'And presto, you have a bank.'

'Exactly. On top of that, there are federal banking incentives that pay six percent of the value of the bank's loans.'

'So, you buy a bank valued at one hundred million dollars for three million dollars and loan out all its loans and the Feds pay you six million dollars.'

'That's a bit of a simplification, but close enough.'

'You would have every incentive to loan money to anybody as quickly as you could.'

'Yes.'

'Is that how money is laundered?' I chose my words carefully.

'There are a number of ways. But think of it like this – less traditional businesses have a large amount of cash. They can't explain how they have the cash, which means they can't explain nice things, nice houses, nice cars. The traditional banks, owned by non-traditional bankers, take that cash in and park the money in Certificates of Deposit.'

'Certificates of Deposit?'

'Think of them like higher interest-bearing savings accounts. The CDs are then used as collateral for construction loans.'

'Oh. But wouldn't anyone be curious about the cash, where it comes from?'

'Like who? The bank it's being deposited in? No, Mr Roark, the only thing anyone is looking at is the profit margin.'

'How does that work?'

'Well, if the money is deposited here, say in CDs and then those CDs are used as collateral on loans in a country like say, Panama or Columbia. For more local clients, the money might get deposited and construction loans are issued. Maybe those loans get sold or refinanced or repackaged with other loans . . . you see where it is going?'

'I think so,' I said.

'Now, let's say some of those construction projects are using union workers and are supplied by union suppliers . . . can you see the potential?'

'Sure. No-show jobs and construction supplies that fall off trucks that no one looks too closely at,' I said. This was a lot closer to my world than anything to do with banking.

'Not only that, but if you have a bank, you have an institution that can move money around to other accounts, to other states and, most importantly, to other countries. Deposit the money in a CD in Boston, New York or Miami, then use it to secure loans in Panama or Columbia. Deposit the money in dirty at one end and withdraw it clean at the other.'

'It's that easy?'

'No, there are a few more steps, even more if you don't want to go to federal prison, but that is the layman's version.'

'So why are we talking? You're a busy man, and I can't imagine you were so impressed by my witty repartee at our last meeting that you wanted to hang out.'

'I have family who want me to invest more in Merrimack Community Bank. I have a fiduciary responsibility to my family. I am doing my due diligence in talking to you.'

'You worried that two murders and maybe some embezzlement issues might bring undue heat?'

'I'm worried that what is being touted as a good investment is actually a very large liability.'

'And you're not a man who likes liabilities.'

'And I am not a man who likes liabilities,' he confirmed.

'I was hired to see if there was any sign of embezzlement.' I didn't want to mention Lintz because that would be as good as shooting him in the head. It might not be that good for me either. I continued, 'I don't know anything about banking, so I approached it by looking at the bank employees, seeing if any of them were living above their means, driving Porsches on Chevrolet salaries.' If he knew I was on the case then he probably knew that much already.

'And did you find anything like that?'

'No, I didn't. I looked at a bunch of employees who seemed to live rather mundane lives.'

'No leads?'

'I wrapped it up and walked away from it.'

'What changed?'

'The bank robbery where the kid caught a .357 Magnum in the melon.'

'You thought that was suspicious? Banks do get robbed and sometimes people get hurt.'

'In and of itself? No. But coming on the heels of being asked to investigate the claims of embezzlement . . . that made me wonder.'

'So, you went back?' he asked.

'I did. I spoke to the bank's president, and he rehired me. I spoke to the dead woman, Karen Marti, and she was holding something back. Then she was murdered.'

'You think she's connected to it?'

'Where there's smoke . . .'

'. . . there's fire.'

'Yes, all of these events happening in close proximity. Two murders. On top of which, it looked a lot like the woman had been tortured. Unless it was the work of a psycho, it looks like someone was interrogating her.'

'Why?'

'You tell me, it isn't my family that owns it. Maybe they are conducting their own investigation into embezzlement?'

'You think they killed the woman?'

'It is one possibility.'

'Are there others?'

'Sure, there might be a violent ex-boyfriend, or maybe she was just the target of violence by being a single woman living alone.'

'But you don't think that's it.'

'No, everything seems to center around the bank. I am not sure if that makes it a good or bad investment for you.'

'That is the question. I don't like all of the exposure.'

'Sure, who would?'

'Will you let me know if you find out more?'

'It depends.'

'Ah, yes, your client.'

'Yes. There are professional ethics.'

'Very Sam Spade of you. Danny mentioned that you have a sort of code you live by.'

'I don't think that I have given it enough thought to call it a code.' I was just trying to exist.

'Well, perhaps you can let me know without compromising your ethics?'

'Perhaps,' I said noncommittally. There were some people who I definitely didn't want to get into bed with. The mob or money launderers for them fit that bill.

'Well, if you do, please let Danny know and I will be in touch.' He held out his manicured hand.

'I will if the situation allows.' I shook his hand. It was nice to work with professionals. Politeness goes a long way with me, even if it is politeness from a gangster. He and his matched set of gun-toting muscle walked out the harbor side of Faneuil Hall into the bright sunshine of May.

I turned and headed back toward Government Center. I was pretty sure that I was going to hear about this from Watts. She didn't approve of people like Danny and The Banker, but I chalked that up to her job. If she could just get beyond that, she might find them quite likeable.

I walked across the brick expanse that was the plaza. Looming over it was one of the single ugliest pieces of architecture in the history of man. Yet, there was something uniquely Boston about Government Center – it was ugly as hell, but it was ours. I liked it a hell of a lot more than the gas tanks with Ho Chi Minh's silhouette on them. That wasn't saying much, as Uncle Ho and I had been, literally, mortal enemies. Uncle Ho and his followers had killed a lot of my friends. I understood why they were fighting, I just didn't need to come home to a picture of him looming over my neighborhood.

I walked back to the office thinking about the meeting I had just had. Something was fishy at the Merrimack Community Bank. Fishy, like it being owned by the mob. What I was curious about was if he was personally involved enough to have had two people murdered?

If we were talking about drug money, mob money and construction loans, we were talking about millions, tens of millions of dollars. That was the type of money that people murder for. Staying out of federal prison was a hell of motive too. I didn't see The Banker doing the dirty work. His muscle certainly seemed capable of it. They were big enough. But I discounted them as being too close to The Banker – he seemed like the type of guy who liked to isolate himself from capital crimes.

I put my trip to Amesbury on hold long enough to stop at a pizza joint near my office. Since old man Marconi had closed his shop downstairs from my office and moved back to Italy, I wasn't eating as much pizza. In all fairness, I had yet to find a pizza joint that lived up to what Marconi made. I managed to get my hands on two slices of thin, New York style pizza. Pepperoni pizza if you were curious. They were greasy and good and all the things that pepperoni pizza should be. They went down quickly, washed down with one of those little glass bottles of seltzer that claim to be from New York. I was a sucker for the blueberry flavor.

When I had finished my not-so-healthy lunch, I went back to the office. The aftereffects of the pizza, the night of drinking and the bad dreams had left me feeling sleepy. I fired up the espresso machine and packed a bowl of tobacco from Peretti's. I opened the office window wide to let the pollen in and the smoke out. When the espresso machine stopped hissing and burbling, I took the tiny cup of the bitter brew to my desk.

I pulled the yellow legal pad that I was using for my case notes over. I started to jot notes on it with a blue felt tip pen. I wrote down everything I could remember about Karen Marti's murder scene. I noted everything that I had talked to the Amesbury cops about. I wracked my brain, trying to see if there was anything from my first two meetings with Marti that I had missed. I couldn't think of anything.

I added notes on my meeting with The Banker. Even though I knew his real name, I couldn't think of him any other way. My notes about The Banker were in two separate categories, the first of which was his very presence and interest in the bank in Amesbury. The second was about the lesson in high-end money laundering. I had never heard of CDs before, never having had enough money to invest in more than a Christmas Club account. I had assumed that construction loans existed, but again, those were far out of my price range.

I drew arrows and linked notes. I wrote down the players' names again. I doodled in the margins and puffed on the pipe. I had finished the espresso an hour before, but thankfully I wasn't sleepy anymore. I was looking at my pad and the words 'construction loans' stood out. Construction loans, real estate and banking were all things I knew nothing about. I wouldn't even know what any of it was worth. Then it hit me like a slap to the head. Construction loans, real estate, finding the value of things . . . you'd need a real estate appraiser.

Captain Muscles AKA Stanley Clark was a real estate appraiser. He did business at the Merrimack Community Bank. He must know Lintz . . . no, not just know Lintz but he could be in on it with him. A real estate appraiser would have to be pretty useful to that type of scheme. I had to believe that someone would have to sign off on the value of the construction loan.

Now, I have to admit that I took an instant dislike to Captain Muscles. He seemed like an asshole in the barbecue joint with Karen Marti. He drove like an asshole in his asshole car, and I could picture him beating a woman. But he was also an asshole with the right credentials to be involved in some sort of illicit banking or money laundering. What if Captain Muscles and Lintz weren't embezzling money but washing it? I could see where maybe Brock might be reluctant to tell me he thought that someone in his bank was laundering drug or mob money. Probably both.

I looked at the pad, and there were a lot more questions than answers on it. The answers to the questions were in Amesbury, the town on the Merrimack River bordering New Hampshire, where I was pretty sure the Chief of Police didn't like me. That meant he wouldn't take too kindly to my presence in town. Unlike Vietnam, no one was going to chopper in so I could get all camouflaged and sneak into town.

It was time to change my look. Not a lot, but enough so that the chief wouldn't spot me in and about Amesbury. I didn't feel like spending any more time in a jail cell there than was necessary. I needed a shave and a haircut. I hadn't much bothered since leaving the cops. Short hair and a bare face reminded me of the Army, but I didn't see any other options. I would also have to see Carney about a loaner. I had spent a lot of time in Amesbury in the Maverick. The cops knew what it looked like, and I was pretty sure that after the night in Cosgrove's apartment, Lintz and Captain Muscles did too.

I packed up my notes and rinsed the demitasse cup out. I put the pipe down to cool and closed the office window. I locked the office up on my way out and realized that I was excited. I had a plan of action, or at least the beginnings of one. The hardest part of a case is trying to figure out where you're going and what you should do when you get there. It's like watching a compass needle spin around uncontrollably. At least now I had an azimuth. I would get cleaned up and start looking into Lintz and Captain Muscles, but hard. They were all that was left, and I had been on the backfoot from the minute that Brock had first hired me to look into the embezzlement.

The nice thing about living in a city like Boston is that everything I need is usually close enough to walk to. Supermarket, tobacconist, liquor store and, fortunately, my little seen barber was no exception. He didn't exactly look up in surprise when I walked in, but when I told him that I wanted a shave and short hair, I was worried that his heart might give out.

'How short?' he asked as though I was playing a joke on him.

'Um, not army short, that's for sure. More like respectable lawyer short . . . Republican lawyer.'

'Gotcha, no Teddy Kennedy for you, then.'

'Nope.'

'All right.'

I sat there in the chair and tried not to wince when he got the clippers out. When I first enlisted in the Army, the gruff barbers had shorn us all like sheep. Then in Vietnam we went into the village and a local lady cut our hair. In the cops, my hair was longish, and then when I went out on my own, I grew a moustache and beard and saw the barber only when I looked like I should be following The Dead on tour somewhere. End of an era, I guess.

After he clipped and scissored my hair down to a poor reflection of its former glory, he switched blades on the clippers. He attacked my facial hair with quick, efficient passes of the clippers. Then he got out the brush and mug of shaving soap. He disappeared into a back room, and I heard water running. Then he reappeared and, using the brush, lathered my face with zeal.

There is no greater sign of trust that one can show another human being than to sit still while they approach your face with a straight razor. They required a bit of skill to be used. My mind flashed back to the time when I was a cop, and there was a kid in his twenties, sitting, holding his hand against his cheek so it wouldn't flop open after someone had slashed him with a straight razor.

When he finished the job, he wiped my face with damp towel to get rid of any excess of shaving soap. Then he took a bottle of Clubman Aftershave and splashed some of it into his hands. He rubbed the stuff into my newly shorn face, and it only stung for a second. He stepped back and spun the chair so I could see his handiwork in the mirror.

I won't be dramatic and say anything silly like, 'I barely recognized myself.' But the effect was noticeable, and I doubted that someone who had never seen me with short hair and no facial hair would recognize me. He had done a decent job, and I looked like I should be handing out religious pamphlets on the street with the other missionaries. My only real complaint was that the short hair highlighted the fact that my left earlobe had been shot off.

I gave the barber a twenty to cover the shave and a haircut. It left him a pretty good tip, but he had earned it. The pile of my hair on the floor around the barber's chair was testament enough to that. I stepped outside into the afternoon sunlight. I had a plan, not much of one but it was a work in progress, and it was a lot better than nothing.

My new state trooper haircut was only part of the disguise. I walked back to my apartment. I needed to go and see Carney. I would need a new set of wheels, ones that were not my slightly battered but fast Maverick. I had only been driving it for a year since my beloved VW Karmann Ghia was blown up by Vietnamese gangsters. In that year, the Maverick had been put through its paces and even been shot with a shotgun. What can I say, I'm tough on my cars.

I got back to the apartment to find it empty except for Sir Leominster, who immediately assailed me with his plaintive whining while rubbing up against my legs. He was a lot friendlier when I was the only one around to crack open a can of cat food for him. There was some sort of life lesson in that. When the cat settled down, I went over to the phone and dialed Carney's number from memory.

'Hello,' he bellowed down the line at me. There was a lot of noise in the background leading me to believe he answered the phone in the bay where they worked on the cars.

'It's Andy Roark.'

'Hiya, Andy. How's the boy?'

'No complaints.'

'Whaddaya need?'

'Who says I need anything?'

'Unless it's Christmas or Easter, you don't call much to say hello.'

'Haha, fair enough. I was hoping to borrow that Ford Escort from you for a couple of days.' A few months ago, I borrowed a shockingly plain Ford Escort from him. It was so uninspiring, I nicknamed it the Ford Breadbox.

'Nix. That's out.' I didn't know if he meant someone else had it or it had been totaled.

'What do you have?'

'I got an '84 T-Bird that should suit you. It's fast, handles well and not too flashy.'

'Can I swing by tomorrow and pick it up?'

'Sure. Come by in the morning.'

'Thanks, it should only be for a couple of days.'

'Sure, no problem.' Unlike most people who said 'no problem' when they meant that something was a problem but they were overlooking it for you, Carney was quite genuine. I hung up the phone and contemplated the silence in my apartment. With Chris crashing on my couch, the place felt a lot smaller and, through no fault of his own, a lot less quiet.

Maybe I wasn't meant for company? Or maybe I just wasn't good company. Either way, it was pretty much the same thing. Maybe that was why I had been single for so long. Chris was good company, though having him around was tough on my liver.

EIGHT

The phone rang while I was contemplating what to have for dinner. I had been at home a couple of hours and Chris was still out. I hadn't decided how long or even if I should wait for him before I made something. I picked up the receiver hoping it was Angela calling to suggest getting together. Had that only been the case. Instead, it was Watts, and she was unhappy to say the least.

'You have a lot of nerve.' It wasn't said as a compliment.

'As in, hi Andy, I think you're very brave?'

'No, as in, you have some set of balls meeting with a known mafia money launderer in Faneuil Hall. Not far from Government Center, where you know my office is.'

'I was invited to meet with him. He picked the spot.'

'I told you to stay away from him.'

'Sure, and what kind of private detective would I be if I stayed away from criminal types?'

'I thought you said he wasn't a criminal?'

'If he wasn't a criminal, you wouldn't be calling me right now. No, he's the criminal of the future – smart, well mannered, well dressed, prefers a computer to a gun. Frankly, I don't know how I feel about it compared to more traditional things like leg breaking and loan sharking.'

'What did you two talk about?'

'Would you believe he was bored and wanted to know my views on the Red Sox shot at the World Series this year?'

'Bullshit. He has a luxury box and frequently gets invited down to talk to the players.'

'OK, he was looking for fashion advice.'

'Only a homeless guy would look to you for fashion tips.'

'Ouch.'

'Is he involved with the bank in Amesbury?'

'He says he isn't.'

'And you believe him. Are you thick?'

'Well, I have put on some weight.'

'Jesus Christ! Don't be stupid. These guys you run with, Angel, your friend with the garage, your Green Beret buddy who likes to hang out with bikers, they're dangerous. They aren't straight businessmen, they're killers. And don't think that your friend the lawyer is any different because he wears a suit.' She slammed the phone down, as was her way.

'But what do you think I am?' I asked into the handset but only the dial tone answered me.

Maybe that was why I was comfortable around guys like Chris and Carney and now Mike Angel. I knew what they were, and I didn't have to pretend to be any different. We might have different motives and different morals but at the end of the day, killing is killing. My hands weren't much cleaner than anyone else's. The only difference was that my motives were purer. It wasn't much of a defense, but it was a hell of a lot better than most.

I decided that the best course of action involved whiskey and a call to Angela. If one has to acknowledge their worst character aspects, it is best not to do it sober. At least Angela wouldn't judge me for my past. Maybe my taste in ex-girlfriends but not much else. Maybe that was part of why I liked her so much? It took some of the pressure off me.

I was at the bottom of my second whiskey when Chris came home. I heated up a can of Dinty Moore beef stew and poured it over a small pot of elbow macaroni. It wasn't fancy, but it soaked up the whiskey in the hollow part of my stomach, and that was good enough. Chris looked at it with an upraised eyebrow.

'You're doing something different with your hair,' he said.

'I thought I needed to change my appearance given the fondness the Chief of Police in Amesbury has for me.'

'You look like a state trooper.'

'Jesus, you really know how to hurt a guy.' I had been a city cop, and my view of the troopers was that, while they were good at what they did, they weren't as good at it as they thought they were.

'If you're gonna sit here being maudlin, not much point tryin' to cheer you up.'

'Maudlin?'

'You're sitting here eating trailer park food and drinking by yourself. Even that annoying cat isn't circling around begging for food.'

'This case is getting frustrating. They have a rhythm, like waves, and this part, this is the trough.'

'Sure, makes sense.'

'I met with a money launderer today and then my FBI friend called.'

'Wanting information about the money guy.'

'Yeah, but not wanting to ask. She's afraid I'm going to get in trouble someday associating with criminals.'

'Seems like that's part of your job.'

'Of course it is. She's convinced that I am too smart for my own good.'

'She sweet on you, 'cause I am pretty sure Angela'd object?'

'No, not sweet exactly. Maybe maternal? And Angela would drop me like a box of rocks if she thought I was entertaining other women,' I said.

'Drop you like a box of rocks? I think she'd cut you.'

'She's not the jealous type.'

'No, Red, she might not be, but there's something about her. She's tough. Maybe tougher than you.'

'Ha! She never ran recon on the Ho Chi Minh trail.'

'Lack of opportunity doesn't mean she isn't tough.'

'Fair enough,' I said, thinking of the warehouse in Southie where Angela had shot and killed a blackmailer.

It wasn't exactly murder – he'd had a gun – but it was as close as you could get. Maybe that was why we were together. She couldn't look at me as a killer without admitting she was one too. Vietnam and my involvement were always an unspoken thing lurking in the background.

'Don't get me wrong, Red, she's good people. Pretty, too. I can see why you're dating.'

'Yeah, she is. Plus, she never criticizes my dinner choices.'

'Red, that's not dinner, that's just pushing calories.'

'We can't all cook like you do.' I was no slouch in the kitchen, but Chris was a fantastic cook. A year ago when I was crashing at his place in San Francisco, he had made the best risotto that I had ever had.

'No, but you don't have to eat canned stew and elbow macaroni.'

'It isn't bad.' It wasn't.

'To each their own. I think I found a place to live.'

'Cool, where?'

'Somerville, above an Irish bar.' He named a local bar that was a Somerville institution.

'Slummah-ville?' I said in my best Boston-ese.

'Yeah, the price is right. Carney helped me find the place.'

'Well, at least you'll be near a bar.'

'It is convenient.'

'You'll like the music. It'll remind you of Bluegrass but less twangy.'

The next morning, Chris and I drove to Carney's in the Maverick. Chris was going to drive my car back and borrow it while I had the T-Bird. We got to the garage as it was opening. Carney moved a little slower than when I had first met him, but he was still big and tough. It had been more than thirty years since he'd been a paratrooper in Korea, fighting for his life in his Asian war, but I wouldn't want to fight him now.

'Andy, got a haircut? Chris.' He offered Chris a casual nod. 'Good to see you boys.'

'Same. How are you doing?'

'No complaints. No one, not the priest nor my wife, listens when I do.'

Carney had a linguistic trait of a lot of Boston Irish men who, schooled by the nuns, spoke at times with a heavy emphasis on good diction and proper grammar. I suspect it had to do with the proliferation of rulers amongst the nuns and their willingness to use them correctively.

'I appreciate the rental.'

'It's a loaner and you know that.'

'I can afford it.'

'Your money's no good, and you know that too.'

'Thanks.'

'Let me get the whip. Wait here.' Carney walked out of the back of his shop. His slight limp, courtesy of some Chinese shrapnel, was barely noticeable.

'Andy, what's up with you two and the money thing?' Chris asked.

'He hired me to help him find his daughter. She was with her drug dealing, pimping, piece of shit boyfriend. She was hooked on H. While getting her out of there, I tossed the guy down a flight of stairs. Since then, he's felt obligated.'

'It makes you uncomfortable.'

'Yep.'

'You don't have to go to him, or you could pay him,' Chris said.

'He's juiced into the parts of Boston that they don't talk about on PBS. That, and it would hurt his feelings if I went elsewhere,' I said.

'He'd know?'

'Yeah, he's that juiced in.'

'Guess you're both lucky, then.'

Any smartass reply that I had was cut off by two sharp beeps of the horn in the parking lot. We went outside to the sight of Carney behind the wheel of a black Ford coupe. It was sharp looking, all beveled edges and none of the boxy, hard angles of most cars these days. It looked fast and sleek and, while I loved the Maverick, I was having serious automotive infidelity issues.

'You like it?' Carney asked as he climbed out.

'Like it? It's a beauty.' It was, with a double pinstripe on each side, a stylized bird emblem above the chrome grill and on the panels behind the half window on each side. It looked fast and modern, and I was impressed. If the Maverick was a P-47 Thunderbolt, this car was like an F-4 Phantom.

'It's got a small block V-8 that I've personally tuned. It's plenty fast. I tightened up the suspension, tweaked the breaks and done a bunch of other stuff that an automotive philistine such as yourself wouldn't appreciate even if I could explain it to you.'

'Philistine, ha,' I objected.

'You loved that garbage Karmann Ghia.'

'That car had style. Like a Porsche 300 series.'

'Yeah, that's all it had.' Carney didn't like foreign cars and, of the ones made in America, he preferred Fords. To each their own, I guess. He didn't criticize my taste in guns.

'Where'd you get it?'

'It's not hot, if that's what you're asking.' With Carney that was a possibility, but no one could change out a VIN better than he could.

'I'm going to a town where the Chief of Police already has it in for me. Me being in a hot car would make him extremely happy.'

'That why you got a haircut like some sort of state trooper?'

'Yep. Where's the car from?'

'A guy had bad luck betting on the horses. He had worse credit. He gave the T-Bird to some guys he owed money to. They sold it to me for a good price. It's got good papers and is as legit as if it rolled off a dealer's lot.'

'Guy'd rather give up his wheels than catch a beating.' Chris stated the obvious.

'Yeah, something like that. Andy, it's registered and inspected. Everything on it is legal, and no one's looking for the car.'

'OK by me.' I didn't love that some guy had lost the car to his loan shark, but that was his business, not Carney's.

'Good. Use it as long as you need it. If you like it, we can talk.'

'Cool.' I lowered myself into the bucket seat, my .38 digging into my side a little. I adjusted the seat; Carney was a little shorter. It wasn't that it was radically more modern than the Maverick, but it was nine years younger and a hell of a lot nicer. The T-Bird had bucket seats, a push-button radio and power windows. It was like going from a Sherman Tank to an M60 tank. Both were tanks, but newer was better.

I pulled out, weaving my way through the city. By the time I was on the highway, I had the radio tuned to a station that was playing The Band, and cool air was coming from the vents. The ride was as smooth as Carney had promised.

The Maverick was fast with an engine that growled. Carney

had tuned the Holley carburetor helped get the most horses out
of the engine. There was something about it that reminded me
of one of those thick-necked bulldogs. The T-Bird was something
else altogether. When I applied a little pressure to the accelerator,
that car responded promptly and smoothly. There was some
growling under the hood, but it was softer. The T-Bird was just
more refined. It's not that I forgot about the Maverick, it's just
that I knew I was going to buy the T-Bird from Carney. It wasn't
as cool as Magnum's Ferrari, but I was never going to have
Ferrari money. But I could probably scrape up quasi-legally
obtained T-Bird money.

I glided into Amesbury, paying attention to the speed limit.
The local cops were probably a little jumpy after two murders,
and I was already trying to avoid them. I wasn't sure that I trusted
Chief Dixon not to throw me in a cell again or otherwise waste
my time. I didn't trust him to find out who murdered Karen
Marti. He didn't strike me as the type to let his detectives do
their jobs without interfering. I was certain that whatever he stuck
his nose into, he would screw up.

Finding her murdered like that had gotten to me. She had died
a hard, horrible death, and I wasn't confident that the local boys
were going to solve it. Even if the rest of the department were
grade A, they still were being led by a boob. Something told me
that they didn't know anything about Lintz and his embezzling.
If they didn't know about that, then they probably weren't looking
at him as the killer. That also meant that they weren't looking
at Stanley Clark, who was mixed up in all of this somehow. If
I found out that one of them murdered her, then I was going to
kill him.

'Young Sergeant, get your ass in my office, *now*!' I remember
Sergeant Major Billy Justice's booming voice like it was
yesterday. I was back in camp from a little R&R down in Saigon.
I had still been drunk when I got on the blacked-out C-123, we
called the 'Blackbird,' that SOG used to shuttle men and equip-
ment around Vietnam. I had walked up the ramp in the back of
the bird in chinos stained with blood, dirt and whatever else had
latched on to them from the streets of Saigon.

It had been an epic R&R, and I had been drunk as a lord. I

didn't pick the fight with the REMFs, and I didn't ask the MPs to join in. I didn't kill anyone, and I didn't use my knife or my R&R gun, which that month was a Smith & Wesson 1917 with the barrel cut down to two inches. It fired a .45 ACP round and held six of them and, though it was heavy, it fit in my waistband under a Hawaiian shirt nicely. I just punched, kicked, Judo-chopped and fought my way through them.

I had made my way through the writhing masses and wandered the streets trying to stay one jump ahead of the MPs. Stopping in off limits clubs and bars, a drink here and there until I was able to make it out to Tan Son Nhat Airport. The guard at the gate took in my tattered chinos and ripped Hawaiian shirt dubiously. He viewed my SOG pass and the SOG 'get out of jail free' card that we were all issued. He thought for a second and then muttered, 'fuck it' under his breath, waving me through.

When it was time to get on the Blackbird, I staggered up the ramp. When we got airborne, the crew chief was cool and let me stretch out on the floor to catch a nap. He nudged me with the toe of his flight boot when we were getting ready to land. I lay there for a second shivering on the cold, metal flight deck. I sat up and realized that I had gone from drunk to hungover in the space of the short flight.

I was walking by the HQ shack when Billy Justice's voice rang out. I did a Right Face and stopped in front of the screen door to his office. I knocked and went in when he told me to. He was sitting at his metal desk that had been redirected from some headquarters element in Saigon. They didn't need it as much as the Sergeant Major did.

'How was R&R, Roark? Looks like you had yourself some fun,' he said, eyeing my Hawaiian shirt with its missing buttons and pocket ripped, hanging down.

'Oh yes, Sergeant Major, it was a good time.'

'Roark, I know you're Irish and your forebears have a reputation for drinking and fighting. I was in the Cav and know all the words to the Garryowen . . . I get it.'

'Um, sure, Sergeant Major.' I wasn't sure where he was going with it, but I was pretty sure I wasn't going to like it.

'It's not your fault. It's a cultural thing, you people just want to drink and fight. The Boston Irish are the worst of all. I think it's those cold ass winters and all that snow. It makes y'all mean. That wanting to fight, it's what makes you good soldiers and average cops. Why, I've been known to drink and fight a little too when I was a youth,' he said paternally, which scared me even more.

'Yes, Sergeant Major,' seemed the safest reply.

'Now, listen here, young sergeant.'

I had no idea how old Billy Justice was, but I had heard rumors that he had been sent to South East Asia as one of the first Special Forces soldiers in Operation Hotfoot, which was to train the Laotian Army, that he had been one of the Green Berets at Fort Bragg when Kennedy had made his famous visit, and that he had been on the ground in the Congo during Operation Dragon Rouge. He had split the last several years between Vietnam, Bragg and Walter Reed. Even if he hadn't been a legend or hulking figure of a man, Billy Justice would be one of the last men on the planet I'd want angry at me.

'The Army has spent a lot of money and time to transform you from some sort of Boston bar fighting trash into a commando, an intellectual and a Special Forces soldier. Not just that, but one fighting in the most secret, dirtiest part of this war. If you get hurt in battle so, be it. Get in a bar fight, fine. Men need to blow off steam. But if you get yourself hurt or killed because you try and take on all the REMFs and all the MPs in Saigon, that means I have one less One-Zero, one less team leader in the fight.'

'Sergeant Major, I'm tired and hungover and not sure I heard you right. I'm a One-Two and assistant team leader, not a One-Zero.'

'Yeah, well, the old man and I had a chat yesterday. You've been moved up; you might stay there if you can stop your natural inclination to fuck up. You gotta watch that anger of yours, boy. It's going to get you in trouble someday.'

'Yes, Sergeant Major.'

He stood up and stuck out his massive right hand. I shook it or, more accurately, had my hand crushed in his massive clasp.

'Go get cleaned up and get some chow. We can talk about your team and the details later.'

I drove up to Amesbury, thinking of how much I wanted to have a 'discussion' with Lintz and Stan 'Captain Muscles' Clark. I wanted to punch my way to the truth of whatever it was they were up to. I told myself that it was about the dead woman, but I wasn't a hundred percent sure that it didn't have something to do with my blowing off the case in the early stages.

I also heard Sergeant Major's voice from the past, cautioning me against my own tendency to be quick to anger. I wasn't a twenty-one-year-old kid anymore. There was a lot more mileage on me now but that was no guarantee that I was any wiser. I would talk to Brock and watch Lintz, maybe even spend some time watching Clark. He seemed like too much of an asshole not to be involved.

I parked in Market Square, which was a nice collection of brick buildings with plate glass storefronts not far from the river. I found a pay phone and called Brock's extension at the bank. He picked it up after a couple of rings.

'It's Roark. Can you talk?'

'Um, this isn't a good time.'

'I can't imagine it is. It might not be, but we should still talk.'

'Roark, really . . .'

'Listen,' I cut him off, 'I found Karen Marti's body and then the local cops threw me in a jail cell for most of the day a couple days ago. I am running out of what little patience I have left.'

'OK, OK, where are you?'

'Market Square.'

'OK, there's a place to get a cup of coffee on Elm and High streets. It's across from the roundabout. I'll meet you there in ten minutes.'

The place was called The Market Square Bakery. Looking through the plate glass windows, I saw a large, open seating area. Beyond that was a glass case that held cakes and pastries and then further along the counter, there were different types of bread on display. Inside, the smell of freshly brewed coffee got my attention. I went to the counter and ordered a cup of coffee and a croissant filled with ham and melted cheese. When I eyed it perched on a pile on a cake stand under glass, I felt instantly hungry and knew that was the only cure.

I took my coffee and pastry sandwich to a table that afforded me a view of the door and the street through the plate glass. I sat with my back to the wall. Amesbury wasn't Saigon or Boston, but lately it was looking a lot more dangerous. Two murders, a bank robbery and embezzlement . . . I was glad that I had my .38 with me.

Looking through the plate glass windows, I saw Brock as he walked down the street in front of the bakery. He had a thin sheen of sweat on his forehead and looked nervously into the bakery. Brock walked in and stopped at the counter to order something, which turned out to be a coffee. I think this country would come to a complete halt if it weren't for coffee.

'OK, Roark, I'm here. What's so urgent?'

'You mean besides two of your employees murdered in as many weeks?'

'There's no need to be flippant. We're all devastated by their deaths.' We both had a talent for stating the obvious.

'It's not flippancy, it's a sour stomach.'

'Sour stomach?'

'You ever spend a night in jail or find a murdered woman?' I asked pointedly.

'No. No, I haven't.'

'I don't recommend either.'

'Why am I here, Mr Roark?'

'Do you know a man named Stanley Clark?'

'Sure. He's a real estate appraiser. Why?'

'He knew Karen Marti, my guess is intimately. Is it possible he's somehow involved in the embezzlement?'

'I am not sure how. He doesn't strike me as a master criminal. He looks at property and based on a simple formula comes up with an estimate. Anyone can do it, Mr Roark. Plus, he doesn't have access to the bank or its accounts.'

'Sure, but Karen Marti did. You told me that she had access

to everything. I saw them out one night. They seemed to be more than casual acquaintances. What if he was using her to access the bank?'

'That's possible.'

'What if she was accessing the accounts for him? Syphoning the money out and something changed, that would be motive to kill her.'

'It would. What about Frank Cosgrove?'

'I haven't figured that angle out yet. Maybe he tumbled on to their activities and Clark set up the robbery to silence him?'

'That seems like a lot of trouble to go to. Why not just kill him in a parking lot or in his apartment? Wouldn't those be less risky?'

'Sure, they would, but a bank employee being killed in a robbery would end any discussion of motive. No one would look closely at the victim's life and activities. Why would they?'

'You think that Cosgrove was the embezzler?'

'Or involved with Lintz in the scheme. A lot of money went missing. I imagine that's the type of thing that is easier to do if you have a partner.'

'Makes sense.'

'You said that nothing happened in the bank that Karen Marti didn't know about. What if she tumbled on to their scheme?'

'Jesus!'

'Yep, that would make a hell of a motive for murder.'

'You think that Lintz is behind all this . . . that he's some sort of mastermind?'

'He was the first name on your list of potential embezzlers.'

'He was.'

'He's also the only person on the list who's still alive,' I said. 'Does seem like a clue.'

It was more of an indicator, but Brock finally seemed to be taking what I had to tell him seriously. 'What can I do?' he asked.

'I need to know exactly how Lintz did it. If it was him.'

'The murders?'

'No, the embezzling. I need to know where the money came from, what accounts, where it went. I have to believe that the money is no good to him if hasn't been washed, unless he's got it in cash. But that much cash seems like it would be its own sort of problem.'

'Sure, you can't take millions of dollars to Atlantic City and turn it into clean money without the authorities noticing.'

'Without a whole lot of people noticing.'

All I could picture was The Banker's associates getting a phone call from New Jersey and bringing the whole house of cards fatally down on Lintz. He seemed smarter than that. He was disciplined, he didn't live like a high roller. His car was nice, but it was older. No, he wasn't the type to take a pile of cash to AC to try and wash it through a casino.

'True, someone would notice, and casinos are heavily regulated. The IRS is involved, as well as the Gaming Commission in the respective states where they are. Bringing duffle bags of cash would raise red flags.'

'So, you've thought of this before?' I said jokingly.

'Sure, it's every banker's worst nightmare, an employee helping themselves to the cash. Thought about it, considered every possible outcome and every angle. The board pays me to protect the bank, and I do it by trying to be one jump ahead.'

'That makes sense.' What I wanted to say was, 'but not in this case.'

'I can go back and see if there is anything linking Cosgrove or Karen to the missing money.'

'Stanley Clark, too.' I didn't say, 'I have a hunch.' That was too much like some two-bit TV detective, and it sounded too pretentious to call it a theory.

'He's a low-rent real estate appraiser. I don't really see him having the brains or wherewithal to pull off a complicated embezzlement scheme.'

'He knew Karen Marti. He's in the bank often enough to have known Cosgrove and Lintz. Is there any way a real estate appraiser could help launder the embezzled money?'

'I don't think so. Real estate appraisers usually don't have access to cash, they simply determine the fair market value of a property and get paid a fee for it. I just don't see where he'd be particularly useful to an embezzler.'

'OK, sure.' I wasn't convinced, and Brock picked up on it from my tone.

'Roark, trust me, this is a lot of money. Too much money for a guy like Clark to know what to do with.'

'Can you think of anything else? Any reason why they were murdered?'

'No, just that the money is missing, and they had access to it. Them and Lintz.'

'Lintz, who is very much alive and well.'

'That's right. Listen, I have to get back to the bank. Call me if you find anything out.'

'Sure, sure,' I said.

He got up and I watched him walk outside and up the sunlit street. Looking out the window at the historic, red brick of the old mill town, it was hard to believe anything bad had happened, much less two murders. I sipped my coffee and took a bite of my croissant.

There was no way that Clark wasn't involved. There were just too many coincidences stacking up. I wanted to talk to him, but it was too soon to brace him. I just didn't know enough about his role in things. Then there was Lintz. He was at the center of this thing and very much alive. If I had learned anything from watching movies on the Movie Loft and reading detectives stories, it was that the guy at the center of things who survives to the last act is usually the villain. There was nothing to make me think that Lintz was any sort of exception to that rule.

I had followed him for weeks and it had led me exactly nowhere other than to and from the bank. Following him hadn't turned anything up, so maybe the next step was to rattle him a little, see if anything would shake loose. Hell, it worked for Robert Redford in *Three Days of the Condor*, it should work for me too. The question was, how do you rattle a very disciplined embezzler enough to get some information or reaction out of him?

In the movie, Redford called Max von Sydow under a pretext. Maybe that could work for me too. I just needed to figure out the right one. What would make an embezzler nervous? Whose phone call would strike fear into his heart?

I got up and went to the phone booth that was in the corner of the coffee shop. I stepped inside the small, coffin-like space, pulling the doors closed. I picked up the handset and dropped a quarter in the coin slot. I listened to the metallic clicks and pings until the quarter reached its destination in the coin box, and the dial tone buzzed down the line to me. Then I pushed the buttons on the number pad, dialing the bank's main number.

When the receptionist answered, 'Hi, I'd like to speak to Frank Cosgrove, please.'

'Oh, um, sir, he's not with us anymore.'

'He quit? You fired him?' I asked with mock incredulity.

'No, no, sir, he's deceased.'

'I'm sorry to hear that. Oh, well, this is awkward. Is there someone else who I could talk to? His supervisor, perhaps?'

'Yes, that would be Mr Lintz.'

'Perfect.'

'May I ask whose calling?'

'Bill Travers, Federal Banking Commission.' I had no idea if there was such an entity, but it sounded official, and that was what I was going for.

'Please hold.' Her voice was replaced by some Muzak version of the Beatles. I didn't quite recognize which song, just the band. If that wasn't bad enough, I was on hold long enough for a Muzak version of 'Light My Fire' to come on. Jim Morrison must be rolling in his grave.

'Hello, this is Mark Lintz.'

'Mr Lintz, this is Bill Travers, Federal Banking Commission.'

'What can I do for you, Mr Travers?'

'Well, sir, we're conducting a survey of banks across the country. Do you believe that embezzlement is on the rise in banks in America?'

'Excuse me?'

I hung the handset up. Now, in the *Three Days of the Condor*, the main character was doing it to find out who Max von Sydow was calling. I wasn't that good or that handsome. I was just trying to rattle Lintz to see what he would do. I left the coffee shop and made my way back to the T-Bird.

I parked fifty yards down the street from the parking lot. It wasn't a hot day, but it was a novelty to have dependable air conditioning. 'Break on Through' by The Doors came on, and I tapped my fingertips on the steering wheel in time to the beat. If I thought that Lintz was going to come tear-gassing out of the parking lot and lead me to his co-conspirators, I couldn't have been more wrong.

I spent the rest of the afternoon reclined in the plush bucket seats of the T-Bird chewing on toothpicks dipped in peppermint oil. They weren't as satisfying as the cigarettes that I craved, but they were better than nothing. The T-Bird was new-ish and nice, and I wanted to return it to Carney in good shape. I waited until the bank closed for the day and watched as Lintz's Mercedes pulled out into the street. He drove home with no haste, stopping at every stop sign and obeying every light. If he was panicked by my phone call, he sure as hell had an odd way of showing it.

Usually when I tail someone, I try to hang back and not get made. I keep cars between us and generally try to blend in. I figured it might help spook Lintz if I made things a little more obvious. After he pulled into his driveway, I cruised slowly past his house at a crawl. He saw me as he was getting the mail out of the mailbox at the end of the driveway. He looked up at me and I did the most TV movie villain thing I could think of doing. I stomped on the gas pedal. I shot up the street with the unmistakable squealing of tires. I drove around for a couple of minutes then made my way back and parked in front of the Lintz house.

'Didn't you think he'd call the cops?' Angela asked as we sipped martinis in a little French bistro she had read about in the Globe and wanted to try. We were, like all civilized people do, seated at the bar. It was more efficient for getting drinks while we dined. Due to the din in the place, it forced a bit of intimacy as we had to lean in to talk.

The remains of a dinner lay abandoned in front of us. She'd had some sort of gratin and cod. I had steak au poivre with frites. Steak and fries sounds a lot classier when you say it in French. The pepper sauce was poured over a strip that had been cooked medium rare and sliced on a bias after resting, minutes before it was placed in front of me. The fries were more of the Belgian double-fried style and served with the obligatory mayonnaise. The French, or more likely the Dutch, had the right idea there.

'You know I don't always think about things before I do them.'

'You do have a reckless quality about you.'

'It is part of my boyish charm,' I said with a smile.

'If by that you mean you need to grow up, I agree.' She smiled back to let me know that it was meant in jest. Her long, dark hair cascaded over her shoulders, her lips had a sheen from lip gloss and her make-up was minimal.

'Well, I might, but I am in no rush. You should have seen the look on his face when I gassed it. I wish I could have seen his face in the bank when I called him.'

'So, you basically crank called him.' She was wearing white linen slacks with a light blue silk sleeveless t-shirt and a navy-blue linen jacket. Her belt was red and matched her heels. She looked like she should be in Cannes or Paris and not slumming in Boston with the likes of me.

'It's a solid investigative technique in which I try and agitate the suspect into making a mistake.'

'Isn't that usually how you get beaten up or shot at?'

'I didn't say it was a good technique.'

'You know one of these days your luck might run out.'

'Doubtful, I'm Irish. We're born lucky or so the legend says.'

'Don't believe everything you read on a cereal box.'

'Speaking of getting lucky . . .'

'Who said anything about getting lucky?'

'Chris found an apartment in Somerville. I am on my own again.'

'Except for that cat.' Angela and Sir Leominster existed in a state of wary détente, fueled by mutual distrust.

'The cat's a hell of a lot less noticeable than Chris snoring away on the couch.'

'Good point. Pay the check and let's get out of here.'

'Yes, ma'am.' Who was I to argue?

Later in my apartment after we had tried to set a record for undressing each other, we were sitting up in bed sipping martinis that I had been dispatched to the kitchen to make. We were sitting, shoulders touching. I was in a slight haze brought on by the combined effects of very recent events and the martini.

'Andy?'

'Emmm.'

'Are you sure that this Lintz is behind all this?'

'No, no, I'm not. There's something hinky about him, though.'

'What do you mean?'

'After two of his coworkers were murdered, he gets a crank call and then some strange dude is obviously following him around, he should have called the cops.'

'Maybe he didn't see you tailing him.'

'Angela, with the tail job I did, Ray Charles couldn't have missed it.'

'All part of your plan?'

'Sure. Then I parked in front of his house for fifteen minutes. If he was legit, then he would have called the cops. Even the Amesbury cops would have gotten there quickly after everything that's been going down.'

'Maybe he didn't notice you.'

'No, someone did. I saw the curtain in the front room move a few times. Someone was peeking out.'

'And all of that has convinced you he's an embezzler and a murderer?'

'No. All of that just convinced me that he's nervous about something and doesn't want to call the cops when he should. Brock gave me three names of potential embezzlers, and Lintz is the last one left standing,' I said.

'So, by process of elimination, he's the villain?'

'That's usually how it works. That and other than a very large, very angry real estate appraiser, I don't have anyone else to look at.'

'All right, I get the process of elimination angle. I just have a hard time reconciling that the guy you described as a boring husband and father as being the type to embezzle millions and kill two people.'

'Is this your way of telling me I should keep an open mind?'

'Something like that,' she said.

'I will, but I definitely need to talk to Lintz.'

'If you haven't scared him off.'

'That is a possibility.'

'You have a tendency to intimidate people.'

'I do not.'

'Ha! You look at everyone like you're sizing them up for a fight,' she said.

'I don't look at you like that.'

'No, you don't, but I have to assume you're not spending time with other people the way you do with me.'

'I'm not.'

'Good.' She kissed me, and then a few minutes later, 'Put your glass down and turn off the light.'

I did as I was told and was pleased to find out that sleep wasn't on her mind.

The next morning, I was up early but not earlier than Angela, who had to go back to her place to get ready for work. We weren't at the point where either of us felt comfortable leaving things at the other's place yet. I went for a run and contemplated my strategy. Today seemed like the day to go have a talk with Lintz. Then, depending on how that worked out, maybe a trip up to Portsmouth to see what Stanley Clark was up to.

The morning was cool but sunny. The pollen was out in force, which didn't make my run any better. At least by the Charles River, the air was much clearer. I got back to the apartment in decent time, and Sir Leominster let me know he was hungry by yowling at me. I opened a can of his cat food and emptied it into his bowl. While he buried his snout in the dish and ate greedily, I did a hundred push-ups and a hundred sit-ups. I wasn't in the same shape I was in when I was in Vietnam, but I was in pretty good shape overall.

After I showered, made coffee and had breakfast, I drove north. Driving the T-Bird was like going from a propeller plane to a fighter jet compared to the Maverick. The Maverick was fast and visceral but also a little sloppy feeling. The T-Bird was all fuel injection and smooth acceleration. I made good time to Amesbury while listening to the news on the local Public Radio

Station. NPR still didn't seem to be a fan of the Reagan administration.

I went to the Lintz house and parked up the street. With the predictability that you could set your watch by, Lintz pulled out of the driveway and headed off to work. I followed him but not as closely as yesterday. I didn't want to make him too jumpy before I braced him. Two people were already dead, and that had to make Lintz jumpy enough. The problem with jumpy criminals is that makes them unpredictable and much more dangerous.

He pulled into his spot, and a few seconds later, I pulled into the one next to his. He was just getting out of his Mercedes. I parked and opened the door. Lintz was staring at me with the wary expression of a gunfighter in a TV Western.

'Good morning, Mr Lintz.'

'Who are you? Why are you following me?' He was taller and better looking up close. He was wearing a tan three-piece suit that someone who had known a thing or two about tailoring had fitted to him.

'Oh, I called you yesterday to talk about embezzlement. You wouldn't know anything about that, would you?' I used the same tone I used to speak to suspects with when I was a cop.

'No, I don't know anything about embezzlement. Who are you?'

'My name's Roark. I'm a private investigator and I think you know quite a bit about embezzlement. Maybe something about two murders, too.' It wasn't exactly subtle, but I have never actually been accused of being subtle.

'I don't have any idea what you're talking about.'

'I'm talking about embezzlement from this bank. Same bank where two of your fellow employees were murdered. I don't think I can make it anymore plain.'

'You think I have anything to do with this?' he said, his voice creeping up in volume and pitch.

'You tell me. You're the guy with access. The only guy left.'

'Mr Roark, you don't know what you're talking about. Good morning!' He stomped off. It seemed like I was getting to him.

My style of investigating involved finding evidence by turning over rocks and seeing what was underneath. I didn't have a crime lab or a computer to analyze anything. A lot of the time the investigation only turns up so much evidence and then I hit a wall. I didn't know if it is a legitimate technique or just immaturity on my part, but that was when I start pushing people's buttons. So far, it worked to an extent.

While Lintz was tall and fit-looking, he didn't look like the beat-a-woman-to-death type of fit. But I knew of a guy across the border in New Hampshire who fit the bill. Stanley Clark and his chemically enhanced muscles seemed just the type to liberally interpret the Live Free or Die thing. I might just be biased because he was driving a newer Camaro. I'd respect him if it was one of the classic ones from my youth.

I got back in the T-Bird and made my way up the highway to Portsmouth. Sometimes I think I spend more time driving around than a traveling salesman. I probably didn't make as much as one. In twenty minutes plus a skosh, I was in Portsmouth, winding my way through the historic Navy town. I nosed my way through the streets with their clapboard and brick buildings that predated America until I was parked with a view of Clark's storefront office.

The local radio station was playing The Who song '5:15,' while I sat low in my seat, chewing on a toothpick soaked in peppermint oil. I might have to buy this car from Carney just so I would feel comfortable smoking in it. I was finding more and more ways of rationalizing buying this car.

I dragged my thoughts back to the matter at hand. Lintz struck me as management, the type of guy who could set up a scheme to embezzle a couple of million dollars from his trusting employer. That was ultimately what embezzlement is – the betrayal of trust. Taking advantage of someone, a system, to fraudulently convert their wealth into your own. While I saw Lintz as the brains, I was having a hard time seeing him as muscle. He wasn't the type to walk in, rob his own bank and murder Cosgrove. Also, he had been working at the bank when it happened. That meant an accomplice, someone used to getting their hands dirty and, despite his job as a real estate appraiser, Stanley Clark fit that bill like it was tailored for him.

I sat in the T-Bird thinking about the next move. What was

Clark going to do? Was I going to have to give him a nudge the way I did Lintz? Or would Lintz reach out to Clark and tell him about my conversation? That is assuming that I was right about them being involved in a giant conspiracy to embezzle from the Merrimack Community Bank and then murder to cover it up. When I said it aloud to myself in the car, it sounded like a stretch. More than a stretch, it sounds pretty farfetched. Maybe the Allman Brothers song 'Dreams' coming from the radio wasn't the best soundtrack for investigative theorizing.

Maybe I was approaching my business all wrong. Maybe I wasn't a private detective, but I was a theoretical detective. I could hear Sergeant Major Billy Justice cackle and say something like, 'Roark, you think you're like some sort of Einstein of detecting? Son, you've been dropped on your head too many times.' I smiled at no one inside the car. No, there wasn't much room for theory in what I do.

The door to Clark's office opened and he stepped out into the pleasant, sunshiny late morning. I waited till he started moving and got out of the T-Bird, following him from across the street, twenty yards back. Even though the weather was nice, it was a weekday and there wasn't a lot of pedestrian traffic in Portsmouth. With the breeze coming off the water, it was about ten degrees cooler than it would have been in Boston. I was glad for my jean jacket over a light polo shirt.

I tailed him from his office down by the waterfront and into Portsmouth's own Market Square. It was smaller, older and a little more neatly laid out than Amesbury's version. Clark walked quickly, light on his feet, not with the lumbering gate that I would have expected from such a muscle-bound guy. It made me think he might have some sort of martial arts background. If we had to fight, given his build and if he knew what he was doing, that would not make things easy. I liked my fights to be easy. It kept me from getting hurt too badly.

If I was hoping that tailing Stanley Clark would be any more interesting than tailing the rest of them, then I was setting myself up for disappointment. I followed Clark as he made his way to a real estate agent. It made sense that he didn't just do business with the one next to his office. I waited outside, sitting on a bench in the square that let me watch the plate glass windows of the office from an angle about ten yards away. I smoked a Lucky and tried to look casual.

Twenty-five minutes and two Luckies later, Clark walked out the front door. He was smiling like the cat who had been at the bowl of cream. It was around lunch time and there were more people walking around. That was good and would help my tailing him seem less obvious. I followed him back to his office and saw him go in. I crossed the street and went to the T-Bird where I could watch his office and at least listen to the radio.

I didn't have to wait long. For Clark, it looked like it was going to be a working lunch. He came out of the office carrying a briefcase and got into his car. He pulled away from the curb with only the mildest of screeching tires that Detroit muscle had to offer. I followed him through the downtown area and then out of town.

I had come into Portsmouth and left by the highway each time. Clark got on I-95 south and I thought he was heading back to Amesbury. Instead, he turned on to New Hampshire Route 101 heading west, which we followed for thirty miles until it crossed over Interstate 93.

In a very short time, the houses on the roads went from smallish lots close together to larger yards and then farmhouses spread out by acres instead of feet. The houses were few and far between as the roads took us over rolling hills. Now it was patches of farmland and trees where the forests edged close to the road.

New Hampshire 101 doglegged to the south-southwest for about fifteen miles then it turned hard to the west. The road had started its life as a collection of deer trails that had grown to routes for carts pulled by horses or oxen. Eventually it was a dirt road with wooden bridges, and then as technology improved, tar and paint were added until it was the road I was on now. It wound around hills and connected the small market towns from coastal New Hampshire all the way to the Connecticut River, which was the border with Vermont.

Clark turned off Route 101 heading south toward a town called Greenville. There wasn't much to see on the drive unless you liked trees. If that was your thing, then this route was a tree lover's paradise. Each time Clark turned off a road, its successor was smaller and more rustic. We were, by definition, in the sticks.

I was curious to see where he was going. Perhaps he was going out to appraise a property. Traffic was light and I gave Clark a good lead. It wasn't especially hard to tail him except that, for him, the speed limit seemed to be purely notional. I had to put some effort into it to keep him in sight. Fortunately, the T-Bird, especially after Carney had worked on it, was up to the task.

After a little over an hour of driving, Clark slowed and turned right on to a secondary road. I slowed down to a crawl to give him a good lead. The road was gravel, and I was pretty sure that he wasn't going to be flying up it in his Camaro. At first the road wasn't bad for a gravel road. It was an access road that went up a hill. There were dirt roads or driveways off it near the base of the hill. I was following the dust that Clark had stirred up.

I passed a logging road that had a metal agricultural gate blocking it; then there was no more dust. Clark had gone up the logging road and shut the gate behind him. A hundred yards up the road, I found another logging road and was able to make a thirty-point turn in an increasingly narrow gravel road. I carefully backed the T-Bird into the overgrown logging road. I turned the engine off and got out, quietly pushing the door shut behind me, locking it.

If my sense of direction was right, I was a hundred yards uphill from where Clark turned up the gravel road. If I started up the logging trail and angled to the left, I should eventually intersect with him. I started up the trail moving carefully, avoiding twigs and dead leaves out of habit. This was New Hampshire not Vietnam, not the Ho Chi Minh trail, but the habits that had kept me alive in SOG were hard to shake.

I moved up the logging trail carefully but faster than I would have ever moved while conducting recon missions on the Trail. I was pretty sure that Stanley 'Captain Muscles' Clark wasn't in the same league as the North Vietnamese Army trail watchers who hunted us. I was pretty sure that Clark's love of loud music in his loud car didn't give him the best hearing.

The trail was steep, and I was thankful that I was still in

reasonable shape in spite of all the cigarettes I smoked. The leaves on the trees and the pine needles were lush, and it was cool with the shade they provided. Even so, I started to sweat a little as I moved up the trail. Somewhere above me and off to my left, I heard a car door slam. I kept moving uphill, pausing every few feet to stop and listen. I didn't hear anything other than birds in the distance. I would pass through an occasional patch of sunlight that broke through the overhead canopy from the trees and see clouds of mayflies whirling in front of me.

After another ten minutes of hiking, the ground started to level off. I could see a clearing in front of me and slowed down. In Vietnam, crossing a large open area was an easy way to get yourself killed. You never knew who was waiting on the other side. All the more so because the NVA knew that any field large enough to put a chopper down in was a potential LZ, so they watched them. Ambushing a team was one thing, but being able to bring down a chopper and ambush a team was a huge prize.

I got to the edge of the tree line and stopped. I wasn't looking at a clearing at all. I was looking down at a pond, surrounded by twenty- or thirty-foot-high stone cliffs. The granite of the cliffs was hewn, bearing the marks of early American industrial effort. I was standing at the edge of an old granite quarry. It was like the quarry in Quincy, Massachusetts, that I had spent some time exploring in my youth.

Off to my left, I heard the Camaro's Detroit muscle rumble to life. Clark punched the gas and the car shot down the road in a spray of gravel. The road that Clark had taken uphill had brought him to a sort of wide gravel open area that was ten or twenty feet above the water. I thought about running back down to my car to try and keep tailing Clark, but there was no point. By the time I got to my car he would be long gone.

Instead, I decided to amuse myself by exploring the quarry. I moved off to the area where Clark had been. He had been there for a reason, and maybe it had nothing to do with the case, but it was worth looking into. I made my way down from my perch by hopping down a series of what seemed like steps carved out of the hillside for giants. Each step, or, more accurately, shelf, was three or four feet high and as deep. This was where they had hacked granite out of the hillside to be used in buildings in cities like Boston, Providence, New York and Philadelphia. Some of it had even been shipped to Europe to be used there.

By the time I made it the hundred or so yards laterally to where Clark's car had been, I was sweating considerably more. The day wasn't hot, but it took some effort to get down from where I was. I looked around, and there wasn't much to see except that the gravel road was in decent shape, albeit a little overgrown. The area where he had parked the Camaro was substantial enough to support a couple of trucks or earth-moving machines. There were discarded crushed beer cans here and there. I was pretty sure this was a popular spot for the local teens to come and party.

Maybe Clark was looking to appraise it for a customer. Maybe they were going to start quarrying it again? I didn't think there was that much money in reviving an old quarry like this. The quarry itself was four or five hundred yards across, and the water was dark, cool-looking and tempting.

I walked across the parking area and made my way through the woods around the quarry. The forest was thick with mayflies, and the occasional mosquito whined next to my ear. I was moving clockwise around the pool of water, moving uphill at a steep angle. New Hampshire was nothing like Vietnam, but for a split second, it felt like I was back doing my thing.

I picked up the logging trail and made my way back down to the car. I got in and started it up, enjoying the cool air coming out of the vents. I eased out on to the road and started back down the way I had driven up. I slowed down by the access road that Clark had driven up. From this angle I could see a rusty metal sign, punctured by the errant bullets of bored teenagers, its original message lost to decades of rust. Spray-painted on it in black paint was the simple message, 'For Sale,' with a phone number beneath it.

NINE

'So, what did he say when you confronted him?' Chris asked and then took a swig from the bottle of Lowenbrau that I had offered him.

'Not much. He seemed more interested in getting away from me.' I had been telling him about my little chat with Lintz in the bank parking lot. We were sitting at my kitchen table splitting a pepperoni pizza and a six-pack.

'He was scared of you?'

'Can you blame him? After all, I once struck terror in the hearts of the NVA,' I said jokingly.

'You were a rough, tough Green Beret,' he responded in kind.

'I don't think that was what spooked him.'

'What, the talk of embezzling?'

'Yeah, his face blanched when I said it.'

'Or being confronted in a parking lot after not one but two of his coworkers had been murdered had something to do with it.'

'Or that,' I agreed.

'Then what did you do after he retreated into the bank?'

'I took a drive up to New Hampshire where I ended up looking at some lovely real estate.'

'Real estate?'

'An abandoned quarry that was guarded by vicious mosquitoes.'

'What brought you up there?'

'I decided to follow Captain Muscles, and that's where he led me.'

'What does that have to do with the case? You think he and Lintz are partners?'

'I'm not sure. I don't think you'd need to embezzle two million dollars in order to buy an abandoned quarry.'

'That does seem a little steep,' he agreed.

'Who knows, it might mean nothing. My hunches don't always

pan out. Besides, it might be perfectly legitimate for a real estate appraiser to be out looking at a piece of property that's on the market.'

'Sure. Makes sense. Maybe they're going to build condos. You know, the ones that look like Swiss chalets to appeal to skiers.'

'Bring the tourist crowd to not-quite ski country, that type of thing,' I said.

'You said he lives near the coast.'

'Yeah, Portsmouth, where the Naval shipyard is, with their version of Leavenworth,' I said referring to the Army's famous stockade.

'And how far away is the quarry?'

'Twenty or so miles inland.'

The first thing I had done when I got home was dug out a folded map of Vermont and New Hampshire. It was printed on thin paper and folded into a rectangle, the type of thing that you could get at any rest stop or gas station. I found Portsmouth on the map and traced our route out of town to where I thought the quarry was. The problem with tourist maps, unlike the army ones, is that it didn't show the contour intervals. On an army map, the irregular red lines would have shown me things like hills and valleys.

I had called the number that was spray-painted on the sign, but it turned out to be disconnected. I could always call around to the real estate agencies in and around Portsmouth, but that was a lot of effort for something that seemed like a bit of a tangent. My time would probably be better served focusing on the case itself.

Later, after leaving the phone number and address of his new apartment in Somerville on one of my pads, Chris left. He seemed to be making the best of his exile to the east coast. I was curious as to what type of shady work Carney had gotten for him. Whatever it was, I was sure that Watts would be horrified and that I would end up hearing about it from her.

The next morning, I got up and went for a run. The sunny weather of the day before had given way to a gray sky that threatened rain. The humidity hung in the air giving a hint of what was to come in July and August. I ran my usual route from

my apartment out to Commonwealth Avenue, working my way
over to Massachusetts Avenue, then across the Charles into
Cambridge and eventually back to my apartment. I didn't know
what else I could do besides following Lintz and trying to shake
something loose. I could try and talk to him again, but without
any leverage, all I could do was try to annoy him to death in
hopes that he'd talk to me.

I made it back home and was met by Sir Leominster, who,
having finished his dish of foul-smelling cat food, was content
to rub up against my legs purring. After I was cleaned up and
had my own breakfast, which smelled a lot better than the cat's,
I drove over to the office. Maybe going through my case notes
could offer some sort of clarity or at least help me focus.

After an hour of reading the Globe, drinking espresso, and
smoking a bowl of good tobacco, I turned to my case notes.
Another hour and another espresso later, I wasn't any closer to
figuring this thing out. The only thing I was positive about was
that I had scared Lintz when I braced him about the embezzling.
On top of that, I had nothing that linked him and Stanley Clark,
other than his being a bank customer. While there was nothing
else linking Clark to the crimes revolving around the bank, I had
a hunch about him. Or he just seemed like an asshole and I
wanted him to be involved.

I was at an impasse and didn't know what to do. Action was
always better than inaction. I knocked the remnants of smoldering
tobacco and ash into the ashtray and rinsed out the tiny cup I'd
been sipping my espresso from. I grabbed my jean jacket on my
way to the door and locked up the office. Outside, the T-Bird
was waiting. Out of habit, I checked for wires on the ground or
any sign of tampering. Have your car blown up once and you'll
become more cautious too.

Satisfied that no one had left me any surprises, I got in and
headed north. I was going to Amesbury to brace Lintz, I decided.
Maybe he'd talk to me or maybe he wouldn't, but either way I
had enough of sitting around, waiting for things to happen. I
drove north, crossing the bridge and watching the sky darken
even more. Rain was coming, and it looked like a pretty good
size storm.

By the time I pulled up to the parking lot of the Merrimack Community Bank, Traffic was on the radio singing about their navigational challenges. Amesbury's finest was no longer keeping the parking lot safe for democracy, and big, fat raindrops were pelting my car. It reminded me of the first day on the job. Which, in turn, made me wonder if I had taken it more seriously if two people would still be alive. Intellectually, I knew that it wasn't my fault they were murdered.

The rain was coming down heavier now, and I decided that I would wait it out. A jean jacket, while stylish, was no match for a New England monsoon in May. While I was contemplating the rain and chewing on one of the peppermint oil soaked toothpicks, a familiar Camaro bumped into the parking lot. I hadn't expected Clark to show up, but now at least I had an idea of how I was going to spend my day, tailing Clark until I found something interesting or it was time to come back and talk to Lintz. I watched Clark run inside the bank, a folded newspaper over his head to protect him from the rain and briefcase in his other hand.

I sat in the T-Bird. There was no way of going in the bank without Clark seeing me. There was also no telling how long he'd be in there. Banks, especially ones that had recently been robbed, were bad places to hang out with nothing to do. They tended to frown on that.

I listened to The Kinks sing about their budgetary woes and then Van Morrison sang about the night's arrival. After a few commercials, more good songs on the radio and about twenty minutes or so, Clark came out of the bank. He jogged to the Camaro, tossed his briefcase in and followed quickly after it. He pulled out of the parking lot with his customary screeching of the tires.

I let a few cars go and then pulled out of the lot. This time he didn't hit the highway but instead headed east on the surface streets and rural routes. The first place we stopped was a small strip mall that wasn't near any road that would bring in a lot of traffic. There wasn't much to the strip mall. A small pharmacy that even from the outside you could tell had seen better days, and next door was a garage that offered low prices on oil changes and tire rotations. Perpendicular to that was a small supermarket, or at least what had been one years ago. Now it was closed and had a for sale sign in the plate glass window.

Clark pulled up next to the supermarket but didn't get out of his car. The rain had eased back to a persistent drizzle so there wasn't much stopping him. He put the car in gear and headed back out on to the road. There wasn't much traffic, so instead of letting cars get between us, I just gave him a decent lead. Ten minutes later he stopped at a lot that once had a building but all that was left now was a pile of bricks. The third and fourth properties were houses that could best be described as 'distressed.'

I had been following Clark around for two hours and decided that I had pushed my luck in terms of being spotted about as much as I should. Also, I wasn't sure how many more rough looking pieces of real estate I wanted to look at. I didn't know how much real estate appraising paid, but if it was based on the quality of the properties, I wasn't sure how he could afford a Camaro. It also occurred to me, not for the first time since I had become a private detective, that perhaps I had gone into the wrong line of work. Though I couldn't see myself having anything to do with real estate, or any other office type of job for that matter. What would Sir Leominster think?

I drove back to Amesbury in time to watch the bank let out. Pretending I was the 'heavy' in a gangster movie, I parked where Lintz couldn't miss the T-Bird. Then I followed him on his ride home, making no effort to avoid being seen. I didn't usually favor being so obvious, but I couldn't think of a better way of pressuring him. He pulled into his driveway, I parked where he could see me. When he walked down to the mailbox at the end of the driveway, he glowered at me.

I put the T-Bird in gear and glided off. I had missed lunch and didn't want to sit in traffic, fighting my way back into town during rush hour. As I drove south, my stomach growled but something occurred to me. That whatever was going on with Lintz, it was possibly some sort of real estate scheme. That would explain Clark's presence and possible involvement. Was Lintz embezzling from the bank to buy up dilapidated properties on the cheap? What would he do with them? The ones I saw couldn't be worth a lot of money, and unless someone was planning on building something bigger and better, I couldn't see where there'd be much in the way of resale value.

Maybe it was my hunger-fogged brain acting up, but I had an idea. Tax records. There were tax records in the tax assessor's office tied to the properties Clark was scoping out today. I could, as can any citizen, go and request them. That should tell me what the properties had sold for. I could then call the real estate agents and see what they were asking for them. With that information, I could finally confront Lintz with what I knew and get him to talk, get him to admit to the embezzlement and maybe find out why two people were murdered. And more importantly, find out who murdered them.

I was starting to feel like a real detective. Maybe my self-improvement plan was working. I had a pet and a steady girlfriend. No one had tried to blow up my car or otherwise kill me in months. I had to believe it was because of my clean living. Life was good. Unfortunately, my new lifestyle choices had no bearing on Boston traffic.

A mile or so from the Tobin, the highway turned into a parking lot. Traffic inched into town past a minor fender bender that brought movement to a literal halt. That was Boston for you. Sir Leominster was not going to be very forgiving about his dinner being delayed. He and my increasingly rumbling stomach would have that in common.

At home, Sir Leominster was waiting, pacing angrily back and forth. I was assailed with plaintive wails as he tried to communicate to me how dire his plight had been, how close he had come to starving to death, not having been fed in mere hours. He didn't let up until I opened a can of the scrapings from the fish processing floor that he considered high cuisine.

Once he was too busy inhaling the disgusting stuff from his dish to harass me, I was able to see to my own needs, which, first and foremost, meant whiskey, two fingers of Powers Irish whiskey over two ice cubes. Then I checked the machine. There was a message from Danny Sullivan reminding me that we hadn't had a drink in some time. The next was a message from Angela suggesting we have dinner tomorrow night. She also had some suggestions for post-dinner activities that would have made a younger version of me blush.

I poked around the fridge looking for something that could be turned into dinner. I found some sourdough bread and a can of tuna. I made tuna salad with mayo and chopped up a few martini olives in lieu of celery. I cut the sourdough into four pieces which I brushed with olive oil and toasted under the broiler. When they came out, I sprinkled salt and pepper on them and spread the tuna on them. From the fridge, I took out half a block of Cracker Barrel cheddar cheese. I cut squares off the block and put them on top of the tuna salad, covering it evenly. It all went back under the broiler. Fancy tuna melts seemed like a decent dinner.

When my sandwiches were done, I transferred them from the baking sheet to a plate. I added more whiskey and ice to my glass. I took my drink and my sandwiches to the couch, turned on the TV and was rewarded by Dana Hersey on the Movie Loft telling me that tonight's movie was going to be *The Maltese Falcon*, the original with Humphrey Bogart. Hot dog! A classic, and I might learn something about being a private detective to boot.

Sir Leominster joined me on the couch, not because he had missed me, but for the chance of getting any stray tuna salad left on my plate. He was a pragmatist. We watched the movie in comfortable companionship, disturbed only by my need to replenish my glass. Later, I went to bed with my .38 on the table next to me and thoughts of Bogey's style in my head.

The next morning found me at Amesbury Town Hall. It was nine thirty, a time that I had picked with care. I wanted the dedicated civil servants in the tax assessor's office to be awake and attentive. I didn't want them to be thinking about lunch or to be burned out on dealing with lots of citizens who had already been annoying them. In short, I was looking to maximize my chances of getting the help I needed.

I also decided to dress like I was a halfway respectable person: cordovan loafers, pressed khakis, blue oxford shirt and a blue blazer from Brooks Brothers, the type with brass buttons. I even had a briefcase that I had picked up a couple of years ago at my local Salvation Army store. It was weathered but not beat up, more of an old friend than a distant relative looking for a loan. With my short hair and clean shave, I looked like a lawyer or maybe a real estate agent. I certainly didn't look like a keyhole peeper from Southie with questionable taste in friends.

I walked up the steps to the town hall and into the lobby. I stopped long enough to look at the directory on the wall. It was the type of affair that used black velvet and white, plastic press in letters. It wasn't cheap or shabby but spoke of municipal budgets. I found the room number of the assessor's office and walked down the hall to it.

Inside was the standard counter with desks and people working at them behind it. I stood patiently, waiting to be acknowledged. The Army had taught me all about patience by providing me with no end of lines to stand and wait in. They all moved glacially, so standing at a counter in a municipal office, other than the Department of Motor Vehicles, was child's play. The DMV was a special kind of hellish torture.

Eventually a tall, thin man in his late twenties, wearing glasses and sporting a ginger beard came over.

'Can I help you?' he asked.

'Yes, I was interested several properties.'

'Interested?'

'Yes, the ownership history, taxes and resale values.'

'OK, do you have the addresses?'

'Here.' I handed him the index card that I had written them on in blue felt tip pen.

'OK, this might take a few minutes.'

'Sure, of course.'

He walked away and I sat down in one of the hard, plastic chairs that seemed to have been designed to discourage any thought of comfort. I would have lit up a Lucky but there was a none-too-subtle no smoking sign. A few minutes was more like twenty. Fortunately, the town of Amesbury believed in computers. The clerk returned with a stack of white and green computer paper with white, perforated edges in them.

'Here you go,' he said.

'Thanks. How much?'

'Five dollars even.'

I slid a portrait of Lincoln across the counter to him. He slid the pile of printer paper over to me. I put them in my briefcase and left with the receipt he offered. After all, I was going to have to bill Brock for my expenses.

Outside, sitting in the T-Bird, listening to Muddy Waters on the radio, I started to look at the property records. Each of the properties that Clark had looked at had been built or purchased decades ago, then had been sold several times over the past year. Each time they were sold, the value went up by fifty percent. They seemed to be sold every two to three months to some new company whose name ended in 'Enterprise,' 'Group' or 'LLC.' Properties that had been worth twenty or thirty thousand dollars to begin with were, at their last sale, worth two hundred thousand dollars.

That should have been the interesting part, real estate quadrupling in value in a year. It wasn't. The interesting part was who was buying it. That was Karen Marti. Even more interesting is that the officer approving the mortgages was the late Frank Cosgrove of the Merrimack Community Bank. If I were a betting man, I would bet that the appraisal was done by Stanley Clark. Somewhere in all of this, Mark Lintz was neck deep in it. I knew he had to be involved. I just didn't see the whole scheme. Brock had screwed up – he didn't need a private eye, he needed a forensic accountant.

I put the T-Bird in gear and headed out to see the properties that Clark had toured yesterday. I was thinking of taking a closer look at them. I wanted to make sure that they didn't secretly have oil on the property or were covering up the entrance to an abandoned but still viable mine.

I spent the next two hours of my life learning just how dusty abandoned properties could be. Other than cobwebs, lead paint and water damage, the only thing the properties had in common was that they were home to spiders. Lots and lots of spiders. I didn't mind them as a rule, as long as they didn't try and shower with me. Also, after the bugs in Vietnam, American bugs just weren't that impressive.

I had taken a quick look at the printouts from the assessor's office and I had seen the properties, but something didn't jive. There had to be some reason why these properties were increasing in value. If it wasn't for the buildings themselves, maybe it was the location. Maybe there was some sort of larger project that was in the works and these properties might be worth substantially more as pieces of the puzzle.

I was getting ready to call it a day when I pulled up to the last of the properties I wanted to look at. It was a run-down house outside of Amesbury. As I pulled up to the property, Clark's now familiar Camaro was parked in the driveway. I drove down the road and around a bend and parked on the shoulder.

Why was Clark back at a house that he had already been at and, in theory, appraised yesterday? Not only that, but one of the houses that seems to have been sold and resold, appraised, and reappraised. Was there something special about the house? Or something in it?

I put the T-Bird in gear and pulled on to the road. Down the road another twenty or so yards was a spot where I could make a U-turn safely. When I was sure there was no oncoming traffic, I banged a U-ey and headed back toward the house where Clark was currently doing whatever Clark was doing. I cruised past the house and banged another U-ey up the road so that I was able to watch Clark's car from forty yards away.

I sat in the T-Bird, watching the Camaro parked in the driveway, listening to John Lennon sing about 'Steel and Glass' on the radio. It wasn't a song of his that often got radio play. After his murder, it seemed like the only John Lennon song that got any airtime was 'Imagine.' Clark came out of the house carrying an AWOL bag, the little gym bag that had gone out of style in the early 1970s. He got into his car, reversed out of the driveway and bombed down the road.

I eased the T-Bird into gear and rolled the short distance down the road to the house. I parked in the cracked asphalt driveway. Taking the penlight that I kept in the glove box, I got out of the T-Bird.

The house was one of the more dilapidated ones that he had

looked at the day before. It had a sagging front porch that had the remnants of decorative woodwork at the tops of the support columns that helped frame the listing railing. The trim had once been brick red, but weathering and cracking paint had left it a dull pink. The window that took up half of the front door had been replaced with plywood, and there were cobwebs in every corner. I was starting to think that this was the house that the local kids dared each other to go into.

Every other window was covered with plywood, and there was no shortage of weeds in the overgrown flower beds. The front lawn seemed to be a collection of rusting car parts and beer cans that predated aluminum cans. As I walked up to the front door, broken glass crunched under my feet. I stepped on to the springing boards of the front porch wondering if I was going to put one loafered foot through the floorboards.

If I had been worried about picking the lock or jimmying the door, I needn't have been. The door had long ago been kicked open. The hardware was rusted and hanging from what little of the door frame was still intact. I pushed the door open with the toe of my loafer, my hand unconsciously resting on the butt of my .38. The door opened with the predictable horror movie creaking, and the smell that made its way out wasn't pleasant. An animal had made its way inside to die and eventually decompose. Looking down at the floorboards, I could see large footprints in the thick dust. Clark's, no doubt.

Taking a last breath of fresh air, I pushed my way through the door and into the house. The light from the few uncovered windows wasn't ideal, but it was enough to see dirt, decay and broken furniture. Anything of value that had originally been in this place was long gone. And unless someone had found a way to turn dust and mold into money, I was pretty sure that Clark's interest in this place had nothing to do with fixing it up to live in it. He might be using it as a stash house. Maybe he was moving drugs, or maybe he had robbed the bank, and this was where he hid the money?

I walked further into the entryway. There was a stairwell leading to the second floor that was sagging halfway up. All the supports for the banister had been kicked or broken off. I thought about going up it, but I noticed it was listing away from the wall, reminding me of something Indiana Jones would have to deal with. I was searching for clues, not artifacts.

To my left was a living room that seemed to be filled with the remnants of furniture. There was a fireplace that had ashes and charred beer cans piled in it. I was starting to think that this might also be a spot where the local high school kids came to party and get up to mischief. In the dim light, I was able to make out graffiti spray-painted on the walls and empty beer bottles in one corner.

I circled back to the entryway and where I had gone left initially, to the right, was a kitchen. It was bereft of furniture and most of the cabinets were open or the doors had been ripped off by vandalistic teens. There was no stove, and the sink was filled with beer bottles and cans that had long been discarded. There was a bullet-shaped refrigerator that dated back to the Eisenhower administration. Knowing I would regret it, I pulled down on the lever-like handle and the door swung open.

The smell wasn't as bad as I thought it would be, but it still wasn't good. What food had been left behind in it had long ago rotted, and all that was left were the blackened, mummified bits. The small ice box in the top right corner with the modern Frigidaire logo on its spring hinged door held nothing more than abandoned metal ice trays. I pushed the door shut and resisted the urge to wipe the greasy feeling off my hand.

There was nothing in what was left of the cabinets. Even the crockery had been smashed or stolen. There were two doors in the kitchen, and one turned out to be a pantry. There were a few cans sitting on the shelf that had burst and leaked out their poisonous contents. There were cobwebs aplenty, but even the spiders had deserted the place.

The second door turned out to lead to the cellar. Panning my flashlight downstairs, I could see fresh footprints in the dust on the treads. Clark had gone down into the basement. If the cellar stairs could hold Clark, they could hold me. I started down the steps, panning the penlight from left to right in front of me.

The basement was low ceilinged with small windows in the

wall. The boiler was gone, ripped out by thieves. There wasn't much else to say about it, except that it was a mess. There were piles of trash and broken furniture everywhere. There was a path that had been cleared, and I was wondering if that lead to some sort of stash? Why else would Clark go to the trouble of coming down in the basement of an abandoned house except to stash something. It smelled bad but not dead-body-in-an-abandoned-building-in-July bad. There had been plenty of those when I had been a cop and heroin had been king.

I made my way further down the path through the decades old detritus. It had been here so long that the rats and roaches had run out of things to eat. That was good for me because it kept the smell down to only mildly nauseating. The other favor that Clark had done besides clearing a path through the trash was that he had cleared away massive amounts of cobwebs.

I made my way down the trash trail which snaked through the basement. To one side of the trail were some steps leading up to what I assumed was a bulkhead. I had to assume because it was so covered by cobwebs and active spiderwebs that I couldn't see much beyond it in the dim light from penlight. I went a few more feet in, and then the trail through the trash abruptly ended. That didn't make sense.

There was nothing that obviously screamed of a stash or that anything had been disturbed. It was a mess, but other than the trail, nothing had been disturbed down here for years. I froze in place, the way I had been trained. If I wasn't in the middle of a giant trash pile and wearing my good chinos, I would have taken a knee.

There was a creak on the floorboards above me. I didn't know who it was, but I was pretty sure that I didn't want to be stuck down in the middle of the trash pile with someone walking around upstairs. It could just be kids, or it could be the cops or Clark. I had reached the foot of the steps when I heard liquid trickling. That was a bad sign because there hadn't been a working faucet in this place in twenty years. Then I heard something heavy scraping along the floor, being pushed or dragged. It could only be the old Frigidaire being dragged in front of the door to the basement.

I started up the steps. I wouldn't have much leverage, but I might be able to get enough force behind the door to push the Frigidaire. It wasn't a great plan, but it was better than nothing. Then the smell hit me – gasoline. I played the light on the steps and saw rivulets of liquid making their way down them. Fuck.

I started to go back down the stairs back into the cellar. Upstairs the floorboards creaked under rapidly shuffling steps. I heard smashing glass, a beer bottle or maybe a jar then a loud whooshing noise almost like a jet engine starting up. A tongue of flame shot out from under the door to the kitchen and the rivulets on the steps were now rivulets of fire. I turned around and headed back the way I came. I crossed the cellar, through the trash pathway at a clip. I looked back and the door to the kitchen was framed in flames.

I made it to the bulkhead and clawed my way through the spiderwebs. They clung to my hands and face, but I barely noticed them. There were six steps and the slanting, rusted double metal doors of the bulkhead. The L-shaped, metal bolt holding the doors closed was rusted. The basement was getting noticeably warmer, and over the gas smell, the trash smell was coming back to life, competing with the smell of melting plastic and smoke.

I grabbed the bolt and yanked on it. It wouldn't budge. I yanked on it again and again. It wouldn't budge. I looked back at the stairs, which were now on fire. There was no getting out that way, and the basement windows were too small to crawl through unless you were the size of a cat. It was unlikely there was another bulkhead, and I was running out of time to find another way out.

There was more smoke in the cellar and the heat was now making me sweat. Two more tugs on the bolt only resulted in me scraping my knuckles and cutting my left hand. The trash bags near the steps had caught on fire while I was trying to get the bolt to move. I was sure that of all the ways I could die, in a trash fire in a basement was last on my list.

I turned my attention back to the bulkhead. I stepped up and bent over at the waist so I could put my shoulder against the metal door. I lunged up into it, battering my shoulder into it over and over again. The fire was growing hotter and closer, and I started to cough in the acrid smoke filling the basement. I wasn't going to go out like this. Again and again, I battered my shoulder into the bulkhead until I felt it give.

I paused, tugging on the bolt, which I had jarred loose from the rust. I gave it a hard pull and it slid back a half inch. Another hard pull and I cleared it from the metal loop it engaged with. I pushed on the bulkhead door, and it gave an inch. I smelled sweet, clear, fresh air and then the door came back down. Something heavy was on it. I pushed again but could only get the hatch to open an inch.

The fire was growing closer, and I was coughing more. If I didn't get out of there, the smoke was going to do me in before the fire would. I backed up to the door, getting both shoulders underneath it and extended my legs, using their longer muscles to push. The door opened a bit more then collapsed back on me. If I got out of this, I was going to feel that in the morning. I pushed up again and the result was the same. I gave one last hard thrust with my legs upward and at first the door started to move. Then the weight on it shifted off and I shot up, falling back on the steps but looking up at the sky.

I crawled out of the bulkhead and on to the grass. I coughed a long, wracking fit and then got up. The heat coming off the house was intense, and I wanted to move away from it. Off in the distance, I could hear the wailing of sirens. I didn't want to be here when the fire department showed up, because close on their heels would be the cops. I was certain that would mean a trip back to the Amesbury PD's finest holding cell.

I managed to stagger, to the T-Bird, coughing the whole way. I unlocked it and collapsed in the bucket seat. I got it started up and reversed out of the driveway, making it around the bend just as the flashing red lights of the fire engine pulled up. I drove the speed limit, winding my way out of Amesbury.

By the time I made it to the highway, the coughing had gone from long, wracking fits to the occasional deep bark. Maybe my lungs were seasoned by years of smoking Lucky Strikes. I noticed that my shoulder had started to throb. I had battered it against a steel bulkhead door god knows how many times. My back also started to remind me that it, too, had taken a beating. All of it, the coughing, the shoulder, the cut hand, scraped knuckles, and aching back were much better than being roasted alive in a basement trash fire.

For once the traffic wasn't horrible and I made good time into town. I made it home and parked in my spot where some Vietnamese gangsters had blown up my beloved Karmann Ghia. After my time in the cellar trash fire, I could empathize with the car.

Walking into the building, one of my neighbors was walking out. He took one look at me and shook his head. I wasn't sure what he did for a living. Most of my neighbors didn't talk to me much, and I was a lot less popular after my car had been assassinated with the girl in it. There had been a lot of broken windows and rattled people.

I caught sight of myself in the mirror in the entryway, and I couldn't blame my neighbor. My face was covered in black, greasy-looking smudges of smoke and sweat. There were cobwebs in my hair and on my clothes. The arm of my blazer was ripped at the shoulder and my pants looked like they had been dragged through dirt and charcoal. There were bloodstains on my chinos from the cut on my hand. At least I was up on my tetanus shots.

My back was starting to ache more. Sitting in the bucket seat for the ride from Amesbury to town after battering my way out of the basement hadn't helped. I was a mess and needed to get cleaned up and get a drink. Probably not in that order.

Later, I sat soaking in the clawfoot tub. The hot water loosened the knots in my back, easing the strained muscles and the pain in my shoulder. I had showered the basement filth and smoke off and then opted for a soaking. The soaking was complemented by a tall glass of whiskey, which did wonders to numb the pain.

I had cleaned the cut on my hand and disinfected it. Chris wouldn't approve of the job I did, but he was a trained professional. I lay in the tub as the aches and pains slowly receded like an angry chorus growing distant. The whiskey started to loosen the cobwebs in my head, and it occurred to me that Stanley 'Captain Muscles' Clark had probably seen me drive by. Maybe he had spotted me tailing him yesterday. I couldn't prove it, but he had trapped me in the basement and tried to incinerate me. From my point of view, as a professional detective, I had made progress in the case.

TEN

'You call that progress?' Chris asked. We were sitting at my kitchen table. He had dropped by late afternoon. I had answered the door in a bathrobe with a pistol at my side, the 9mm Hi-Power instead of the .38 snubnose. People trying to kill me has that effect on me.

'Sure, I went from shaking trees to see what would fall out to someone actually trying to off me.'

'Sure, that makes sense,' he said, and to him, maybe it did.

It seemed a lot like what we had done in Vietnam. Show up on the Ho Chi Minh trail and try and find the NVA. If they started to shoot at you, you found 'em. Chris was one of my few friends who would understand that. Most of the ones I had served with were dead and the ones who hadn't been there wouldn't get it.

'It had to be Clark.'

'Did you get sloppy tailing him?'

'He must have spotted me. It is hard to follow someone on the back roads around Amesbury or New Hampshire. I thought I had been careful, but it's always a risk.'

'And then you went into the creepy abandoned house?'

'Of course.'

'Don't you watch horror movies, or at least Scooby Doo?'

'I'm a detective. I detect things. I look for clues. Sometimes that leads me into dangerous situations. It's not like your job is safe.'

'It's a hell of a lot safer than yours. No one ever tried to burn a house down around me.'

I would have said, 'yet,' but there was an angry buzzing of the doorbell, someone stabbing a finger into the button repeatedly.

'Shit,' I said.

'What?'

'I was supposed to meet Angela. We have a date. I forgot, with the potential immolation and all.'

'Now you're in danger.' He got up and went to let her in. I couldn't say that I minded, as sitting at my kitchen table, the muscles that had loosened up in the bath had stiffened up. I heard angry voices. Well, one angry voice and Chris's deep one. Then the sound of high heels aggressively treading on the floors, and then Angela was standing in the kitchen door.

'We had a date. I waited for you and now you're here getting drunk with your shitbag buddy.'

'Ange . . .'

'You're not even ready, you're just wearing a robe.'

'Ange.'

'Someone tried to kill him today,' Chris said from behind her.

'Someone tries to kill him a lot,' she said with controlled fury.

'Ange, I was in a house. Trapped. A guy lit it on fire, and I almost didn't make it out.'

'Jesus.'

'I was in the bath getting cleaned up, and Chris dropped by. We got to talking and I lost track of time. Let me throw some clothes on and we'll grab dinner.' I stood up and moved creakingly toward the door.

'Is your hand OK?'

'Yeah, it's fine. I cut it trying to get out of the basement.'

'Are those bruises?' she said sharply, spying my shoulder where the robe had flopped open.

'Uh, yeah.'

'What happened?'

'I was trapped in the basement of a house that someone torched hoping I wouldn't get out. I had to batter my way out of a metal bulkhead.'

'You're hurt?'

'Bruised and scraped, but nothing serious.'

'He'll be right as rain after a couple of days of rest,' Chris offered.

'Are you a doctor?'

'No, ma'am.'

'Ange, he's a Special Forces medical sergeant. They trained him to do surgery in the field and treat most illnesses. I'd rather have Chris than most doctors.'

It was true, SF medics were supposed to see to an A-team's medical needs in austere conditions in the field. They were taught to do everything from treating gunshot wounds to surgery to providing basic healthcare to the locals to include delivering babies, in the strange places SF went. Chris was one of the best.

'Oh, OK. Well, as long as you two are in your cups, you could offer a girl a drink.'

'Absolutely,' I said enthusiastically.

'Why don't you go put on some clothes. We can order in.' Then to Chris, 'You know anything about making martinis?'

'Yes, ma'am. I do know a fair bit.'

'Think you could rustle one up for me? Something tells me I'm going to need it to listen to you tell war stories over dinner.'

It wasn't the best peace offering, but it was progress. I didn't hear Chris's reply because I had stepped into the bedroom. I found a pair of old, comfortable jeans and t-shirt from a Dutch paratrooper outfit that I had picked up in my travels. I took the Hi-Power and locked it up behind the swing-out panel in the living room closet. Then I joined them in the kitchen.

They were sitting at the table, Chris with a bottle of Lowenbrau he had gotten from the fridge and Angela with a martini that was showing just a hint of condensation on the glass.

'How'd he do?' I asked, nodding at the martini.

'Not bad. Do they teach all you Green Beret types how to make martinis?'

'There's no point being an elite commando if you can't make a good drink,' Chris said.

'Yep, forget all that jumping out of airplanes, scuba diving and demolitions, it's all pointless if you can't make a good martini.'

'You two are pair of clowns. You're perfect for each other.'

'Ha, ha, well, Chris can do better,' I said without irony.

'Plus, you're the first woman Red's talked about in a long time that lasted more than a couple of weeks.'

'What can I say, I'm a glutton for punishment . . . and he does make a good martini.'

'Better than mine?' Chris said, mildly aggrieved.

'Yes, but yours is a close second.'

I smiled. I'm a sucker for compliments from pretty women.

'What's for dinner?'

'We ordered Chinese food.'

'Yep, the lady and I had fun picking out your food. I told her there was nothing too gross for you to eat.'

Later, after dinner had been eaten and Chris had gone, we were lying in bed. In spite of the day's events and the toll it had taken, we managed to make love, slowly and gently. I had no complaints.

'You still smell like smoke.'

'Cigarette smoke?'

'No, it's subtler, underneath that, and worse, like melted plastic.'

'The garbage bags in the basement probably. I tried to wash the smell of it away, but sometimes it takes a couple of showers.'

'You did a number on your shoulder.'

'I wasn't going to die down there . . . not like that.'

'I don't blame you.'

'Yeah, I mean not just that.'

'What then?'

'There were a few times in Vietnam. We were sent to the sites of aircraft, usually helicopters but sometimes planes, that had been shot down.'

'And?'

'Usually with the jets there wasn't a lot to see. Maybe the fuselage was mostly intact, but there would be a lot of debris scattered around. But with the helicopters, there were a couple of times when they crashed, they caught fire. I will never forget the way the bodies looked. The ones that died on impact, that was one thing . . . but sometimes they survived that only to be killed by the bird catching on fire. Especially if there was a lot of fuel or ammunition left on board.'

'Jesus.'

'That's what I was thinking of in that basement. That it wasn't going to be me. I wasn't going to die like that.' I spared telling her about the times we found corpses that had been caught in the melted windscreens of the helicopters, grotesque sculptures that had once been men.

'Oh Christ, Andy.' She pulled me close to her and held me tightly. My shoulder hurt but I wasn't going to say anything, it was a small price to pay. I felt warm liquid on my shoulder.

'Hey, hey, it's OK. I made it out. I'm OK.'

'You made it out this time. You might not next time.'

'That's true. But that applies to all of us. We don't know from one moment to the next. Car accidents, heart attacks, earthquakes, there are a lot of ways to die.'

'Those are all random, you put yourself in these situations.'

'Well, yeah.'

'Why?'

'I'm not sure I have a good answer or an answer you will like.'

'Try me.'

'I was a kid when I enlisted in the Army. I spent two years training to go to war, to be in combat. I wanted to test myself. I spent three years in Vietnam doing really, really dangerous stuff. Most of my friends were killed, and when I came home, I couldn't stay in the Army. It would have gotten me killed, and I couldn't hack it in the peacetime Army.

'So, I joined the cops, kind like going from smack to methadone but still dangerous. I was almost killed a few times in the cops which was in some ways better and worse than the Army. I finished my college degree in night school. I quit the cops and knew I couldn't work a straight job or an office job. I'd have ended up putting a bullet in my head or drinking myself to death like my old man.

'In the end, this is it. This is the compromise I made with myself. Most of the time my job is boring, watching people and writing reports. Sometimes there's some violence, fights and the like. Sometimes people try to kill me; no one's succeeded yet.

'I might get banged up a little, but I am still here, and I can still function in this world. Live in it. I am not sure I could do that any other way.'

I hadn't ever explained it to anyone like that. I had lived with a woman named Leslie and dated a girl named Sue, but I was never able to explain it to them. Maybe I hadn't really felt the need to.

'When we first started dating you told me about it, but not like that.'

'I probably didn't do a good enough job explaining.'

'Andy, it isn't about explaining. Someone locked you in a building today and tried to burn it down with you in it. That isn't or shouldn't be a normal part of a person's day-to-day life.'

'I know, I was there. It isn't a "normal" part of my life. Days like today are the exception, not the rule.'

'Sure, but you are so damned casual about it.'

'I don't know any other way to be. I can't do what I do and lose my shit every time someone takes a shot at me.'

'No, but I can. I like you.'

'I've noticed.'

'I like the thought of you being around long enough to really get to know.'

'That's my plan,' I said. I meant it, I really did.

I slept in the next morning. When I woke up, the sky was overcast. It was one of those rare, stormy days in May, the kind that are cool and the hours are punctuated by downpours and storms. I was in no rush to get up and decided to read another chapter of *In Cold Blood*. Sir Leominster hopped up on to the bed when I was a few pages into the chapter. He purred and butted my head with his. When I put the book down, he began to whine to let me know his breakfast was long overdue. No rest for the weary.

I swung my feet over the edge of the bed and stood up. The aches and pains, the chorus of bruised and strained muscles was immediate. I took a few shuffling steps and started to loosen up. I got the damned cat his food and started to worry about myself. Coffee was the first priority. I lit a Lucky off the burner and took a deep drag and immediately started coughing. When it passed, I took another, shallower drag and felt the nicotine working its magic.

The stovetop espresso machine started to burble away, and I decided that after yesterday, I needed more for breakfast than yogurt and wheat toast. I found some bacon in the fridge and put it in a pan, letting the pan heat up, releasing the magical smell of cooking bacon. It might not have made my aches and pains feel better, but it was good for morale. When the bacon looked not quite done, I pulled it out of the pan and put it on some paper towel. It would continue to cook out of the pan but wouldn't overcook. I poured most of the bacon grease off into the can I kept in the refrigerator.

I put two slices of bread in the toaster and put the bacon pan back on the flame. I cracked two eggs into the pan. I dusted them with salt and pepper and, using a fork, began to scramble them. I moved the yolk and white around quickly, mostly incorporating them the way I had watched my father do a thousand or so times when I was a kid.

As I ate my breakfast, I thought about the events that led me into that basement. Had Clark spotted me or had Lintz told him that I was onto the embezzlement scheme? I had shaken the hornet's nest enough to get a reaction, but had I shaken it enough to find out why two people had been murdered?

After I had put the dishes in the sink and taken a long shower to loosen the knots in my back, I dressed and made my way to the office. I pulled out the legal pad my current case notes were on. I updated them with the recent turn of events and then wrote down a series of questions about the case. I was no closer to proving anything other than two people were dead, to date, I had been sapped and almost, quite intentionally burned to death.

The only people who might have answers were Lintz and Clark. Lintz seemed like the brains to Clark's obvious brawn. Bracing Clark would mean fighting him, and that didn't seem like the best idea this morning. Lintz, on the other hand, didn't strike me as a tough guy. Maybe he just needed more direct pressure to talk.

After the fire, I thought about bringing a bigger gun, my Combat Commander in .45 or my Hi-Power. But in reality, a gun hadn't made any difference yesterday, so it didn't make sense to opt for a bigger one now. It looks great in the movies when the hero shoots the lock of a door but in reality it just jams the lock or sends bullets ricocheting all over the place. Not to mention the discomfort that comes from toting around a large, heavy automatic.

When I got in the T-Bird, it still smelled of smoke from yesterday. I rolled the windows down halfway. It had stopped raining, but looking at the sky, I could tell that was just temporary. I drove over to the office, taking a couple of extra turns and looped back a couple of times. If I had a tail, he was good – the cops, the Feds, the pros all use at least three cars. Someone like Clark probably didn't have those types of resources.

I found a spot in front of my building ten yards down from my front door. I fed some quarters into the meter. A cop might give you a break, but the meter maids were heartless. Normally I would've parked in the spot in the alley behind my building, but I was ambushed there a few months ago. The Maverick took the bulk of the shotgun blasts, but I was in no rush to see if anyone was waiting for me. I locked the T-Bird, went into the building and upstairs.

I checked the door to my office by opening it a crack. I know I sound paranoid, but last spring, the Vietnamese gangsters who shot off my earlobe had left a fragmentation grenade wired to my door. Every fresh attempt of my life brought out my inner instinct for survival.

There was no one waiting for me inside. No nasty surprises either, just dust and the smell of old pipe smoke. It wasn't the nicest office, but it was functional. I fired up the espresso machine out of habit but decided to pass on a pipe. I was still coughing up smoke from yesterday's basement trash fire.

I sipped my espresso and thought about everything that happened yesterday. The more I thought about it the more questions I seemed to have about Clark and Lintz. I was curious to see how they were connected. Lintz obviously had access to the bank's money and Clark was clearly muscle. He was also a real estate appraiser so that had to figure into their scheme somehow. Marti and Cosgrove had been involved and they were now dead.

Had Lintz gotten greedy, preferring to split pot with one person instead of four ways? That made sense to me. It also meant that whatever role that Marti and Cosgrove had played, they weren't needed anymore. But Lintz and Clark still had business together or they would have turned on each other. Why take the chance that one or the other would rat if they got caught? Two murders and millions of dollars was a hell of a lot of incentive.

It's like the old saying about the minimum number of people who can keep a secret . . . one. In the end, they would turn on each other. I just had to figure out how to help them on the way. I'd rather have one adversary to deal with than two. Let them turn on each other, do the heavy lifting for me. The yellow legal was a mess of names, circles, arrows and doodles.

Maybe it was time to talk to Stanley Clark. I took a small blackjack out of my desk. It was eight inches long with a one-pound lead weight at the tip of a spring steel handle, all of it wrapped in leather, with a teardrop-shaped head and slim handle. At close range, it was a fight stopper, and in my battered condition, I wanted an edge if I was going to talk to Clark. Shooting him seemed impractical.

I dropped the blackjack in the inside pocket of my jean jacket, locked up the office and headed out. I had a knife, a blackjack and a gun. I was as prepared as I could be.

I got in the T-Bird and headed north on a drive that I'd made so many times lately I could do it in my sleep. I realized, singing along to The Rolling Stones and their choice of colors while painting doors, that I was happy. I was looking forward to meeting with Clark and having a frank exchange of views.

I followed the highway north to Portsmouth. It might be nice to check it out with Angela sometime when I wasn't working. I didn't think she'd appreciate my interrupting a romantic weekend to put pressure on a guy who I was sure was involved in not one but two murders. She might not think of that as romantic. Who could blame her?

By now, finding my way to Clark's office was a familiar route from the highway. I had to circle the block a few times but found a spot that was a few doors down from it. I got out and put quarters in the meter. I got the feeling that the meter maids in Portsmouth were every bit as heartless as the ones in town. I slipped the blackjack in the back pocket of my jeans with just the tip of the handle sticking out so that I could get to it in a hurry.

I walked up to Clark's office, took a breath, and pushed open the door. His secretary looked up from her desk. She smiled at me as she said, 'Hi, how can I help you?'

As smiles go it was pretty great, 1,000 watts. Her perfume was light and alluring and made its way to me, and I started to have unprofessional thoughts about her outfit.

'Hi, I was hoping to talk to Mr Clark about doing some work for me if he's available.'

'Sure, who can I say is asking?'

'Kees, Tim Kees.'

'OK, Mr Kees. Just give me a sec.' She got up and walked to a door that was behind her desk where I assumed Clark had his office. I watched her walk and my curiosity about her outfit and what might be under it grew even less professional. I snapped my mind back to the business at hand.

'Mr Kees, you can come this way,' she said from the doorway. I walked over and she stepped aside so I could walk in. I was pretty sure that she wasn't oblivious to my curiosity. It was impossible to believe that I was the first man to walk through that door with that level of curiosity. She'd probably had to deal with attention both wanted and unwanted since high school.

'Mr Kees, what can I do . . .' Clark started to ask, but then his face froze. I had read and heard a lot about people reacting like they'd seen a ghost, but this was the second time in my life that I had actually seen it firsthand. The last time had been at Fort Devens when a good friend of mine thought I'd been killed, but he'd been decent about it and sported me a couple of glasses of expensive scotch. I was certain that Clark wasn't that generous.

'Hello, Stan . . . surprised to see me?'

'Amanda, call the police.'

'Yeah, Amanda, call the police and we can talk about two murders, an attempted murder, arson and embezzlement. I am sure that they'd be interested. Come to think of it, I am sure the Feds would be interested, too,' I said with heavy sarcasm.

'Mr Clark?' Amanda was smarter than most men would ever give her credit for.

'Yeah, Mr Clark, what should we do?'

'Amanda, why don't you go to lunch early.' It clearly wasn't a question.

'Are you sure you'll be all right?'

'Yeah, it'll be fine.'

'OK.' She walked out, high heels clicking on the wide-beamed wooden floor.

'What do you want, Roark?'

'See, you should have said Kees or not used a name at all.'

'Huh?'

'You shouldn't have told a man you've never met that you know his name.' I might have said it menacingly. I had reason enough. I walked over to one of the chairs in front of his desk and sat down.

'I am not afraid of you.'

'Stan, something tells me you're too fucking stupid to know when you should and shouldn't be afraid.'

'Hey, asshole.'

'Stan, you tried to kill me yesterday, and today I walk through your front door. What does that tell you?'

'Uh, what are you talking about?'

'I've survived a lot, people who were really skilled trying to kill me, felons taking their shot, gangsters, spies and soldiers, and I'm still here, motherfucker. So, some fucking juicer trying to burn a building down around me isn't exactly impressive.'

'I didn't . . .'

'Stop. Just stop.'

My voice was cold, and I realized that I was angry. He must have heard it too. He reached down toward something on the floor, my guess was a gym bag. I started coughing, leaning forward into the fit. When I straightened up, he was grinning and holding up a very big gun.

'See this, asshole, this is a Tec-9. It holds thirty rounds of nine-millimeter. More than enough for an asshole like you.'

The Tec-9 was a marriage of plastic and steel with a perforated sheet metal barrel shroud. It was designed by a Swede and was supposed to replace a lot of other submachine guns. When that didn't work, the American gun market was the next stop. Criminals and gangbangers loved it because it was compact and held a lot of bullets. It was also easy to convert to fully automatic. The problem with a lot of bullets is that they are heavy.

'Not so tough now, are you, asshole?' Clark asked.

'That's a big gun, Stan.'

'Sure is. I can pump thirty rounds into you before you pull out your gun. What do you carry, a snubnose .38? Ha, garbage compared to this.'

'Oh, easy, Stan, we might have gotten off on the wrong foot.'

'Sure, sure we did. Not so tough now.'

'As you? No, Stan, I am definitely not tough like you are.'

He smiled and put the Tec-9 down on the desk, still holding on to it.

'That's right, asshole, you aren't as tough as me.'

I started to reply but started to cough, and I doubled over, leaning forward. My right hand snaked into my back pocket, and I wrapped it around the handle of the blackjack. I sat back, started coughing some more and leaned forward again. Then my hand shot out and brought the head of the blackjack down on his hand that was wrapped around the grip of the Tec-9.

He screamed in pain, then screamed again when I hit his hand a second time. It only took two and he jerked his hand away from the gun like it was electrified. I thought I saw a knuckle that looked wobbly.

'No, Stan. You're right, I am not as tough as you, I'm a whole hell of a lot tougher. Not to mention meaner.'

'Jesus, you broke my hand.'

'Your hand isn't broken. A couple of your knuckles are fucked up, but your hand is fine.'

'You broke my hand,' he repeated.

'You locked me in a building and torched it. Do you think we're even? More importantly, do you think that I think we're even?'

'I didn't do anything . . .' I smashed the blackjack into the desktop hard enough to make the phone jump.

'Don't fucking lie to me. I get really upset when people try to kill me and then lie about it.'

'Man, I didn't.' I smashed the desk again and he unconsciously leaned away from me.

'I've only hit your hand twice. Imagine what else I can do with this thing. All the places you can get hurt.'

My mind drifted back to the interrogation class we took before shipping out to Vietnam.

'Remember, young sergeants, the application of pain is nowhere near as effective as the credible threat of pain.'

The instructor in the Modern Interrogation Techniques class looked like he should have been selling insurance instead of teaching a class of newly minted Special Forces NCOs how interrogate America's Communist adversaries. His starched fatigues and spit shined jump boots seemed out of place given his otherwise professionally nondescript appearance.

'The problem with inflicting pain is that after enough of it, the subject will tell you anything, whether he likes boys or girls, likes to wear ladies' underwear or has a thing for his cousin.'

Somewhere someone in the class snickered. We were at Ft Bragg; enlightenment and the sexual revolution hadn't breached the barbwire of the fort yet.

'The problem with introducing pain to the subject is that they'll eventually tell you everything, anything to make you stop. They'll tell you what they think you want to hear whether or not it's true. You didn't want to beat lies out of them, you wanted to elicit intelligence from them, young sergeants. There will be times when you might not even be looking for answers, but you might be priming the pump, getting them in the right frame of mind to do something that fits your plan. Prime the pump, and while they're worried about question-and-answer time, you are setting something in motion.' His eyes were cold, but he smiled with genuine pleasure. You could tell he was a man who loved his craft. Those were the guys who scared me the most.

Looking at Clark now, wide-eyed, it was time to switch gears. I pushed the Tec-9 out of reach of his good hand. He wasn't going to be doing much with the injured one for a day or two. I leaned forward.

'Stanley, why'd you make me hurt you?'

'What? I didn't.'

'Stanley,' I said as though I was talking to a little boy, 'I didn't hit your hand randomly. Why did you make me do that?'

'I didn't, man, c'mon.'

'Stanley, you locked me in a basement and lit a house on fire on top of me.'

'I didn't.' I brought the blackjack down on the phone on his desk, smashing it into several large pieces.

'Jesus!'

'Stanley, I have every reason to hurt you.'

'No, no you don't, man.'

'Stanley, two people are dead. You tried to kill me, and what do you think the law of the jungle says about that? That I should kill you?'

'No, man, don't.'

'Maybe you want to tell me what's going on.'

'I can't,' he said anxiously. Beads of sweat started to course down his face.

'That's a shame. It really is.'

'Listen, man, you can beat me or kill me. I won't talk.' His right eye developed a sudden tic and it occurred to me that Stanley was scared. Very scared, but not of me. Something or someone else scared him a lot.

'Naw, no need for any of that.'

'Good. I won't tell anyone about this. Not the cops.'

'I know. You don't want them poking around in your business.'

'No, man.'

'Besides I don't need you.'

'Huh?'

'Sure, I'll go talk to your partner, the banker with soft hands. I'm positive that he's not as tough as you. How long do you think it will take before he's singing?'

I stood up and picked up the Tec-9. I pulled the magazine out and then racked the bolt back to make sure there was nothing in the chamber. I threw the oversized handgun into the corner of the office.

'Be seeing you, Stanley.' He didn't say anything. He probably was used to being the bully more than the bullied. I dropped the magazine of shiny 9mm bullets in his secretary's wastebasket on the way out of the office. Even if he moved fast to retrieve it, I was pretty confident that his hand was too banged up to facilitate a fast reload.

I hadn't learned anything other than Clark's taste in guns was like his taste in cars, overcompensation. At least he was going to be a little slower on the draw. I realized, walking to my car, that I was whistling part of a Dire Straits song about a Western fairy tale. You could take the boy out of Southie, but you couldn't take the Southie out of the boy. It wasn't combat or even a fight, but it was enough to satisfy that ancient instinct.

The sun was trying to fight its way through the dense clouds as I steered the T-Bird south to Amesbury. I had to go see a banker about a series of felonies. I was grinning as I pushed down on the accelerator, rocketing some of Ford's best down the highway. It felt good to be decisive, active for the first time in the investigation. Too much of it had been passive, sitting, watching and waiting for something to happen. Now it was my turn.

ELEVEN

I drove south down the highway with an eye in the rearview mirror. I was confident that Clark wasn't going to call the cops, but my confidence had gotten me in trouble more than once. I pulled off the highway and wound my way into Amesbury. I wanted to talk to Lintz.

I was angry. I hadn't liked being in that cellar, feeling like a trapped rat, scared. I didn't mind the fear. That was a natural response to danger. It was manageable. I couldn't stand the feeling of mounting panic as the flames and smoke had worked their way toward me. I had been in bad spots before, really bad spots, but I'd never been that close to panicking.

I hated the feeling, and that hatred had turned to anger. I couldn't hit or punch the feeling in the basement. I could only strike the men who put me in that position. I was certain that Clark was the one who locked me in and torched the place. But Clark just wasn't smart enough to be the brains of the operation . . . any operation for that matter. Lintz was the management type. The type to come up with an elaborate plan to embezzle millions, a plan to kill his fellow conspirators, a plan to kill one better than average-looking private detective.

Lintz and I were going to have to discuss what went down. The way I felt now, beating the truth out of him was OK by me, maybe even preferable. He didn't look like he was tough, certainly not as tough as Clark. I would have to take a different approach.

I pulled into the bank parking lot and found a spot in the back. I could watch the bank exits from there and would be well placed to follow Lintz if he went anywhere. I couldn't brace him in the bank. There would be too many people around. After everything that had gone down, I was sure the cops would be called. I was certain that wouldn't go well for me.

Also, I couldn't confront him at his house. His family would be there, and that would make him less likely to talk and more likely to fight. I could see Mrs Lintz calling the local cops pretty quick. I didn't want to force him to talk. I wanted to encourage him to talk to me. There's a difference.

I sat watching the door, and my stomach started to rumble. Sometimes I think that my cat and my stomach are soulmates. While I was contemplating all of the things that I could possibly have for lunch, the bank door opened and Lintz walked out. He walked across the parking lot to his Mercedes and got into it.

I started the T-Bird and eased out of my spot only when I saw him turn into the street. I was able to follow him at a distance with a few cars between us. Unlike the other day, I was actually trying to be subtle. He headed out of town toward the highway, which made me wonder if he was going to meet Clark. My suspicion that he was meeting someone looked more promising when ten minutes later, he pulled into the parking lot of a Friendly's restaurant.

I drove by and headed down the road a hundred yards to give him time to get out of his car and into the restaurant without seeing me. I turned into a strip mall and then doubled back to Friendly's. It was lunchtime, so the place was, not surprisingly, busy. I walked in and found a seat at the counter that gave me a decent view of Lintz's back.

Friendly's was the type of restaurant that had menus and condiments in little clusters along the counter. A waitress drifted up to me when she saw me sit down. I took the menu from the metal holder that was attached to a rack that held the standard diner condiments: ketchup, mustard, relish, salt and pepper.

'Get you something to drink?'

'Unsweetened iced tea?' I liked iced tea, but spending time around army bases in the South had convinced me that there was such a thing as too sweet.

'Sure.'

The door opened and Mrs Lintz walked in with her son, holding hands. He walked with a strange rolling gait, and now, seeing him closer than I ever had, he wasn't what I had expected. His eyes were almond shaped, and his face was round. His hair was on the long side but stylishly so. He was dressed neatly and there was something about him I couldn't place. He looked at me, blew a raspberry out and giggled. Mrs Lintz tugged on his hand and said loud enough to ensure that I heard, 'Mark, honey, that's not polite.'

I could hear him giggling as they walked over to Lintz. The boy, who I had initially thought was about eight or nine but was maybe older, lunged into the booth where Lintz was sitting. He gave his father a hug and then climbed up next to him. Then he grabbed Lintz by the head and planted a kiss on his cheek. Mrs Lintz slid into the seat opposite.

I looked at the menu. There was little chance that either the ice cream or burgers were as good as Brigham's. I decided that the turkey club looked safe enough. You have to get up pretty early in the morning to mess up a turkey club sandwich. Friendly's sweetened the proposition by offering it with coleslaw and French fries. The waitress arrived with the iced tea and departed with my order.

I spent the next several minutes watching the Lintz family order – coffee for the embezzler, some sort of soda for the wife and the boy had milk. Their son would occasionally blow kisses at the waitress who seemed amused, even if his parents weren't. I sipped on my iced tea and pretended to be interested in a discarded copy of the Globe. My sandwich came cut into triangular quarters on an oval plate with a pile of French fries and one of those paper cups of coleslaw.

Their waitress brought a hot fudge sundae over for the boy. He clapped his hands and licked his lips in an exaggerated manner, like something he'd seen once on a cartoon. It looked like Lintz was having a cheeseburger, and she opted for what looked like a sandwich of some type. It was a celebration of some sort or maybe a reward for good behavior.

I watched Lintz laugh with his son and wife. Watched them eat their lunches and watched Lintz wipe fudge or melted ice cream from his son's face. Watched him ruffle his son's hair, and it occurred to me that I was having a hard time reconciling him with two murders. I had known a lot of killers in my time and more than my share of murderers, and Lintz didn't seem to fit that bill.

He certainly didn't seem to act the way I'd expect a man who was involved in killings to act, a man who embezzled millions and had a private eye breathing down his neck. Unless I was losing my touch, and he didn't take me seriously. Maybe it was time to put aside the BS and just talk to the guy instead of trying to shake him up.

I finished my lunch and dropped a ten on the counter. It was a generous tip, but I was more concerned with getting out of the place before Lintz got up and saw me. I was sitting in the T-Bird listening to Skynyrd playing something that wasn't 'Free Bird' when they walked out. The boy was holding his father's hand, and Lintz looked like a happy man. They walked over to Mrs Lintz's car, and he helped the boy get in, put on his seatbelt, then bent down to kiss his forehead. He kissed his wife before she got in and drove off.

I got out of the T-Bird and walked over to Lintz's car while he was watching his wife and son pull out of the Friendly's parking lot. He turned and started back to his car, his face darkening when he saw me leaning against the door. I couldn't blame him. He walked over to me with his shoulders set.

'What do you want? More wild accusations?'

'Actually, I was hoping we could talk for a second.' I held my hands up in front of me in the universal sign to indicate my intentions were peaceful.

'About what?'

'I don't think you had anything to do with the murders.'

'Of course, I didn't!'

'No, but after I talked to you, I followed Clark to an abandoned building. I went to check it out and someone locked me inside.'

'So, you're accusing me of conspiracy to inconvenience now? You know, you're really not a very good detective.'

'That has occurred to me. No, someone went beyond inconveniencing me. They set the building on fire with me in it.'

'What? Who?'

'I think it was Clark. Up until an hour ago I thought that you two were involved in conspiracy and I was on my way here to ask you some pointed questions about it.'

'What changed?'

'I saw you with your family. Your son's retarded.'

He took a deep breath and let it out slowly. 'We don't like the word, Mr Roark, any more than a minority likes a racial slur. My son was born with Down syndrome. His development is different from yours or mine but that's what it is. It certainly doesn't deserve a negative connotation.'

'No, sorry. I didn't mean to offend. It's just that's the only term I know.'

'You and most of the world. Just don't use it again, especially in front of my wife. She'll take your eye out.'

'He seems like a very affectionate boy.'

'He is.'

'Watching you two together, I couldn't see you being involved in a murder, much less two.'

'No, the only way would be if someone hurt my family, then all bets are off.'

'Fair enough.'

'Why did you think I would be?'

'Brock hired me because someone is embezzling money from the bank. Your name was on the shortlist; so were Cosgrove and Karen Marti.'

I watched the blood drain out of his face, and I knew he had done it. Innocent men protest or get angry. Guilty guys offer over-exaggerated anger or fear.

'Maybe we should go inside, have a cup of coffee and you can tell me about it,' I suggested gently.

'Uh, yeah . . . sure.'

He reminded me of someone punched in the gut, wind knocked out of them and struggling to breathe again. I couldn't blame him. We walked back into Friendly's and found a booth in the smoking section that was away from the few late lunch customers. I took out my pack of Luckies, shaking one partway out and offered it to Lintz, who shook his head. I lit it and took a drag. When the waitress came by, I ordered us two coffees.

'You wanna tell me about it?' I asked him.

'Not really. Brock knows?'

'No, Brock suspects.'

'You haven't told him anything?'

'Up until now, I didn't know anything. Brock hired me to watch you three and see who was living above their means,' I said.

'Ha! That's a good one.'

'None of you seemed to be, and that's what I reported.'

'Then why are we talking?'

'Cosgrove was murdered but everyone assumes that was a robbery gone wrong. Then Karen Marti is murdered. One murder might be unrelated, but two people who work at the same bank and in town like this . . . this isn't exactly New York City or Chicago.'

'No, it isn't.'

The waitress brought our coffees and left. Lintz took a packet of sugar out of the holder on the table but didn't tear it open. He just sat, fiddling with it.

'Why don't you tell me about it. It might make you feel better to get it off your chest.'

'Catholic guilt and confession?' he said, smiling wanly.

'Exactly.'

'I met my wife, Stephanie, in college. Up in New Hampshire. I knew I wanted to marry her on our second date. You ever have that happen to you?'

'Sure.' I hadn't, but there was no point in telling him that I wasn't the marrying kind.

'She's from Amesbury, and I didn't have any desire to live in Maine where I was from. We moved down here after graduation, and I got a job at the bank. It was a good job and pays well. I got promoted and promoted again.'

'What happened?'

'After a couple of years trying to have child, seeing specialist after specialist, we had given up. We could still be happy. Then we found out that Stephanie was pregnant. We were overjoyed.'

'Sure, but lots of people have kids and they don't embezzle money from their employer.'

'True. I never wanted to. I am not a criminal.'

I didn't feel the need to point out that, actually, he was. 'How did it start?'

'Do you know much about Down syndrome?'

'Um, not much.'

'My son was born with an extra chromosome. That means his development, physically and mentally, will be different from his peers. He also has health issues as a result. Those two factors mean special schools, special doctors, surgeries and a whole other boatload of things. My wife gave up her career to take care of him. My job pays well, but somehow it's never enough.'

'So, you started dipping into the till?'

'I'm not proud of it.' He didn't say it defensively, which was a bit of a surprise. I had heard criminals defend their actions for years. 'Nope, not proud. Desperate. I love my son. I don't want him in some state hospital.' He shuddered.

'He could get the care he needs.'

'No, Mr Roark, they are worse than you think. There are horror stories about them. What my son needs is his father and mother, to live in a loving home. He needs to go to a school where he sees other kids and not inmates.'

'Come on, they aren't that bad.'

'Have you ever seen one?'

'No,' I had to admit.

'Given the choice of raising and caring for our son at home or potentially going to jail, I started to take money from the bank.'

'But two million dollars, it's that expensive?'

'Two million?'

'Yep.'

'Mr Roark, I've probably taken three thousand a year for the last four years.'

'What?'

'Yes, I've taken money to keep our heads above water. That's it. Pigs eat, but hogs get slaughtered. You want to get caught embezzling, steal a lot. I just wanted to help my family.'

'How the hell did Brock come up with two million?'

'Search me. You're the detective.'

'What about Stanley Clark?'

'He's a real estate appraiser.'

'Could he be involved in embezzling?'

'From the bank? No. He doesn't have access to accounts.'

'I noticed that he, Cosgrove and Karen Marti were all involved in some sort of scheme where he appraised property, Marti bought it with a loan from the bank, and Cosgrove approved the loans. Then it was resold and reappraised at a higher rate until the value of the property was three or four times higher than it started out.'

'Shit. Land flipping.'

'What?'

'It's called land flipping and it's not good.'

'You don't say.'

'No. How much do you know about banking?'

'I have a savings account and checking account.'

'Ugh, and Brock hired you to investigate embezzlement?'

'That was my reaction.'

'OK, what do you think of when I say the word inflation?'

'The nineteen-seventies, gas lines, Jimmy Carter.'

'Exactly. So, one of the ways that the Fed—'

'The Feds?'

'No, *the Fed*. The Federal Reserve Bank. Think America's savings bank.'

'OK.'

'What they did was ease off certain banking regulations to encourage mortgage lending. People buying homes is good for the economy.'

'OK, and . . .'

'Well, that was good for smaller Savings and Loans or Community Banks. Community Banks and S&Ls were limited to certain types of loans. The problem with restrictive rules is it limits profits. So they made it easier for us to loan money, which meant that more people were building homes or commercial real estate. Which in turn meant we could also be more profitable. All of which would help with inflation. I am grossly oversimplifying this, but you don't strike me as a guy with a strong grasp of economics or banking.'

'So, they're committing fraud of sorts, not embezzling?'

'Not exactly. See it's in the bank's best interest to lend money.'

'Sure, that's how banks make money, isn't it?'

'Well, sort of. The Fed also offers tax incentives and other, for lack of a better term, bonuses. For instance, if the bank has all of its credit extended in the form of loans, then they can get tax breaks based on their anticipated tax returns for three years in advance.'

'Like they get three years of tax returns.'

'In one year. It can be a lot. Not to mention the money made on interest on our loans.'

'So, there is a lot of money coming in and out of the bank.'

'Yes, both in terms of actual cash and in terms of credit. For instance, when someone sends their mortgage payment in, it's sent in the form of a check, not actual dollars. That frees up liquidity, money the bank can lend or pay off its own debts with. Get it?'

'OK, so how would someone embezzle two million plus dollars?'

'There are lots of ways. I would look to move the money around so much that when currency valuations fluctuate, I would shift a small amount, a penny or two, into another account and then move it to another and then just park an amount in a dummy account.'

'You make it sound easy.'

'It is and it isn't. It's easy if you have access to the bank and the accounts and know what you're doing. It isn't if you are missing any of that.'

'So, a guy like me should stick to holding up liquor stores.'

'Someone can only embezzle if they have access. No access to the money, no embezzlement.'

'How did you do it?'

'I collected up scraps.'

'Scraps?'

Lintz took his wallet out of his back pocket and from that took out a dollar bill. He put it down between us.

'What's this worth?'

'A dollar.'

'Sure, but is a dollar always worth a dollar?'

'Of course it is.'

'Wrong. Can you buy as much with a dollar as you could five years ago or ten or twenty?'

'No. Everything gets more expensive.'

'Right, through the magic of inflation and the cost of living and cost of resources going up or down.'

'OK, so how does that help you embezzle?'

'Much of the money that the bank deals with isn't cash. We don't keep a hundred million dollars on hand in case we have to cover our debts. We keep a tiny fraction of that on hand and the rest is tied up in banks, investments, etc. When someone sends their mortgage payment in, that check is just a credit, it's as good as monopoly money. It counts toward the bank's available credit.

'The value of the dollar is changing, or more accurately, the value of the bank's dollars changes and shifts based on interest rates, movements in the stock market, etc. I would carefully wait, and if there was fluctuation in an account that pushed it a little over the face value, I would move that fraction into a dummy account before the money was noticed. It wasn't that I was stealing the money, I was just moving a statistical anomaly into a holding area. I would move it around to other accounts and then withdraw some cash on a Friday.'

'Why a Friday?'

'Fridays are busy. People are cashing their paychecks; we have lots of cash on hand. More importantly, we'd be too busy for anyone to notice an extra transaction.'

'It's that simple?'

'No, I am still grossly oversimplifying it for you.'

'I would never have found anything like that.'

'No, that's the point. A private eye wouldn't be likely to. But you did find me out.'

'Only because of the murders. If it weren't for them, I would have given the case up.'

'Thanks, I guess. How come?'

'I have known a lot of killers and a handful of murderers, the murderers usually don't make good family men.'

'Because I love my family?'

'A man willing to murder two people wouldn't be the type to hang around and raise a child who's re . . . different,' I said, catching myself.

'I am sure there are murderers with families.'

'Sure there are, but in a case like this, they wouldn't be likely to stop to buy their kid a hot fudge sundae. Instead, they'd be scrambling to save their skins.'

'What are you thinking?'

'I think Clark has or had some scheme with the bank. Cosgrove and Marti were involved and outlived their usefulness. It wouldn't make sense to kill them if they are still making money.'

'How does that explain the missing millions?'

'One, it's you and you're lying to me.'

'It isn't and I'm not,' he said in an aggrieved tone.

'Or two, Clark has some leverage on someone else in the bank.'

'Like who? No one's left.'

'I am thinking it is Brock.'

'Brock?'

'Sure, he has access, but he doesn't strike me as the type to beat a woman to death. Also, he was in the bank when Cosgrove was murdered,' I said.

'Sure, he was.'

'What if Clark has something on him?'

'Are you thinking he's blackmailing Brock?'

'It's possible and would certainly explain a few things.' It was also possible I was seeing blackmail everywhere after wrapping up a blackmail case a few months ago.

'Jeez, I'm not sure what there would be to blackmail Brock about.'

'What do you mean?'

'I've known him for years, and he's just not that interesting.'

'Not the type to cheat on his wife?'

'He's not married. There was office speculation that he might be gay, but there was also speculation that he and Karen had something going on,' he said.

'Does he gamble?' It was funny how debts to the type of lenders who bring baseball bats to collect can erode one's judgment.

'Not that I know of. No, he is passionate about golf and banking. He's a stickler for the rules and regulations. He runs a tight ship.'

'No other hobbies?'

'He hunts, but around here, that's about as exotic as Wonder Bread.'

'Hunts?' Growing up in Southie, there were kids whose dads took them hunting. Not my dad. After the war, he had enough killing. If he was hunting anything, it was the next bottle.

'Sure, deer and duck hunting. Though I always thought he did it to rub elbows with the local business owners. You know, to help him get in, get their business.'

'That's a tough way to make money if you're not into it, freezing your ass off in a duck blind.'

'That's Brock. Everyone always said that he's married to the bank.'

'So, you don't think he's wrapped up in all of this?'

'Not willingly, no.'

'Unwillingly?'

'That's the only way I see him being involved.'

'Yeah, that makes sense.'

It did, given he was in the bank when Cosgrove bought it. Also, if he was involved with Karen Marti, killing her didn't make sense. It made more sense if someone like Clark was trying to send a message to Brock.

'Roark?'

'Yeah.'

'What about me?'

'What do you mean?'

'Are you going to tell Brock?'

'Shit. I don't know. Probably not.' I didn't either. I'd been hired to prove he was embezzling, and he'd confessed. On the flip side, he was stealing to support his family, keep his kid out of an institution. I could only guess what type of pressure that put on a man.

'Roark, I know I don't deserve it, but I'm begging you. Please don't turn me in.'

'Lintz, right now, I am worried about who murdered two people. Your thing . . . that's a distant concern, at best.'

'Oh, OK.' He offered a faint smile that spoke of hope. I had been around long enough to know that hope will kill you as sure as cancer.

'Here, take my card. If you think of anything or anything pops up, call me.' I wrote my home number on the back. 'That's my home number in case it's after hours.'

'Thank you.'

'No problem.' I put two singles under my saucer.

'What are you going to do now?'

'Try and figure this whole mess out.'

'What should I do?'

'Go back to work. Act normal. Do what you'd normally do.'

'What are you going to do?'

'I'm not sure.'

Which was my way of saying I would sit back and see if anything came from stirring up the hornet's nest. Someone, either Brock or Lintz, was lying to me. Just because he was a family man didn't mean Lintz wasn't involved. He wouldn't be the first criminal I'd met who admitted to a lesser crime to weasel his way out of trouble.

'You won't tell Brock?'

'There's no point.'

'That's good.'

'No, I mean he already knows.'

'What?'

'Sure, why else would he hire a private detective with no background in financial crimes, unless he already knew. What I want to know is why he hired me if he already knew you had taken the money.' And why would he tell me it was millions of dollars when Lintz admitted to taking several thousand?

'Why wouldn't he call the cops if he knew?' Lintz asked.

'My guess is that you're right, and he's being blackmailed by Clark. Clark has his hooks into your bank and how. Maybe he figured if I was poking around, looking at all of you, that it might spook Clark or at least buy Brock some time to figure things out.'

'Things like what?'

'Like how to keep his job. Or how to keep the FBI out of his bank. Those seem like pretty important things to a guy like Brock.'

'OK, that makes sense.'

'You should get back to the bank. I assume that people will notice if you are late getting back from lunch.'

'OK, yeah . . . Roark.'

'Yeah?'

'Thank you.'

'Don't thank me, you aren't out of the woods yet.'

TWELVE

I drove back to the office, listening to Creedence's cover of 'I Heard it Through the Grapevine.' I liked it a lot. It lacked the smoothness of Marvin Gaye but there was something a little raw about it. I circled the block once out of habit to make sure that there was no one obviously waiting to try and kill me. I parked the T-Bird and went into the office. I needed a pipe and maybe an espresso and some time to think.

Inside, I checked the machine. There was a message from Carney on the machine. 'Hey, if you like that T-Bird, I'll give you a good price and take the Maverick off your hands on top of it. Give me a call.'

Well, hell, things were looking up. I called him back and we talked about money until we agreed on a price that was a lot less than the T-Bird was worth but still at the high end of what I had in the bank. I liked the Maverick but not as much as I liked the nearly new T-Bird.

I picked up my pipe and scraped the ash and unburnt tobacco from the bowl into the trash. I ran a pipe cleaner down the stem. Once I was satisfied it was clean, I fit the stem and bowl together and began to pack it with a mellow blend of Virginia and Latakia from Peretti's. It lit on the second match and was drawing nicely in no time, filling the office with pleasant-smelling smoke.

I opened the office window but decided against an espresso. I had plenty of coffee and iced tea and wasn't sure I needed any more caffeine. I hoped to get some sleep tonight. I pulled the legal pad with my case notes over and began to write down what I had learned today.

Lintz was an embezzler, but, by his own admission, a pretty cheap one. He was just a guy trying to take care of his family. Brock was the only other person left with access to the money, but he didn't strike me or Lintz as the type to embezzle millions, much less orchestrate two murders. Clark was brutish enough and certainly his waving a Tec-9 around his office spoke to his capacity for violence. It's just that he didn't have access or, frankly, the brains to pull it off. At best, he was a thug involved in a campaign to artificially inflate real estate prices.

There wasn't anyone left at the bank I could think of that could be behind it. Murder was a business technique for the Mob. If they caught wind of the real estate scam that Clark, Cosgrove and Marti were involved with, that might be reason enough. Maybe that's why Brock had hired me? He suspected Lintz but that wasn't what he was worried about. He was worried that the bank's 'actual' owners had caught wind of something and maybe he hired me to sniff it out before he got hurt. That would explain his insistence it was Lintz, his annoyance when I quit. Hell, it would even explain why he hired me back. It would explain a lot of things.

I added to my case notes. The felt tip pen made a half scratching, half squeaking noise as it moved across the page. If it was the Mob, then they wouldn't care that Lintz was stealing from them for the sake of his family. He was as good as dead. The minute he took a penny of their money, he had sealed his fate, as certainly as Karen Marti and Frank Cosgrove had. I couldn't agree with how he chose to support his family, but I could respect his motives.

I sat back in my chair. My pipe had long grown cold, and evening was nibbling around the edges of the Boston skyline. I was stiff from sitting, and the bruises from my battering my way out of the cellar were making themselves known. It was time to go home. The office phone rang and when I picked up the handset, I was rewarded by hearing Angela's voice.

'Hey, you're in the office. I just left a message on your machine at home.'

'Yeah, I was just finishing up some case notes.'

'Did you solve it yet?'

'Yes and no.'

'That doesn't sound very definitive.'

'No, I guess not. What's up?'

'I was hoping we could get a quick drink?'

'Sure. My place or yours, or did you have something else in mind?'

'There's a place not far from your office.' She named a place a couple of blocks away and not too far from the courthouse.

'Sure, I know it.'

'Fifteen minutes?'

'Great, see you then.' The night was looking up!

I locked up the office and decided to walk to the bar she had mentioned. It wasn't far and it would take me longer to find parking than it would to walk. The weather was nice, and if you've never seen Boston in the spring then you're missing out.

The bar was small and tucked into an odd corner of a larger granite office building that had been built when Otis's elevators were high tech. It was three steps down into a room filled with smoke. The long, oak bar was directly in front with the standard mirror behind it reflecting liquor bottles and taps. There were half a dozen small tables to my right, each surrounded by either two or four wooden chairs. The far wall to my right held two banquettes finished in black leather, and to my left was the exterior wall with a bunch of bookshelves.

It was late enough that the crowd of after work drinkers had thinned out, but it wasn't quite time for the pre-dinner out crowd to roll in, which suited me fine. I like a bar that's sparsely populated. Actually, I just like a bar, populated or not. I have spent a significant portion of my adult life in them.

Angela was sitting in one of the banquettes and smiled at me when I walked in, which I didn't mind. I walked the short distance to her. The place was tiny, bordering on a fire code violation. She was still dressed in work clothes, which in this case were navy blue slacks, modest heels and a cream-colored blouse. There was a strand of pearls around her neck and denim jacket on the seat next to her.

'Hi,' I said, bending over to give her a kiss. 'Can I get you anything from the bar?' It was one of those places that only had bar service.

'Sure, vodka rocks.'

'Stoli?'

'Yes, please.'

'Be right back.'

It didn't take the bartender long to pour her drink, uncap my Lowenbrau or take my money. I brought our drinks back to our table and sat down at the short edge of the table, my back to the wall, perpendicular to Angela.

'Cheers,' I said, raising the green bottle of beer. She replied without much enthusiasm, and we touched glasses. She took a big sip of her drink and put the glass down.

'How was work? Seems like you had a tough day,' I asked.

'It was OK. Andy, we have to talk.'

If experience had taught me anything it was that nothing good has ever come from your significant other starting a conversation by saying, 'We have to talk.'

'About what?' I said, certain that I knew.

'Andy, I can't . . . I can't go on like this with you.'

'Like what?' I asked with forced politeness. I had been on the receiving end of this conversation more often than I had given it.

'Like this.'

'What, because I was almost killed yesterday? That's part of the job. You certainly knew that when we first got together.' Someone had tried to kill me when I was working for the judge she clerked for.

'It's not just that. Though for the record, I don't like it.'

'Well, as long as it's not just that.'

'I owe . . . I feel like I owe you. That I owe you so much that it feels claustrophobic.'

'Huh? Where is this coming from?'

'I owe you my very freedom. That's a tough sort of obligation for a girl to take into a relationship. It makes me feel like I'm paying a debt, like we're a transaction.'

She had shot a man, a man who deserved it, and I had elected to not tell the police about it.

'I've never asked for anything based on that or used that against you.' I tried to make my tone a reasonable one.

'No, you haven't. That doesn't mean that I don't feel a sense of obligation.'

'Are you saying that I've taken advantage of the situation?'

'No, of course not. It's not about you or what you do.'

'It's not about me but you're breaking up with me?'

'I'm not breaking up with you. I just need some time apart from you. I need to figure this, us, all out.' She waved her hand in front of her in an all-encompassing gesture.

'I suppose there's a distinction in there somewhere.'

'If I am with you out of a sense of obligation, that poisons everything. It makes me feel like I'm with you to pay a debt, not because I'm choosing to be with you. It makes me feel like I'm a whore. I can't explain it more plainly than that.' She finished her drink in one belt and got up. She walked away quickly and didn't look back.

I watched her walk away and was not exactly sure of what I had or hadn't done wrong. The only thing that I was certain of was that my luck with women was still lousy. I know, I should have gone after her, told her it was true love or at least it could be. The guy she had killed deserved it, but that wasn't the only reason I had reinterpreted events for the cops. For the first time in a long time, I had met someone, and it had felt like there was a possibility of it turning into something.

The bartender was good enough to pour a shot of bourbon and then another in exchange for my cash. He was a professional, he didn't ask any questions or offer any advice. He'd seen a guy get dumped by his girl more than a few times. It wasn't a new show for him. I appreciated his quiet professionalism almost as much as I appreciated the bourbon. I left him a five-dollar tip and went home to get drunk by myself. It was a lot gentler on the bank balance.

I woke up at six with a headache. The bright sun of mid-May was streaming through the window, and Sir Leominster was walking on my chest and meowing. This morning he decided I was an early riser. He was hungry and was not sympathetic to my romantic misadventures. I got up and opened a can of his foul-smelling food. Then and only then did he leave me alone.

I had come home and had a few drinks, but alone in the apartment, I just didn't have it in me to get polluted. I went to the faucet and poured myself a big glass of Boston's finest tap water.

It probably wasn't the healthiest, but I was more concerned with dehydration than fluoride or lead.

I opted for a run instead of sitting around feeling sorry for myself. When I got outside, regardless of what happened last night, I had to admit it was a beautiful morning. It was cool but not cold, sunny and everything was in bloom. I ran down Commonwealth Avenue, listening to the birds chirping, which were audible only because it was early and traffic was light.

Running over the Smoot-annotated bridge, I thought about the case. It was possible that Lintz was playing me, and it was also possible that Brock was more involved in this than I thought. I had kicked at some hornets' nests enough to get a couple of reactions but nothing that broke the case wide open. I had been knocked out and almost burned to death but nothing that put me any closer to solving things.

By the time I was running in Cambridge, heading back toward my apartment on the wrong side of the Charles River, I had a thought. Maybe it was time to do what recon men do best . . . surveil the target. I needed to go back to Amesbury and watch the bank. Watch Lintz, see what he was up to. Or should I watch Clark? He was up to his neck in this whole thing.

I couldn't be in two places at once. The problem was that Clark was probably jumpy, and he might be on the lookout for a certain handsome, big city private eye. Plus, I wasn't sure about the bank. I needed help, and there was only one person who I trusted to ask. Chris.

I trusted Chris with my life. He was a recon man and was already trained in surveillance. I knew he was tough enough to deal with any bullshit that Clark might try and pull. Also, I wouldn't have to bring him up to speed on the case. Hopefully Carney could spare him for a couple of days.

By the time I walked up the steps of my building, I was feeling generally better. The bruised muscles had loosened up. When I stopped, I had a coughing fit and coughed up some black crud that I assume had to do with the smoke from the basement trash fire. I had sweated out much of what I had to drink last night. More importantly, while I wasn't thrilled about Angela breaking up with me, the weather had been sufficiently beautiful to take my mind off it. Also, I had, for what felt like the first time in this case, a plan.

Upstairs, while the coffee was bubbling away in the stove top machine, I called Chris. He answered sleepily, after a few seconds.

'Hey man, I was hoping you could help me out for a couple of days,' I said after he had woken up enough to understand what I was asking him.

'Doing what?'

'I was hoping you could tail Clark for me. He knows me and obviously knows what I am driving. A different face and car, though . . .'

'Why don't we just go down there and beat the shit out of him until he talks?'

'Because we're not a bike gang. Also, I will be following Lintz.'

'I could just do it. Seems a lot easier than just watching him all day.'

'It probably would be, but this isn't that type of job.'

'OK, but he's the one who tried to kill you in the burning building, right?'

'Yeah, most likely.'

'So why not off him and be done with it? He's earned it.'

'Because I don't operate like that.'

'Anymore,' he said, with emphasis.

'Right, all that law of the jungle shit went out the window when I came back to the world. I have to work mostly within the law.'

'OK, I get it. I'm just sayin'.' His Southern drawl became a little more pronounced.

'Get a pen. I'll give you his details.'

'Andy, I'm bringing a gun.'

'I would expect nothing less.'

'OK, send it.'

I told him what Clark was driving, where his office was and his home address. I told him to stop at a bank and get two rolls of quarters then gave him the number of a pay phone near the Merrimack Community Bank. We would touch base every hour, on the hour. It sounded hokey saying it. I had been a solo act my entire time in business and wasn't used to working with a partner.

After I hung up the phone, I ate my usual, uninspiring breakfast of wheat toast and yogurt. At least the coffee was strong and flavorful. Then I showered and dressed, my mind alternating between the case and my meeting with Angela last night. I made a thermos of coffee which went into a nylon backpack, along with a paper bag with a couple of apples, a plastic-wrapped block of cheddar cheese and a package of those flat crisp breads from Scandinavia.

I dressed in old blue jeans, running sneakers and a Lowenbrau t-shirt that they were giving away as a part of a promotion one night in a bar I was in. I tucked the shirt in and threaded a leather pancake holster on my belt. Things had been getting weird lately, with arson and Tec-9s being introduced. When things get weird like that, my response is to get a bigger gun. The 9mm Browning Hi-Power was in the safe where I left it. I slapped a thirteen-round magazine into the grip and chambered a round. I flicked the safety up and on. I popped the magazine out and topped it off with a single round before slipping the full mag back into the pistol. Then I holstered it and snapped the retaining strap over the gun.

I had a nifty magazine pouch that held two spare magazines. I snapped the matching leather pouch on my belt and put two thirteen round magazines in the pouch. I put a faded plaid shirt over it all. It wasn't as heavy as my leather duty belt when I was a cop, but it was a lot heavier than a .38 snubnose and five spare rounds. That was the price of prudence. I pulled on a lightweight, green nylon L.L. Beans anorak over my t-shirt. It hid the gun, and the kangaroo pouch in front was very convenient for things like car keys and cigarettes.

I was about to close the safe when my eye fell on the 12 gauge Ithaca Model 37 shotgun. It was an old police surplus gun that held four in the tube and one in the chamber. It was a lightweight model, and if you held the trigger down and kept pumping it, it would fire. It wasn't a Tec-9 bullet sprayer, but it might level the playing field if I had to go up against one.

I took the Ithaca out and slid it into a soft, zipppered canvas case that I had picked up somewhere. I threw in a box of buck-shot and, as an afterthought, a box of one ounce shotgun slugs. I wasn't expecting to need them, but I also hadn't expected the flaming basement treatment, either. It would most likely spend the day in the trunk of my T-Bird, but it was a comfort to know they were there just in case.

I put out some extra food and water for the cat. I locked the apartment door behind me and headed downstairs. One of my neighbors was just leaving his apartment at the same time. He saw the canvas rifle case and his lip curled.

'Is that a gun?'

'Fishing rods,' I answered flippantly.

'Fishing rods?' he said dubiously.

'Sure.'

'It looks like a rifle case.'

'I get that a lot.'

'I don't believe you.'

'That I don't get that a lot? Nice talking to you. Have a good one,' I said cheerfully.

I left him standing there with his mouth open. Outside the sky was still blue but there were clouds nibbling around the edges of an otherwise nice day. It was one of those cool May mornings that could go either way – chilly and raw or a near approximation of summer.

I opened the trunk and put the shotgun in, then got in the car and started the now familiar drive north. I wasn't looking forward to more surveillance, but I had stirred up so much shit I had to think that something was going to happen in the next day or two. It might be a hunch, but I had learned to trust my instincts.

I drove north out of the city, the same route that I had taken many times now. I was whistling to J.J. Jackson's 'But It's Alright' playing on the radio. The sky was clear as I crossed the bridge and watched the city skyline grow smaller in my rearview mirror.

The now familiar to the point of being boring drive up to Amesbury passed quickly. I pulled into the parking lot of the Merrimack Community Bank and parked near the pay phone. Lintz's almost ten-year-old Mercedes was parked in its spot.

Brock's car was also parked in its assigned spot. The only person we were missing was Clark.

When the change of the hour was close, I got out of the T-Bird and walked over to the pay phone. It rang on the hour, and I picked it up.

'Hello.'

'Red, it's me. Your guy is in his office chatting up his secretary.'

'OK. Nothing much on this end. Give me the number of the pay phone in case I have to call you.' He did and we agreed we'd only call if something came up. I went back to the T-Bird and settled in. The Allman Brothers' 'One Way Out' was on the radio.

The morning crawled by, and I was reminded again how tedious surveillance was. I tried to smoke sparingly and got out of my car when I did. I wasn't too concerned about Lintz seeing me. He knew I was on the case and my watching the bank wouldn't shock him. By the time the hands on my Seiko dive watch showed me it was noon, I had finished one apple and half of the thermos of coffee. I was contemplating the second apple with some cheese and crisp bread when Brock walked out of the bank.

He walked over to his big American-made car and got in. He fired up the domestic land yacht and, easing into traffic, left the bank. In all the weeks off and on that I had been doing surveillance here, I had never seen him leave before three-thirty in the afternoon. I thought about tailing him, but I decided to stick with Lintz. He was, after all, an embezzler by his own admission, and he might have spun all that stuff about Brock being blackmailed to throw me off the trail. He had a couple million reasons.

At one, I made a quick run to the nearby deli to pick up a couple of bottles of blueberry flavor New York seltzer and to use their men's room. Back in the T-Bird, I used my Buck knife to open the block of cheese and cut off several slices, then I carefully cut the apple into thin wedges. I put pieces of cheese and apples on one of the crisp breads.

It wasn't a Reuben, but it was still pretty good. I repeated the process, washing it all down with one of the blueberry seltzers.

I ended up eating four of them when all was said and done. There wasn't much crisp bread. By the time I was brushing crumbs off my shirtfront, it was only an hour from the bank's closing time.

Brock still hadn't come back. Either it was a late lunch, or he had split early for the day. I couldn't blame him; the weather was beautiful. It was a perfect day to play hooky or go fishing or just not be in a stuffy bank. I drank more coffee and stopped in the deli one last time for more seltzer. The bathrooms were only for customers. I was back in my spot by three fifteen, which was good, because if I missed Lintz because I was in the restroom, I might have to surrender my license.

A few minutes later, Clark came walking up to the bank from up the street. He was wearing jeans and an untucked button-down shirt. He had a gym bag in his left hand, and the way he nervously tapped his waistband with his right hand, I was pretty sure he had a gun tucked in it. People carrying guns in their waistbands have to worry about them shifting or working their way out. They tend to tap them nervously. That's why holsters were invented.

I hunched down in my seat so that Clark wouldn't see me if he looked over. He wasn't that interested in much except for Lintz's car. Clark went over to it and leaned against it. He put his gym bag on the hood, and I wondered what was in it. A Tec-9? He certainly wouldn't stuff that in his waistband and walk around with it.

A little after three thirty, the bank employees started to trickle out and make their way home. I recognized a few of tellers, but there were a couple of newer, younger faces mixed in with them. Ten minutes after they left, Lintz walked out and made his way to his car. He stopped in front of Clark, they had a short discussion and then Lintz unlocked the car. They got in, Lintz driving and Clark riding shotgun. They looked pretty chummy from my vantage point thirty yards across the parking lot.

I started the engine and was about to put the T-Bird in gear when Chris tapped on my passenger side window. I hit the button unlocking the door and he slid into the seat. He winced as the Magnum revolver he was wearing in a shoulder rig under his arm collided with the bucket seat and dug into his armpit.

'I was wondering where you were.'

'I trailed him down here but I didn't want to draw attention to you, so I had to work my way around a couple of buildings to the back of the parking lot.'

'No worries. Anything interesting going on with him?'

'Other than a Tec-9 and bunch of stick magazines in the gym bag?'

'Yeah, other than that.'

'He's got a piece in his waistband, and I couldn't see what else is in the bag.'

'That's a lot of artillery.'

'Yep, somebody's gonna be in some deep kimchi if he opens up.'

I smiled; I hadn't heard the term 'deep kimchi' since I left Vietnam. I pulled out of the lot and picked up Lintz's car as they made their way out of town.

'Where do you think they're going?' Chris asked.

'Not sure. It seems like a meet of some sort. Why else would Clark have a piece in his waistband and a Tec-9 in the bag?'

'He's expecting trouble.'

'Sure, just like we are. You've got that hand cannon in your armpit, I've got a Hi-Power and a twelve gauge in the trunk.'

'No rifle?'

'I don't have one right now and didn't think to call Carney to see if he had anything laying around.'

'Well, at least you're carrying something better than that snub-nose .38.'

'Listen, that's an upgrade, I used to carry a Colt .32 automatic.'

'Wow, were you hoping whoever you shot would die of infection?'

'It was flat and carried well.' I didn't bother to point out that I had killed a man with it four years ago.

I followed them out of town, heading generally north and occasionally turning to the west.

'I think I have an idea where they might be going.'

'Where?'

'I think we're going to an abandoned quarry.'

'The one you followed Clark to.'

'That's the one.'

'That's an out of the way place for a meeting.'

'Might be a good place to divvy up two million dollars.'

'Might be a good place for someone to get greedy.'

'And double-cross their partner.' I said what we were both thinking.

'Sure, criminals aren't known for their loyalty.'

'Not with that much money on the line.'

'It is a lot of money . . . there is nothing to say that we couldn't . . .'

'There isn't, but I can't.'

'Cause of the FBI lady?'

'No, not that she isn't important.'

'Then what? Angela? You don't owe anyone anything. You did three tours in-country and for what?'

'No, she broke up with me last night.'

'Shit. I'm sorry, you seemed like you liked her.'

I shrugged noncommittally. I didn't really want to talk about how much I had liked her or thought that maybe we might have the makings of something that had potential.

'If it isn't her, then what is it?'

'For the same reason that I can't take any of the money if it's up there. For me. A man has to stand for something, and money isn't the thing I want to stand for. Don't get me wrong, I like the stuff and never seem to have enough of it, but every morning I have to look at myself in the mirror. Money isn't a good of reason to make that any harder to do.'

'OK, John Wayne, OK. I get you.'

'Thanks.'

'Red?'

'Yeah, Chris.'

'That loot would buy you a pretty nice fucking mirror.'

We both laughed and, like the moments after a thunderstorm had passed, everything was right again.

We crossed into New Hampshire, following Clark and Lintz at a distance. I explained the layout of the quarry to Chris, the parking area and the high ground around it, and the shelf of steps. Terrain was important to guys like us who had lived and died by its idiosyncrasies in the war.

'So, the parking area is basically the low ground.'

'Pretty much.'

'And if there's gunplay there, that doesn't leave a lot of options to run to or take cover.'

'Nope, not many.'

'The water's not an option.'

'Not on a month of Sundays. It's deep and cold and water isn't cover.'

'And if there's anyone up in the high ground, anyone in over-watch with a long gun, you're sincerely fucked.'

'Well, when you put it like that, it doesn't sound good.'

'Is there a part of this that's good?'

'Sure, these guys aren't exactly a crack NVA unit.'

'Fair enough.'

'Also, I don't think there's anyone in overwatch if they're going to divvy up the money. My guess is that the double-cross will happen at the cars if there is one.'

'If?' Chris said dubiously.

'Well, we're assuming that there'll be one.'

'Why the hell else would they be going to an abandoned quarry?'

'Yeah . . .'

'It's a ready-made body dump. Out of the way location, deep cold water that no one is going to go scuba diving in.'

'You have a point there.'

'Why else would Clark have a bullet hose like a Tec-9 and pistol in his waistband unless he was expecting trouble, or he was gonna be trouble?'

'Your logic, sir, is unassailable.'

'Usually is.' Then after a minute, 'How do you want to play it?'

'I'll drive up and park at the access road I parked at the first time. You work your way around and make sure there's no one waiting in the woods to ambush us.'

'And you?'

'I'll walk down to the lower area where Clark parked last time.'

'And what then?'

'I'll brace them and see what they have to say.'

'OK, simple enough.'

'You take the shotgun.'

'Nah, I'm better off with the long-barreled Magnum. You take the shotgun.'

'OK.'

'We should have brought rifles or at least carbines for this sort of thing.'

'Woulda, shoulda,' I said dismissively, but he was right. I drove up the hill and passed the access road that led to the parking area. Further up the hillside, I eased on to the logging trail and went a few yards up it, parking where I had a couple of days before. We got out and I popped the trunk.

'I'll leave the keys on the back tire, driver's side, in case something doesn't work out.'

'Like you get shot and I don't?'

'Exactly.' It was nice working with professionals. No sentimentality.

'OK.' Chris checked the cylinder of the Magnum, patted his pockets where he had a couple of speedloaders. He put the Magnum back in its shoulder holster and took the Spanish 9mm automatic out of a holster in his waistband.

'Two guns?'

'Sure, not as good as a rifle but better than nothing.'

'Can't argue with that logic.'

'Probably won't need 'em. These guys are just office types.'

'Sure, probably won't.'

'See ya in a few.' Then he was gone, quietly moving up the logging trail and quickly absorbed by the forest.

THIRTEEN

I took the Ithaca out of the trunk and opened the box of slugs. They were one ounce of solid lead that were rifled for accuracy. I could hit a man-sized target at a hundred yards with them. At close range, they'd be devastating. I thumbed one into the tube, and, holding the shotgun in the trunk to muffle the noise, I racked the round into the chamber. I thumbed four more into the tube. I took my lighter and cigarettes out of the kangaroo pouch in my anorak and dropped them in the trunk. I took a handful of shotgun shells and put them in the pouch.

I gently pushed the trunk closed and put my keys on the tire. Then I started down the road with the shotgun held down at my side. I didn't want to startle anyone driving by who might not be an embezzling murderer. The air was humid, hinting at the summer to come, and the mayflies were everywhere. Five minutes later, I was sweating a little as I walked up the access road toward the parking area. The metal gate was open, and I knew better than to think it was an invitation.

The first thing I noticed as I quietly eased up the road was Lintz's Mercedes. The engine was still ticking. The late afternoon sun danced off the chrome and glass of the car. I heard voices but couldn't make out what they were saying, and a mosquito buzzed in my ear. I ignored it, even when I felt it land on my ear and help itself to my whiskey-thinned blood.

I also realized that I had gone from casually carrying the shotgun in one hand to its now being at the low ready, stock pressed into my shoulder. Keeping my finger out of the trigger, I pushed the safety off and laid my index finger against the trigger guard. I moved slowly up the road, the muzzle of the shotgun dipped just enough that I could look over the top of the brass bead sight.

I went around the Mercedes and saw that Clark had his back to me. He was at the edge of the quarry. He was bent over and looked to be binding Lintz's hands and feet. The bindings around Lintz's ankles were tied to a metal rim from a car's wheel. It was old and rusty and would make one hell of a weight for pulling a body to the bottom of the quarry. The Tec-9 was slung over his shoulder and resting against his back. I inched closer and when I was five yards away, I said softly:

'Hey. Clark. Hey, Clark,' I said a little louder. 'I'm pointing a twelve-gauge loaded with slugs at you. Move and you're a fucking dead man.'

'Roark . . . that you?'

'Who else.'

'How do I know you've got a gun on me?'

'I can shoot you if that will help you figure it out.'

'Naw, but I'm betting I can dump this guy in the quarry before you get a shot off.'

'You probably can, but then I'm definitely gonna shoot you and you'll join him with most of your chest blown the fuck out.'

'I might risk it.'

'You might, but you'll get just as dead.'

'OK, so what do you want to do?'

'I want you to straighten up slowly and carefully. Put your hands up. High. If you go for the gun, I'll drop you where you stand. Got it?'

'Yeah, tough guy, I've got it.' Something told me that I wasn't his favorite person. He straightened up and stuck his hands up but they were level with his head. He was dumber than I gave him credit for if he thought he could get to his gun first. He was facing me, eyes blazing with anger. The next few minutes were going to be interesting.

'Clark, what are you doing with Lintz? A double-cross?'

'A double-cross, him?'

'Why else would you be about to roll your partner into quarry?'

'He's not my partner.'

'You aren't smart enough or connected enough to embezzle two million from the bank on your own.'

'Fuck you. I was making plenty from that bank.'

'Good. With two fingers take the strap of the Tec-9 and lower it carefully to the ground.' It was an open bolt gun and if he dropped it, the bolt could slam forward firing the thing. He seemed like the type to convert it to shoot full auto. I didn't feel like getting shot by accident.

'What makes you think I have two million dollars?'

'Brock hired me to find out who embezzled that much from the bank. He said it was Lintz, and Lintz said he only took a few thousand. But you were doing business with Cosgrove and Karen Marti.'

'Sure, we were doing business,' he still hadn't unslung the Tec-9, 'good business. I would appraise a piece of garbage real estate, Marti would get a mortgage from the bank that Cosgrove approved, and then Marti would put it back on the market. I'd reappraise it at a higher price, then Cosgrove would buy it, I'd reappraise it and he'd sell it back to Marti. Each time, the bank would underwrite the mortgage. Eventually the property would sell, but by then we'd doubled or tripled the price, with the bank paying for it. It was a great scheme, and everyone made money.'

'Why'd you kill Marti and Cosgrove?'

'He got spooked and wanted out.'

'What spooked him?'

'He thought people were onto us. That someone was following him.'

'So, you set up the bank robbery?'

'Sure, I knew a guy who just got out of the brig at the Naval Shipyard. He needed money and wasn't picky about earning it. I suggested the bank job and he agreed.'

'Who shot Cosgrove?'

'Me. I figured no one would think it was anything other than a robbery gone wrong.'

'And Karen Marti?'

'What about her?'

'Why'd you kill her?'

'I didn't.' He was lying. There was something in his eyes when he denied it.

'I saw you two arguing one night at that roadhouse.'

'Sure, I wanted to go back to her place, but she had a boyfriend and wouldn't. I figured, what the hell, I was putting good money

in her pocketbook. She could show a little gratitude, you know?'
His answer sounded hollow.

'Sounds like a good reason to go to her place and take it out
on her.'

'Naw, not my speed. I don't mind a little rough stuff in the
sack, but killing women . . . I draw the line, you know.' He piled
it on.

'Who was her boyfriend?'

'I dunno.'

Behind him, off to one side birds were flushed from cover by
some animal. The broke cover, making a racket, in a rush of
beating wings and chirping. My eyes started to track them auto-
matically, and that's when he made his play. He reached back
with his right hand, pivoting his hips a little and clawed at the
pistol grip of the Tec-9. He brought it around, grabbed the magazine in his left hand and started firing from the hip like he was
in some World War II training film.

The Tec-9 had been converted to full auto. Dirt and rocks in
front of me started to spit and break up. He was pulling his
rounds to my left and I stepped to the right, lining the brass bead
up on his chest. Taking the slack out of the trigger and, after
what felt like an eternity, the Ithaca bucked hard into my shoulder.
What seemed like forever after that, the shotgun boomed loudly.

In the movies, Clark would have been blown ten feet back in
a spray of blood. Instead, he spun in a clumsy pirouette, letting
go of the Tec-9, and he dropped like a box of rocks. The one-
ounce lead slug had been designed to drop bears and made short
work of Clark, who was now lying in a crumpled heap on the
ground.

I went over to make sure he wasn't going to be a threat; he
still had the pistol in his waist. There was no need to worry. The
slug had done its work with remarkable efficiency. It had entered
a little below his heart and punched through his chest cavity,
making a nasty exit wound in his back. Blood was pooling on
the grass, leaking out of the massive exit wound in his back. His
chest wasn't rising or falling, no last automatic reflexes of life.
The rifled slug had worked as efficiently as a light switch.

I walked over to Lintz, took out my Buck knife and cut his

bindings. He stood up, rubbing his wrists where he'd been tied. He looked at me for a minute and said, 'You killed him.'

'Yes. It was him or us.'

'Good. He told me that if I didn't go with him he'd kill my wife and son,' Lintz said.

'That's why you got in the car with him?'

'You were watching?'

'Good thing for you I was.'

'Yeah, he said if I did anything my family was as good as dead. He showed me the gun in his waist.'

'What happened then?'

'We drove here. He had me turn off the car and drop the keys out the window. We got out and then he punched me in the face. I blacked out and he was tying me up. Then he got that submachine gun and loaded it. He was dragging me over to the quarry when you got here.'

'Did he say anything?'

'Only that I was going to go for a swim. The sick bastard said it like he enjoyed it.'

'Lintz, I know who really owns the bank?'

'Really owns . . .'

'Listen, man, too much weird shit has been going on. Too many dead people and someone has gone to a lot of trouble with these deaths.'

'Some guys from Boston own it.'

'Some guys?'

'Mob guys.'

'Oh, those type of guys?'

'Sure, they own a lot of smaller banks.'

'So, if a lot of money, two million dollars went missing, they'd want to know who took it?'

'Mr Roark, even the small amount that I took . . . if they knew about that, I'd be a dead man. You don't steal from these people. They don't care what your excuse is.'

'OK, I get it. Let's get out of here.'

'What about him?'

I was about to answer when the birds flushed again on the other side of the quarry. There was a flash of sunlight on glass, and I heard the crack of a rifle round and then the boom of the round going off. I dove rolling to my left ending up in some brush. I looked over and saw that Lintz had taken cover behind the Mercedes.

'You OK?' I called over to him.

'No. Not really. Someone is shooting at me.'

'Yeah, I picked up on that.'

Another rifle round cracked over my head and then report of the rifle firing. I was in a bad spot and was going to have to do something. I could try to make it to Lintz's car, but I got the feeling the guy pulling the trigger would figure that. Ten yards to my front and to the left was a boulder that was three feet high and a couple feet across. That was going to be my new home.

'Lintz, sit tight.'

'Where am I going to go?'

Another report, this time I didn't hear the round cracking as it came at me, but almost immediately the sound of something striking metal. He was shooting at the Mercedes. I jumped up and fired the Ithaca in the general direction of where I had seen the flash of light. I held the trigger down, pumping the action, the shotgun bucking against my shoulder until it was dry.

I dove behind the boulder and lay on my back feeding rounds into the Ithaca's action. I pumped a round into the chamber and then rolled out to the left of the boulder and fired a round a little below where I had seen the flash of light. My chances of hitting him were next to nothing, but at least he had rounds coming at him. It was one thing to shoot at people when no one was returning fire. It can be a bit disconcerting when your targets are shooting back. I rolled back behind the boulder.

He fired another round at the car. It was a high caliber rifle, a .308 or a .30-06 and the rounds punched through the door panels of the car with ease. I rolled out to the left and fired off two quick rounds in his direction, then rolled back behind the rock. I looked over at Lintz, who was lying on the ground. His shoulder was red with blood.

'Lintz! Are you OK?' I called over.

'Yeah, I'm hit, but I think I'm OK.'

'OK, stay down.'

I rolled to the right and fired my last two rounds at the shooter. I rolled back in just as a round cracked and hit the dirt where I had been. Then it was quiet. I dropped the shotgun and pulled out my Hi-Power. I thumbed the safety off and waited.

The mayflies kept up their whirling dance unconcerned by the gunfight going on, and I felt a mosquito bite the top of my head. There was a familiar ringing in my ears and all the sounds of a late May afternoon sounded as though they were being filtered through that ringing. Through the ringing, I heard Chris calling.

'Red . . . Red. It's all clear, we're coming over there.'

'Chris.'

'Yeah, I got him. I'm walking him over, don't plug me by accident.'

'OK.'

I peeked out and then raised up on one knee, using the rock as cover with the Hi-Power outstretched at arm's length. Eventually a man appeared in the wood line. He was wearing a camouflage jacket and matching hat. Not the kind that the Army used, but the stuff they sell at L.L. Bean's or Eddie Bauer, the splotchy stuff that makes hunters think that they can sneak up on deer or ducks. Behind him, a rifle slung muzzle down over his shoulder, was Chris. Based on the grunts and sudden steps forward now and again, he was urging my would-be sniper along by poking him in the back with his Magnum revolver.

I stood up, holstered the Hi-Power and went to check on Lintz. He was pale and sitting up. His shoulder was red with blood that had soaked through his shirt.

'How are you doing?'

'I've had better days.'

'Yeah, me too. Let me take a look at it.' I peeled his shirt away to reveal a pretty good-sized cut where his neck and shoulder met.

'It looks like you were cut with some shrapnel from the car. It isn't too bad, just a bit on the bloody side. Give me your handkerchief.' He was the type to have one.

'Here. Do I need to go to a hospital?'

'You'll need some stitches, but you'll be fine.'

I folded the handkerchief into a thick square and pressed it against the cut.

'Hold this into the wound. That should stop the bleeding.'

The air was heavier, and the sky had darkened. An afternoon storm was on its way. It was late May but was starting to feel more like late July.

'Hey Red, look who I found up in the hills lining you up in his sights.'

'Hello, Brock.' He looked at me with hatred in his eyes.

'Roark.'

'I guess I found my embezzler.'

'Guess so.'

'When you hired me to follow Lintz and the other two, you already knew he was stealing from the bank didn't you?'

'Yes.'

'What about what Karen Marti and Cosgrove had going on with the late Mr Clark over there?'

'Of course I knew. Karen was my lover.'

'She told you about it.'

'Who do you think set it up? I knew that Clark was shady as hell. I told Karen about the plan, and she convinced Cosgrove to join in.'

'If you were getting cut in on this, why embezzle from the bank? The people who own it wouldn't be too happy about that.'

'No, they wouldn't. They wouldn't be too happy if they found out about our scheme either.'

'You didn't give them a cut?'

'No, they just want the bank as a way to clean drug money.'

A drop of rain, then another plipped on to the roof of the car.

'How did Clark get involved in all the killing?' I knew the answer but I wanted to hear him say it.

'Cosgrove panicked, went to him and told him he wanted out. Clark thought he was going to talk.'

'So, he staged the robbery and shot Cosgrove. Is he the one hit me in Cosgrove's apartment?'

'Yep. He must have gone there to find my second set of ledgers.'

'Why'd he kill Marti?'

'Cosgrove had told him that there was money missing from the bank. Clark knew that Marti would know something, so he went to her and beat it out of her. She gave him my ledgers.'

'Is that why you hired me to scare him?'

'No, I knew that the embezzlement would come to light sooner or later. I figured if I had hired a PI to look into it and then Lintz disappeared forever, everyone would stop looking for the money. Stop looking at me.'

'How did Clark end up here today?'

'He was worried that you were onto him, that it would all unravel. He wanted to trade the ledgers for half the money. I agreed, but told him he'd have to make Lintz disappear. He told me about this place, and we came up with a plan.'

'He was going to double-cross you, wasn't he?'

'I have to assume so. That was my plan, to pick him off from a couple hundred yards away after he took care of Lintz.'

'Jesus, you people are really something,' Chris said, jabbing him in the back. Brock cried out. The rain had gone from a drizzle to a steady drumbeat. Thunder rumbled off in the distance.

'Don't feel too bad for him, he murdered Karen,' Brock said coldly.

'Then what were you going to do?'

'My plan was to walk into work tomorrow morning and eventually call Stephanie Lintz asking where Mark was. Then the police would be called, and I'd report the money missing. There'd be an investigation, I'd tell them about your unsuccessful efforts, and everyone would blame Lintz.'

'And you'd go on living your life, two million dollars richer.'

'Yes.'

'Well, it was a hell of a plan.'

'Except for all the dead people,' Chris said acerbically.

'Listen, Roark . . . it can still work. We're all reasonable men here. Businessmen. I have the money in the trunk of my car. We can split it three ways and never bother each other again.'

'Three ways . . . oh, you want us to take care of your Lintz problem.'

'It's the only way it works. Lintz has to go. That's almost

seven hundred thousand a piece. I bet that's more money than you've ever seen in your life.'

'You're right about that.'

'That's a good split.'

'There is one problem.'

'What's that?'

'I don't know if I'm more insulted that you think I'd do it or that you called me a businessman.' Big, fat raindrops started coming down in earnest now.

'Roark, don't be stupid.'

I would have answered him except that the air suddenly was alive. I could feel my skin tingle and the hair on the back of my neck and arms stood up. There was a flash and the sound of an explosion and a tree twenty yards away blew apart where the lightning struck it.

Brock was a banker, but he moved like a commando just then and dove for Clark's Tec-9 that was lying in the grass. He got to it and clawed it off the ground as I was stepping to one side, drawing the Hi-Power. Brock stood, holding the Tec-9 in two hands, one on the grip and one on the magazine. He pulled the trigger and the gun started to jump, spraying bullets, which made him pull down on the magazine.

I flicked the safety off as I brought the Hi-Power up, and the front sight lined up on Brock's chest. My mind processed the fact that his gun wasn't working anymore. He probably jammed it pulling down on the magazine while shooting, trying to control the recoil.

Off to my left there was another flash and loud boom as Chris shot Brock in the middle of the chest. Actually, Christ shot him three times in quick succession, which is tough to do with a .357 Magnum firing full power loads. But Chris was good, frankly, better than me and I am good with a gun.

I holstered my pistol. I didn't have to check to see if Brock was dead. There was a neat cluster of three holes that you could cover with a baby's fist in Brock's chest. Chris had been using hollow points. Brock was just as dead as a man could be. Nobody said anything for a few minutes, and then, through the ringing in my ears, I heard Lintz.

'Roark, what now?'

'Now?'

'Yes, can you let me break it to my wife and son that I have to go to prison? I'd rather they hear it from me,' Lintz said.

'You're not going to prison.' I went over to Brock's body and dug in his pockets until I found his car keys. I tossed them to Chris. 'Can you get his car and bring it around?'

'Sure, I saw it while I was playing around in the woods.'

'Thanks.'

'No worries.' He dropped Brock's rifle in the grass next to his body and started off into the woods.

'Can you trust him not to take off with the money?' Lintz asked.

'Yeah, he's not a banker.' Lintz winced and, momentarily, I felt bad for the slight. I was edgy. Gunfights and killing have that effect on me.

'Give me a hand with these guys.' We packed rocks in the dead men's clothes. I collected their guns and threw them in the quarry one at a time. I took the old rim that Clark had tied to Lintz's leg and tied that to Clark's leg. Then I used what was left of the bindings and tied their wrists together.

I heard a car bumping up the logging trail. Chris arrived in time to help us drag the weighted bodies to the lip of the quarry and we managed to get them over the lip. They splashed into the water below. We watched the bodies slip under the surface and disappear.

'Won't they float up eventually?' Lintz asked.

'Probably not. Floaters usually happen when the body starts breaking down and the resulting gases blow it up like a balloon. Those boys have some big holes in them. Lets the gasses out,' Chris said.

'What now?'

'Now you take the money that Brock stole. It should be enough that you never have to worry about your son having to go into a state institution. You don't tell anyone, not even your wife, what happened here. You don't live above your means. No flashy cars, no furs for your wife or expensive vacations. When you get tempted, remember that your life, your family's lives, depend on your being disciplined. The people who own the bank won't care that Brock stole it first. They'll only care that you stole from them.'

'I know.'

'Tomorrow morning, you drive your wife's car to work. Put the Mercedes in your garage. Go to work and when Brock doesn't show up, start calling his house. Then send someone to his house. When he doesn't show up by noon, call the police and report him missing. There's been enough weird shit at the bank that it will seem normal. Then don't ever worry about Brock again.'

'What will you do?'

'We're going to leave his car in long term parking at Logan. Eventually the Staties will find it. By then everyone should know about the missing money. Maybe you find something amiss and report it. Maybe the bank sends an auditor. Who knows? Either way they'll find his car, and everyone will assume he took off with the money.'

'You're using his plan?'

'Why not? It beats you going to jail or getting killed. You have a nice family, a kid who really needs his parents.'

'But it's stealing.'

'The money's dirty. What do I care if the mob is out of some drug money?'

The rain had picked up.

'Roark, how can I thank you?'

'Don't screw it up.'

Chris had gone down to Brock's car and moved the money to the Mercedes. It turned out to be three large duffle bags' worth. I quickly outlined the plan for Chris after the money was transferred. Chris headed back down to Brock's car and eventually for Logan. I stood with Lintz going over it all again.

'Tomorrow morning, casually tell people that you had to take your wife's car to work because yours is acting up. You're thinking of trading it in for something more sensible, a Chevy or a Ford.'

'You told me not to buy a new car.'

'You aren't tomorrow or the next day. Chris is going to come by your house with a car. You'll give him the keys to this thing, and you will have yours traded in. Until then, keep your car in the garage. The bullet holes will draw attention. You'll pay him what he asks for the car, and I suggest five thousand for his trouble today.' I was sure that Carney had a car that would fit the bill and that he'd take the Mercedes and some of the bank loot for a trade-in.

'Do you want that much, too?'

'No, I don't want anything.'

'Why are you doing all this?'

'Your kid needs a father.'

'That's it?'

'Yep, pretty simple.'

We shook hands. Then, with my empty shotgun in hand, I walked back to my car to begin the long night of driving back and forth to Boston, shuffling cars between Boston and Amesbury in order to frame a guilty man.

It was late and I was exhausted by the time I made it home. There had been a lot of driving back and forth. I was damp from the rain. My clothes had grass stains and mud on them. I itched from a hundred mosquito bites, and I was pretty sure that I smelled bad. I dragged myself and the shotgun, back in its case, up the stairs to my apartment. Mercifully, I didn't run into any of my neighbors. I was pretty sure I didn't have any pithy comments left in me.

Sir Leominster met me at the door, meowing and prancing back and forth in front of me. I would like to think that he missed me, but I knew that he had really missed his evening can of cat food. I put the guns on the kitchen table and stuffed the miserable beast. That done, I poured myself two fingers of Powers whiskey and felt the warmth of it hit me. I drained it in one go and poured another.

The light on the machine was blinking. It could wait until I had a shower and another drink. In the shower, the hot water stung the scores of scratches and tiny little cuts that you pick up in a fight without ever registering them. When I closed my eyes, I could see Clark's face as the slug hit him in the chest. It would be more fuel for yet another bad dream in the kaleidoscope of bad dreams.

Once I had cleaned myself up and put on some shorts, I thought about food. I hadn't eaten in hours and was starting to understand how Sir Leominster felt. On the plus side, the whiskey was working that much more efficiently. I thought about making something but poured a large whiskey instead. The rain was beating against the windows when I remembered the blinking light on the machine. I went over to it and pressed play.

'Hi, Andy, it's me.' Angela's voice from the machine's speaker sounded brittle. Or maybe it was just me. 'Andy, I feel terrible about how things . . . how things ended up. Please call me. I want to talk to you . . . OK, I hope you're all right.'

Outside, the rain was beating down and the street was filled with large puddles. The rain on the glass made the lights from the cars and the streetlights into stars. I took a big sip of whiskey and thought about calling Angela right then, but there'd be time enough tomorrow.